LAURA THALASSA

D1268780

The QUEEN of TRAITORS

BURNING EMBER PRESS

A Burning Ember Book
Published in the United States by Burning Ember Press, an imprint of Lavabrook Publishing Group.

THE QUEEN OF TRAITORS. Copyright © 2016 by Laura Thalassa
www.laurathalassa.blogspot.com

Grandpa Hall,

I'll always be your little sister

I LOVE YOU as certain dark things are to be loved, in secret, between the shadow and the soul ...
    —Pablo Neruda

CHAPTER 1

CONFUSION.

Am I conscious? Everything's dark.

A moment later, pain flares my body to life. I'm awake, I have to be to acutely feel every inch of throbbing skin.

I grind my teeth together against the agony, but I can't stop the tears that leak from my eyes. I'm lying on my side, my weight pressed against my bad arm, my wrists bound behind my back. If not for the pain, I wouldn't even know I had a bad arm.

I can hear people talking, and I smell oil and steel. But I can't see any of it. Something covers my face. I try to shrug it off with my shoulder, but I don't make any progress.

What's going on?

I search my mind, but there's nothing to grasp onto. I cannot remember a moment before this. What actions led my life here, cuffed and wounded. My past and my identity have been cleaved away, along with my freedom, and I have no idea what any of it means.

The floor dips and rises, and my bodyweight is thrown against my injury. The agony is instant and all-compassing. I can't hold back my gasp, but it cuts off as the pain overwhelms me and my mind shuts down.

I wake off and on to voices, pain, and jostling. I should know what's happening to me, but the explanation is a wil-o'-the-wisp; the more I chase it, the farther away it gets.

My entire existence is a series of shallow breaths drawn from damp, recycled air, my world contained within the bag that covers my head. I do not know my name, the color of my eyes, the shape of my face. Most importantly, I have no idea what's going on.

And now I'm being jerked to my feet, and now we're walking. I hiss in a breath at the pain. My legs can't hold me up. They keep wanting to fold under me, but my captors grip my elbows and force me to remain upright.

I can hear cheering as I'm carted away. A migraine pulses behind my eyes and along my temple, and the noise stirs it.

A crowd must be watching this procession. People begin to boo.

At me, I realize. The entire mass of them are booing at *me*.

Who *am* I?

Something smashes into the side of my head. I stagger,

2

and my headache unfurls the full force of its power. I have to swallow back the bile that rises up in my throat.

"Move!" an angry voice shouts. A booted foot kicks the back of my knee, and I stumble forward.

Beneath the pain and the confusion, anger simmers. My cuffed hands curl into fists. If I wasn't restrained, I'd gladly endure more suffering to land a few good blows on my captors. I'm no helpless thing.

The air cools as I'm directed indoors. That doesn't stop the booing crowd or the objects flung at me. Whatever's happening, I'm supposed to be humiliated. They're wasting their efforts. I'm in far too much pain to care about what they think of me.

This goes on for a while, and I resign myself to enduring this for the time being. It's not until I hear the heavy turn of locks and I'm pushed forward once more, that my situation changes.

Now the noise from the crowd dulls and the thump of dozens of footsteps break away. I can't say how much farther we walk, or how many turns we take. I'm weaving on my feet.

The men holding my arms halt. Ahead of me, locks tumble and then another heavy door creaks open. A tug on my injured arm has me moving forward. We only walk a few steps forward before I'm stopped again. Behind me, the thick thud of a door cuts the last of the sound off completely.

Someone rips the bag from my head, taking some strands of my hair along with it.

The overhead light blinds me, and I squint against it,

gnashing my teeth against the new wave of pain behind my temple. I sense more than see the men on either side of me.

I finally breathe in fresh air, and it shakes off a bit of my weariness. The last time air was this crisp ...

I stand in a moat of bloody bodies. Men in dark fatigues creep closer. I don't know who they are, but I know I need to fight them.

The memory's blurry, and I can't be sure it's real.

I blink, my earlier confusion roaring back to life. Why can't I place where I am? Who I am? I know I should remember these things, so why can't I?

And then there are the things that I inexplicably know. The fact, for instance, that I'm in a holding cell. The kind with a one-way mirror. I have no memory of this place or any like it, yet somehow I recognize exactly what it is. A room for prisoners.

That's what I am. I can't say what my crimes are, though I'm obviously someone important. Someone infamous.

As my eyes adjust, I notice three men in uniform standing around me. Soldiers of some sort. They appear wary of me, like I might get violent at any moment.

I think they're wise to be wary.

One of them shoves me to my knees. Roughly, he grabs my bound hands behind my back and unlocks the cuffs. Pain slices through my arms as they're released and sensation flows back into them.

I pivot on my knees, primed for attack. I may not know what's going on, but I have muscle memory, and it's leading me now.

4

I lunge for the nearest of my captors. Clumsily my arms wrap around his calves as I slam into him, and God, does my injured arm burn. The pain almost stops me. Almost.

He loses his balance and falls. Not good for him.

My instincts are directing me. Before he can recover, I move up his body and slam the fist of my good arm into his temple. Again and again.

I was right. It is absolutely worth every bit of agony to pummel one of these men.

Just as quickly as I find myself on my captor, I'm dragged off of him by the other two. The entire time they curse at me.

Like I actually give a shit.

I struggle against them, and even injured as I am, I still manage to slip their hold. One tackles me to the ground. "Your gun, man, your gun!" he shouts to his comrade.

I don't understand the order until I see the hilt of some military grade weapon raised above me. The butt of it slams into my temple, and I'm out cold once more.

WHEN I COME to, I'm cuffed to a chair in my cell. Across the table I sit at, an enemy soldier watches me with obvious disgust. That one-way mirror looms behind him. Someone's watching us. I can practically feel their eyes on me.

I catch sight of myself in the mirror. It's brief, just a flash of blood-matted hair and skin that looks more like overripe fruit.

I can taste blood in my mouth, and a tooth is loose.

I don't think I have a concussion, but that's sheer luck. They hit me hard and repeatedly.

A chill slithers up my spine. Perhaps I already have a concussion, and that's why I can't remember anything about myself.

Standing guard next to the door of my cell is another soldier, a military-grade rifle in his hand. His finger loosely cradles the trigger. I can read nothing from his face. That, more than anything, convinces me that if I so much as flinch the wrong way, he'll shoot me.

Looks like my situation just went from bad to worse.

"I'm Lieutenant Begbie. Do you know why you're here?" The man across from me wears dark fatigues, and he has a gristly look about him, like he's held together mostly by sinew and anger.

"You want answers from me," I say.

"Yes, ma'am." He settles a bit more into his chair. "And you're going to give them to us."

"And if I don't?" But it's not *if*, it's *when*.

Begbie studies me, sucking on his teeth while he does so. "We're going to try this the civilized way first. If you answer our questions, we won't use force to get them out of you."

I raise an eyebrow, even though my heart pounds like mad. Torture.

"We'll start off easy. Tell me your full name."

I can feel the burn of the cuffs on my wrist, rubbing my skin raw. My body is a mass of wounds, and my head feels as though it's ready to split open. These are all injuries this man and his people gave me. Perhaps this little tasting

6

of their wares is supposed to scare me.

I don't feel scared. And I don't feel very talkative.

But I am angry. I'm very angry.

"What's your name?" he repeats.

I lean to the side and spit out blood. Answer enough.

My interrogator's scowl only deepens.

The door to my cell opens, and angry voices from the hall trickle in.

"–*I don't give a damn. I need to see her for myself.*"

My eyes flick to the man that enters.

Old, strong, his hair cropped close to his head. His features are hard, even his eyes. A man used to making tough decisions. I can already tell he'll show me no more kindness than the rest of them.

"Serenity," he says to me, "what happened to him?"

Serenity—is this my name? It doesn't sound like a name. I stare at him curiously. Does this man know me?

"Kline." Begbie says the word—another name perhaps—like a warning.

The older man stalks across the room and leans over me. An intense pair of blue eyes fix on mine, and I see a mixture of anger and grief in them. "What did you and the king do to him?"

He rests his hands on the metal backing of my chair and shakes it to emphasize his point.

Air hisses out of me as the movement jostles my already screaming gunshot wound. The headache that's been pounding behind my temple pulsates with pain.

"For the love of Christ, Serenity, what did you do to my son? I want to hear you say it."

This man might know me, but he's no friend of mine.

"General," Begbie rounds the table and grabs the man's upper arm, "that's enough. We're in the middle of an interrogation."

The general—I assume this is a title—shrugs off Begbie's grip and gives a jerky nod, his gaze trained on my face.

"Get her to talk," he says. And then he turns on his heel and stalks out of the room, the door slamming shut behind him.

I stare at the space he took up. Whoever that man was, I did something to his son—me and this king they keep asking about—something that broke a hardened man.

I search the empty halls of my mind for a memory—even just a fragment of one. Nothing comes to mind. And now I have the general's cryptic words to add to my already addled state. The whole thing makes me weary.

I'm injured, locked up like the world's deadliest criminal, and being questioned about a past I can't remember. They're going to torture me, then kill me, and at the end of it all I'll have no idea why. It seems so pointless.

My interviewer runs a hand over his cropped hair. "Why don't we start where we left off?"

"What do you really want to know?" I ask, leaning back into my seat.

There's no use in me stalling. Torture's coming, either way.

"Where is the king?" the man across from me asks.

This mysterious king whom I can't recall. I must work for him. It makes sense.

"I don't know," I say, still distracted by my own thoughts.

My interviewer leans forward. "Surely you know where he would go."

"Maybe," I hedge, shifting my weight as the injury on my calf begins to burn. The movement causes the pain in my arm to flare up.

Would it be wise to reveal how little I know?

Begbie must read my expression because he says, "If you're not going to cooperate, Serenity, then we'll force the answers out of you."

Serenity must be my name.

"That I'm well aware of," I say.

My reflection catches my attention once more, and I shift my eyes away from Begbie. Aside from the bruises that cover my face, and I have a deep scar that runs from the corner of my eye down my cheek.

I look ... sinister. And hardened. Oddly enough, that gives me courage.

Begbie tries again. "What do you believe you're worth to the king?"

"I don't know."

The Lieutenant leans back in his seat and studies me. "Alright," he finally drawls, coming to some sort of decision, "what locations in the WUN do you believe the king will select for his armories?"

"I don't know."

Begbie touches his lips with two fingers; he taps one of them against his mouth as he watches me. I know he's trying to figure out the best way to crack me.

"I don't want to hurt you, Serenity," he says, "I really don't, but you have to give me information for this to work."

Contrary to his words, this man wants to hurt me very, very badly.

We stare each other down. I'm going to be killed either way, and that knowledge settles on my shoulders like a cloak. Whatever else happens, my words won't get me out of here.

He leans forward in his chair, his hand coming to rest on the table. "What *do* you know?"

This is one question I can answer.

"That my name is Serenity, and my memory is gone."

CHAPTER 2

Serenity

LIEUTENANT BEGBIE ENDS the interview shortly after my admission, promising me "advanced interrogation techniques" if I can't come up with answers soon.

Suffice it to say, the man doesn't believe me.

After he finishes questioning me, he unlocks my cuffs, and this time I'm wise enough not to attack. The guard with the assault rifle looks ready and willing to use it. If I want to rebel, today won't be the day.

I make note of the fact that the lieutenant has a gun holstered to his hip, and he likely has another weapon somewhere on his person.

If what I know won't save me, then my actions must. I'm going to have to hurt people to leave this place.

That should bother me more than it does. I add heart-lessness to my growing list of character traits.

Until then, I'll bide my time and figure out what, exactly, is wrong with my mind. Specifically, why I don't know who I am.

Once Begbie and the guard leave, I lean against the cement wall of my cell, my legs bent in front of me. I rub my wrists.

I haven't changed clothes since my capture. I wear black leather boots, fitted pants, and a crimson shirt.

At least, these were the original colors I wore. Blood and dust now cake them. My outfit's ripped in several locations, and the back of one boot's burned away. I can't remember how I got this way, which makes my past all the more intriguing.

I finger the material of my shirt. I have nothing to compare it to, but its softness, weave, and saturated color all scream *wealth*.

While I'd been unconscious, someone cut away the fabric covering my injured arm and leg. Gauze covers both wounds; these enemy soldiers went to the trouble of patching me up. I'd assume it was a small kindness, but after seeing the way they've treated me, they probably just wanted to make sure I live long enough to be of use to them.

Eventually I'll need to check the wounds and let them breathe. Even if they were tended by combat medics, staunching the blood flow and wrapping a wound up is no permanent remedy.

How do I know any of this?

I'm still absently rubbing the material of my shirt when light glints off my hand. My body stills as I hold it up.

I don't know which surprises me more: that I'm wearing jewelry, or that my captors haven't yet confiscated it.

If I'm someone important, they will eventually. Another truth I inexplicably know.

I study the two rings that adorn my hand. One is a band of yellow diamonds. Expensive. The other is a polished piece of lapis lazuli. Tiny flakes of gold shimmer amongst the dark blue of the stone, reminding me of the night sky. This one doesn't seem so expensive, but meaningful perhaps.

My heart thumps loudly in my chest.

I'm married.

I let that sink in. I don't think I like that. Even without the aid of memories, there's something constricting about the prospect.

Still, that means someone's missing me right now.

Around my rings, the skin is scarred—particularly my knuckles. Apparently the guard wasn't the first face these fists have dug into. My hands, however, are free of even the hint of wrinkles.

I add up what I know: I'm young, female—I gleaned that much from the mirror—married, dangerous, and valuable to these people's cause.

It's an unlikely combination.

Who am I to be so young and so experienced in the darker deeds of men?

I hold my hand up again, letting the rings catch the light.

And what kind of man would marry a woman like me?

TIME TICKS BY slowly in this place. No one's come for me again, but they will.

I lean my head back against the cool cement wall and close my eyes.

I'm at the back of the room. Cornered. Enemy soldiers creep closer to me. Between us, bloody men and women lay unmoving.

This is the first memory I have, and it's a struggle to hold onto it. I try to focus on the wounds of the fallen, but my mind won't give up those details.

The hiss of scraping metal snaps my eyes open. A tray slides through the slot at the bottom of my cell's door. Those crafty soldiers use the end of a broom to push it through; by now they've figured out that I'll take out a finger or two if given the chance.

I'm not a very nice person. I wonder if that's the result of nature or nurture.

My stomach cramps painfully as I stare at the food, and only then do I realize just how hungry I am. Adrenaline and pain had distracted me up until now.

I get up and grab the tray. The sight of the food tempers my appetite somewhat. If I were less hungry, perhaps I'd simply skip the meal. Instead I pick up the plastic utensil and try what can only be described as gruel.

It's over salted, and the more I eat, the queasier I get.

I set the food aside and steady my breathing. I'm all right, just a little too battle worn. It doesn't help that my arm wound pounds like it has its own pulse.

The memory of those dead bodies flash through my mind again, only now, when I don't bid it, do I see their injuries in all their gruesome detail.

I barely reach the toilet in time.

My entire body shakes as I vomit, and all the awful food I just forced down leaves my system. I feel weak, so weak, as I hunch over the toilet bowl. My stomach didn't just purge itself of food. There's blood in the mix as well.

From my injuries?

Behind me, the door creaks open. I don't bother glancing back. I'm too tired to defend myself, and I've already accepted the fact that torture will come. If it's right now, then there's not much I can do about it.

Instead, a chair scrapes back. Someone's taken to watching me.

"You're sick."

I recognize the voice. It belongs to the general, the man who knows me.

I'm not surprised he's come back, but I am surprised at the shift in his temperament. His voice even has a modicum of control to it.

Experience that I can't remember tells me not to trust his calmness. There's always a calm before a storm.

I reach a hand up to flush the toilet, then drag myself to the wall, leaning my back against it. I'm sweating, either from sickness, like the general mentioned, or my injuries.

"I hadn't realized ..." the general starts, taking me in. "When you were sick before, we assumed you and my son ..." He lets the sentence trail off. His Adam's apple bobs.

I try to process all that he is and isn't saying. Apparently this nausea is more than just fatigue, and the general's known me long enough to have some insight into this. More surprising, this man who opposes the king is father to a man I was once close to.

"Will?" I ask, remembering the name he threw out at me yesterday. There's something downright spooky about learning of a relationship and having no recollection of it.

The general bows his head and nods.

I'm afraid to ask what happened to Will. Afraid of what else this man knows about us.

"You really don't remember who you are?" he asks.

I stare at the rings on my left hand. "No."

I am a woman unmade. Something of skin and meat and bone and consciousness, but not a person, not in the truest sense. I have no opinions, no past, no identity. It's been stripped from me. And even here I can feel the wrongness of it.

"That bastard," the general whispers.

I glance up at him. All the earlier heat in his expression is gone. Now he just looks old and defeated.

He studies me, something like pity softening those hard features. "Our sources believed he'd been working on a memory suppressant. Never thought he'd turn it on you."

A memory suppressant. So that's why I lack an identity. Someone deliberately erased my memory—the king, if the general is to be believed.

He could be lying. About everything. For all I know this entire situation was concocted for some purpose I'm unaware of.

16

"Who are you?" I ask.

"I'm the former general of the Western United Nations—the WUN." He says this as though it should ring a bell. It doesn't.

"Who am I?" I ask.

"You were our former emissary."

Past tense.

"But I am no longer?" The cell is proof of that. Still, I want to know what changed between then and now.

The general rubs his face.

"No, Serenity," he sighs out. "No."

White whiskers grow along his cheeks and jaw. He doesn't strike me as a man who forgets to shave. Everything about him screams defeat, despite the fact that once he's done here, he'll be the one walking out that door a free man.

"What happened?" I ask.

I don't think he's going to answer me. I'm stepping out of line, the prisoner asking questions of her captor. But then he does speak. "The WUN surrendered to the Eastern Empire and you were part of the collateral."

I furrow my brows. What he says makes no sense.

"It's my fault," he admits, leaning forward in his seat. He threads his hands together and rests them between his legs. "I made the call to give you to King Lazuli."

Lazuli, like the stone on my finger. My stomach drops.

"'Give'?" He makes it sound as though I was nothing more than a commodity. Little more than what I am now—a means to an end for these people.

"It was the only way," the general says. He's pleading

with me, and I can tell this long ago decision cost him. "The king was prepared to rip apart the WUN. You were the only bargaining chip we had, and God, he wanted you so badly. He was willing to give us everything we wanted."

Bile rises up in my throat again, and I swallow it back down.

"Why did he want me?"

He bows his head, staring at his clasped hands. "You left ... quite the impression when you and your father negotiated the terms of our nation's surrender."

"So you gave me to him ... in return for peace?" I say, making sense of his words.

He rubs his eyes. "Yes, I did."

Outrage flares up in me. I may not recall this decision, but I had to live through it at some point. This general offered me to our enemy. Never mind that it saved countless other lives. This was the same man I must've worked with—whose son I had some sort of relationship with—and yet he threw me to the wolves.

I stare at my ring as an even more terrifying idea takes form. "I don't work for the king, do I?"

The general sighs and meets my eyes. "No, Serenity, you don't work for the king. You're married to him."

CHAPTER 3

Serenity

GIVEN TO THE king like a war prize.

"Do I love him?"

The general squints at me. "He killed your parents, razed your hometown, and if that sickness is what I suspect it is," he nods to the toilet, "then you have him to thank for it as well. No, I don't think you love him, but I do believe he's poisoned your mind."

I frown. This story is getting more and more twisted and harder for me to believe. This king sounds like the devil. Yet here I am, prisoner to the very people whose side I once fought on. I have to be missing something. No matter how heartless I might be, one doesn't go from hate to love or swap loyalties without a good cause.

"Why would I marry him?"

"You were forced to."

To be married to my parents' killer ... a shudder works its way through me. I may be heartless, but even I don't deserve that kind of fate.

"Who are these people?" I glance at the one-way mirror.

"They're the last soldiers willing to fight the king. The world is now controlled entirely by him. The Resistance and other grassroots organizations are the only ones that stand in his way. Us and you."

Someone knocks on the door, and the general stands.

He hesitates, then says, "Perhaps it would do to take you outside and show what your husband has done to our world."

I raise my eyebrows. "I've never heard of a prisoner getting that type of privilege." Not that I've heard much of anything since my memory was wiped. It's a mystery how I know what a typical prisoner's experience should be, and the source of the knowledge left no maker's mark.

"You're not a typical prisoner," the general says. "For better or worse, you're the queen of this entire rock."

He pauses at the door. "No one here is going to torture you. Not if I can help it. But the reality of your situation is that your life is no longer in your control."

"Was it ever?" I ask, searching his eyes.

I genuinely want to know. Did I choose to do wrong by these people, or was I forced into it? The distinction matters.

The general hesitates. "No," he finally says, "it wasn't."

I FIND I miss the general once he leaves. I don't want to miss him. I have no illusions that he likes me, and by the end of our discussion, I'm not so sure I like him all that much either.

However, he knows me, and he's been civil enough, which is more than I can say about the rest of my captors.

I begin moving around the room.

Blanket, bed, wall, ceiling, floor. Rings, shirt, pants, shoes. The names of each item come without hesitation, but I have no memories to attach to each of them.

I move onto current events. Here I brush up against a barrier. Part of me wants to say that the world is suffering. Food's scarce, land's contaminated, war's prevalent. I don't know how much of this is me guessing from the snippets I've heard and how much is actual knowledge.

What year is it? I begin to pin dates to historic events. The 1700s, 1800s, and 1900s are all distinct enough from the present that I can write them off as the past. But the 2000s ... my knowledge of this century is muddled, and when I think of 2100s and later, I can't conjure anything. I actually huff out at a laugh. I've narrowed the year down— give or take a century or so.

I know what people look like, but I can't picture up anyone I know besides Lieutenant Begbie and the general. My head begins to pound from the effort.

I don't have a concussion after all, at least not one responsible for my staggering memory loss. The king did this.

The king, my husband. A man willing to tear apart the world to satisfy his own need for power, a man who forced me into marriage. This is not a man fit to rule over others. This is not a man fit for anything, really, except a swift, bloody death.

It's not until much, much later that anyone returns. By then I'm dozing on the thin mattress. The door to my cell opens, and Lieutenant Begbie enters, followed by a soldier.

I shiver as I'm roused awake. This type of chill comes from the inside out. I know without looking that my arm wound is worsening.

"'Morning," he opens.

I swing my feet out of bed and bite back a groan. Movement's agonizing. I roll my shoulders, crack my neck, and push the pain back. I can lick my wounds later.

Begbie rounds the interview table in my cell and takes a seat. The table's bolted to the floor, but the chairs aren't.

I've already considered everything in this room as a potential weapon. The sheets can choke, the chairs can bludgeon, my pillow can smother. Those types of deaths require intimacy and strength, neither of which I have at the moment. Hence, I've taken to assessing the soldiers that come into the room.

This time they pulled in a greenie to guard the door. I can see it in his jaw; he's forcing himself to look stoic. The more experienced soldiers don't have to force anything. They've seen and done it all, and if it hasn't broken their mind or their will, they become a whole new type of lethal, and sometimes they'll let you see the emptiness in their eyes.

This soldier's eyes are not empty, despite all his valiant

efforts. I tear my gaze away from him before either he or Begbie notice my interest.

"We're in negotiations with the king at the moment," Begbie says.

The king. I don't want any part of his madness.

I take a seat across from Begbie. "He knows I'm here?"

"The way I see it, I'm the only one who should be asking questions."

Begbie leans back in his seat and folds his arms, getting real comfortable. "There's a rumor out there that the king is immortal, that he can't die. We have a clip of the king getting shot in the heart. Another of a grenade clipping him. Both were killing blows, but that fucker is still alive."

The general never mentioned this. Despite myself, the hairs on my arms rise. Memory wipe or no, I'm pretty sure immortality is impossible.

"He's responsible for the deaths of your friends and family, he's taken over your country, and he wants you back. If the rumors are true, you do realize there's no killing him, don't you? You'll have to live with him, the man responsible for the death of your countrymen, and he'll want things from you—sex among them.

"You'll continue to be dubbed a traitor, all while sleeping with your parents' killer. And, frankly, I don't see any end in sight for you."

I'm glaring at Begbie, though my vitriol is not aimed at him. Not really.

I don't believe him, however. Not entirely. The king may have killed my family, defeated nations, taken my memory and forced my hand in marriage, but I don't believe he's figured out the riddle to immortality.

I lean forward. "You're wrong, Lieutenant. Everything can die."

Love, hate. Even kings.

BEFORE HE HAS time to respond, a soldier cracks open the door and leans in. "Get the prisoner ready."

Lieutenant Begbie stands. "Put your hands behind your back," he orders me.

I could escape now. By the time the lieutenant figured out my motives, it would be too late. I'd steal that gun holstered to his side. I'd gamble the greenie wouldn't shoot me before I got a chance to fire at him.

I could do it, there's a confidence to my assessment and I already know I have the muscle memory. Yet every fiber of my being recoils from the thought. Whatever else, I'm not a monster by design.

Just necessity.

"Put your hands behind your back," Begbie says more forcefully.

I've missed my opportunity.

I do so, and he cuffs me rougher than needed. I run my tongue over my teeth, clenching my jaw as my raw wrists and my bullet wound sting. It doesn't help that the lieutenant jerks me up.

Pain is a warm companion. I must've known it quite well before today, whether at the hands of the WUN or the king. Probably both. It seems like they're two sides of the same coin.

Begbie and the soldier escort me out of the cell, and I get my first good look at the outside of my prison. More cement walls and fluorescent lights. No windows.

"Where are we going?"

No one answers me.

I might be walking to my death. Or to an interrogation chamber, the kind that leaves behind teeth and blood-stains. Now I know why I was so ready to kill, despite my disgust. Being soft doesn't save you in this place. Power does, fear does, and pain does.

If I have the chance to act again, I won't hesitate.

THEY MARCH ME down the narrow corridor. We make several turns, and I memorize each one. The drabness of this prison doesn't exactly change, but the atmosphere does. An increasing number of people wander the halls. When their eyes land on me, I see them react. Sometimes it's just recognition, other times it's fear or anger or pity.

They know of me.

What had I been expecting? I am the king's wife. Likely a public figure.

We stop in front of a door, and on the other side I can hear murmurs.

An execution, then. Torture doesn't require so many people, I think.

Only, when they open the door, my presumptions melt away. In front of me rests a camera and a chair, the latter currently occupied by a soldier.

But that is not what captures my attention.

At the back of the room is a large screen. My breath catches when my eyes land on it, and suddenly my pulse is in my ears.

The soldier sitting in front of the camera turns, then stands when he sees us. My guards march me forward and force me into the relinquished seat.

The entire time I stare at the man whose face takes up the screen.

I expected an abomination.

Not *this*.

Evil is supposed to be ugly, but he isn't ugly. In fact, this man—my *husband*, if my assumption's correct—is more than just a little pleasing to stare at.

Unlined, olive skin, dark hair brushed back from his face, a strong, straight nose, eyes that draw you in, and a mouth that promises secrets and slow seduction. Was that why I married him? God, I hope not. I don't want to know who I was if that were the reason.

My heart thumps faster. He is gorgeous, but it's not his looks that have moved me.

I recognize myself in his eyes. Even as fogged as my mind is, even as unaware of my past as I am, something about him resonates deep within me. I don't know what it is I feel or what it means, but already I can no longer think of him objectively.

"Serenity." He doesn't say my name the same way my captors do, like I'm the scourge of the earth. He says it like we're lovers.

We *are* lovers.

He wants me back. I can read it plainly on his face, in

the way his pupils dilate. This is the man they all fear and hate. A man, if they're to be believed, that *I* fear and hate.

"King Lazuli," I return.

Why would he want me back, this man who's so willing to ruin my life?

"Montes," he corrects. I get the impression he's done that before—corrected me.

His gaze scours my face, and I realize his cool exterior is hiding a well of emotions. A vein in his temple pulses. "What've they done to you?"

This abomination of a human being *cares* about me. It doesn't add up with what I've learned of him.

And now, one wrong word and this house of cards will tumble. That's the kind of power I sense I wield, being the king's wife. He'll kill them all, and unlike me, he'll enjoy it thoroughly.

"I'm okay."

His jaw clenches ever so slightly. That and the throbbing vein are the only signs he feels. The king's tells are subtle, but I'm still shocked at how genuine his emotions towards me are. Whoever Montes Lazuli is, at the moment he's more man than nightmare.

Odd that right now, of the two of us, I am the colder one. My heart is made of steel and ice and I cannot muster emotion to match his.

"I'm going to get you out of there," he says. "You need to stay alive for me."

I can't go back to him. I can't. He has power over me, power that has nothing to do with pain and punishment. I'm enthralled by him, and considering the way he tracks my every movement through the screen, the feeling seems mutual.

"Time's up," someone calls. "We've proven she's alive."

"Alive and injured," the king says. A dozen threats lace his voice. I fear that if I live long enough, I'll see each one of them carried out.

At my back, several soldiers approach. I take in the handsome man on the other side of the screen a final time. "Whoever you are, I hope you were worth it." After all, torture and death are still on the table for me. I hope the Serenity who had a past was satisfied with it.

They drag me away after that.

"Serenity! Wait—" I can hear him at my back, his voice rising as he shouts at whoever will listen that he isn't finished talking with me.

Yes, my husband wants me back, and he'll guard me like a dragon does its treasure. I doubt very much that I'll enjoy that kind of protection.

An ache starts up in my chest as I stride back to my cell. I'm trapped between the king's wishes and this organization's, and there's no room for my own. As the ache grows, I realize it isn't fear or sadness.

It's rage.

Other people got me into this mess; they're not going to get me out of it. I will.

And I *will* get myself out of it, or I'll die trying.

CHAPTER 4

Serenity

INFECTION'S BEGINNING TO set in.

My hands shake as I unravel the gauze over my arm. A shiver racks my body. I need to see just how bad it is, but I don't want to. My skin's already swollen above and below the bandages. It won't be pretty.

I hear nothing from outside the walls of my prison. If soldiers are watching, they've decided not to interfere.

My eyes burn, and as I remove layer after layer, I can tell I'm worse off than I thought I was. A foul smell emanates from my bandages, and it gets stronger the more I unwind.

The last layer of gauze is the worst. The material's fused to the wound. I clench my jaw as I peel it away. The pain blazes so brightly my vision clouds. I can't stop the agonized cry that slips out. My breath comes out in pants. Sweat beads along my forehead. With a final tug, I remove the last of the bandages.

I'd prepared myself for the savage sight of my injury, but it's still hard to look at. Blood and puss cover the wound. The dirty skin around it is so swollen it looks ready to burst.

Reaching over to the untouched tray of food I received a short while ago, I grab the cup of water. Taking a fortifying breath, I pour it over the wound.

As soon as the first drop hits my skin, the pain explodes. My teeth are tightly clenched, so my cry escapes as a hiss of air. My vision clouds again, and I'm blind for a couple seconds as I fight to stay conscious.

The empty cup slips from my hand, and I spend the next several minutes shivering and clutching my arm to my chest.

In the hallway outside my cell, I hear raised voices. They sound panicked, and they're getting closer.

Don't let the enemy see your weaknesses.

I need to rewrap my arm. The thought tightens my stomach.

Reluctantly I crawl over to the discarded bandages. Using my teeth, I rip off the soiled section of cloth. The agony's even worse this time around, so bad that I have to pause twice to vomit. The wound doesn't want to be bound, and my cheeks are wet by the time I'm tying the knot.

BOOM!

The earth quakes, and I nearly fall on my injured arm. I

brace myself against the wall. I glance above me.

The voices in the hall turn to shouts.

BOOM!

The door to my cell opens. A soldier runs in and grabs me, cursing the entire time. I scream as he squeezes my injured arm. Before I consciously decide to hit him, my good arm shoots out and slams into his nose. I hear it crunch, and he cries out, releasing me to clutch at it.

The time for compliance has long since run out. If I don't want to die in this prison, now's my chance.

While he's distracted, I grab his gun from its holster. Flicking off the safety, I cock it and shoot him in the thigh. There's no hesitation to my actions. No uncertainty.

He howls, falling to his knees. I watch him dispassionately, and my lack of reaction terrifies me.

As he writhes on the ground, another soldier begins to enter my cell. I clench my jaw against the pain in my arm as I lift the gun and fire. The bullet clips him in the shoulder.

Not only can I injure without remorse, I know how and where to shoot a man without killing him.

I shake my head, more than a little curious just what kind of ball-busting broad I was before I lost my memories.

Before the door can click shut, I force my way out, ignoring the burn of my injuries as I step over the man and push my feverish body into action.

BOOM!

My back crashes against the wall. The fluorescent lights flicker.

Out here I hear shouting and the echo of dozens of

pounding footsteps. Somewhere in the distance, rounds of gunfire go off.

A uniformed man runs past. Only after he passes me does he pause to glance back. I point my gun at him.

"Keep moving," I say.

This one is either smarter or less courageous than his comrades because he does.

I need to get out of here before someone decides I'm worth the trouble. I begin to jog, clenching my teeth against the pain in my calf. I hook a right, then a left, following the sounds to their source.

In the chaos, no one I pass stops me, though several of them pause when they recognize my face. The gun in my hand seems to deter them from doing anything more.

BOOM! The screams increase in number and volume.

The lights flicker again. We're going to lose electricity soon. I welcome the possibility. At the moment, I'm too recognizable.

Ahead of me, people herd into a stairwell and from my vantage point, they seem to be descending the stairs. Most, but not all, wear fatigues. I hesitate. Either escape or shelter is down there, but so are my enemies.

Making a spur-of-the-moment decision, I head into the mass of people, keeping my head ducked.

We shuffle into the stairwell, and the current of bodies tries to drag me down the stairs, but I don't want to go down. I want to go up.

It's as I try to extricate myself that I get noticed.

"Hey," a soldier next to me says, bending to peer at me, "are you … ? Shit, it's Queen Lazuli," he says, more to the people around him than to me.

People look over, and the murmurs begin.

"Queen Lazuli." "It's the queen!" "Someone grab her!"

I straighten; no use hiding now that my cover's been blown.

Just as the first hand reaches for me, I raise my good arm in the air, the one holding the gun. I aim it at the bare bulb lighting the stairwell, and then I pull the trigger.

The bulb shatters, and the stairwell goes dark. Around me, the crowd shouts and covers their heads.

"The next one goes in someone's brain!" I yell over the noise.

People fall away from me like I have the plague.

Pushing myself the rest of the way through the crowd, I head upstairs. No one else tries to stop me, too intent on saving their own lives.

The higher I climb, the more distinct the noises of battle become. I can hear shouted orders and the thump of machine gun fire—the kind that's mounted to a vehicle rather than a person. It's louder, you can hear the force of the kickback.

Again, I wonder how I knew that.

I lean heavily on the metal bannister as a series of shivers course through me. My eyes burn. It probably doesn't matter whether I manage to escape or not. I'm pretty bad off. I give myself another day before my fever takes me completely, and then it'll be up to Mother Nature to decide my fate.

The next floor is where the noise is loudest. Ground floor. I brace myself for the onslaught of soldiers, readying my gun, but the only people who enter the stairwell carry injured men, and they have no time for me.

I follow the stairs up two more flights to the top. All's quiet here.

Running on instinct, I slip out.

I understand immediately why no one's here. Building materials, broken furniture, and a couple bloody limbs litter the ground. The floor outside the stairwell slumps, and less than twenty feet away from me, it's crumbled away completely. In several places fires sizzle. I welcome the heat against my feverish skin.

The place got firebombed. No wonder nobody's here.

Beyond the gaping remains of this building, another building smolders across the street, lighting up the dark night. Between the two, I hear more than see the fighting. The air is filled with hazy smoke, and it smells like gunpowder and charred bodies.

Hell has come to earth.

The whine of a jet shakes the building as it swoops by, and I grab a wall for support.

My stomach clenches at the noise, like it knows something I don't.

It does.

When the explosion hits, the sound consumes me. It shrieks across my skin and as my body's thrown back, the last thought I have is that out of all the ways I thought I might die, this one's the most preferable.

I FIGHT AGAINST consciousness. Everything already hurts. I

don't want to face it.

My body doesn't give me a choice. I moan as I stir.

I'm on fire. I must be.

The fever's fully set in, and I'm being cooked from the inside out.

I peel my eyes open and lick my chapped lips, tasting soot and plaster on them.

Where am I?

Trash and debris litter the ground I lay on. I remember the mad dash I'd made up here and the sounds of fighting.

All's silent now.

The rays of early morning light stream in from the gaping hole, and my throat tightens. It's the most beautiful thing I've seen since I can remember.

I crawl to the edge of what remains of the room, where the floor drops away. I lay directly beneath a beam of that early morning light. It touches my skin and all the depravity of this place can't ruin this moment. I close my eyes as a tear trickles out.

I'm not going to die here. Not amongst my enemies.

I crawl back to the stairwell, grabbing my fallen gun from the debris. I must've dropped it during the explosion. Shakily, I push myself to my feet and tuck the weapon into the small of my back, flicking the safety on.

Everything hurts. God, does it hurt. I won't allow myself to focus on the pain or the unsettling silence.

When I make it to the ground level, nothing stirs. Only the dead live here now.

I make my way towards what must be the front of the

building, ignoring several bodies that are slumped against the wall or splayed out along the floor. The bombs missed this section, and the front door ahead of me is still intact.

Only a fool would head towards the carnage, but I'm beyond playing it safe.

I step into the light on shaky legs. I blink away some of the fever-induced haze to take in my surroundings.

The pink rays of dawn touch scattered bodies. Dozens of them. Maybe hundreds. The morning light doesn't seem so peaceful anymore.

It's just like my first memory, only worse. A sea of soldiers surround the building I just exited. All dead. I don't even hear moans or their death throes.

My skin prickles, and I can't say it's from my fever this time.

Someone attacked them so thoroughly that none survived, and none of the living have come to collect them.

The king.

They've been picked off like fish in a barrel. It's not just from the explosions either. Their bodies are riddled with bullets, and some look bloated, their vacant eyes bulging from their sockets.

Snow hits me, tangling in my hair, and I'm distracted from the graveyard of bodies. It's snowing. Only, heated air blows on me like the devil's breath.

I catch a flake in my cupped hands, cradling it like I've captured a butterfly. I open my hands wide enough to peek at my find. It's gray and paper thin.

Not snow. *Ash.*

I glance above me. The sky looks bruised, as do the

clouds. And it smells ... it smells the way hell should smell. Of sulfur and spent kindling.

My gaze moves from my hands to my feet. Between bodies, piles of the ash swirl like fallen leaves. Up my eyes move. Up, up, until I see mounds of rubble and tilted phone poles. Crumbling streets, some with large sinkholes, stretch off towards the ruins of a city.

My carefully crafted memory never showed me this. It wouldn't know how to string together so many awful sights.

None of the skyscrapers are completely intact. Some looked chewed upon, like a giant creature came, got a taste, and found it lacking. Others look like they're decaying, slowly shedding their sleek chrome exteriors and tinted windows for steel cables and concrete skeletons. One skyscraper looks as though someone took a giant axe to it and felled it like a tree. Its upper half leans against another.

Then there are the gaping holes between some of them, like some of these behemoths have already collapsed.

Do people still live there? What sort of existence must they eek out?

I take a few more steps forward. The sight of this world— my world, the one I don't remember—robs me of breath.

The drone of an engine has me tearing my eyes away from the ruins and towards the sky. In the distance I can make out several aircrafts.

I was wrong to think there was any safety in the silence. The jets are not nearly done with this place. I begin to move, though all I really want is to collapse.

I catch sight of a military vehicle partially buried beneath the rubble. I stumble over to it. As I get closer, I can hear the low purr of an idling engine. The machine gun responsible for the earlier noise is welded to the bed of this vehicle. The body of a soldier slumps over the weapon.

The driver side window is shattered, and when I open the door, another body tumbles out.

I'm numb to the sight of death. I step over the dead soldier without giving him a second glance and hoist myself into the car.

The key's already in the ignition, so all I have to do is shift the car into reverse and press on the gas to get it going. I hear a sick thump as the body in the bed of the vehicle hits the metal wall that separates us. More sick thumps come as I drive over the bodies littering the ground. I white-knuckle the steering wheel as each one jostles my injuries and shakes my unsettled stomach.

My hands tremble, sweat drenches my clothes, and self-preservation alone sustains me. I maneuver the car out of the graveyard, and then I floor it.

The vehicle tears down the street that leads into the city. Wind gusts through the shattered windows, whipping my hair around my face.

I can no longer see the encroaching aircrafts, but there's no way I escaped undetected. The streets I drive are utterly abandoned. I've made myself a target simply by being on them.

Now that I'm free of my captors, I could simply pull over and flag down one of these jets. They're likely the king's. But I have no way of knowing whether they'd recognize me. They might mistake me for an enemy and gun me down.

And then there's a larger matter of returning to the king. If I want to live, he's my last chance. But what would a depraved king want with an injured, soon-to-be amputated woman who has no memory? I can't imagine I'd like whatever he has in store.

No, better to die on my own terms than to live on his.

A bottle of amber liquid rests on the seat next to me, and I grab it, unscrewing the lid and lifting it to my nose. The astringent smell of alcohol burns my nostrils.

I bring it to my lips and take several swallows. I grimace at the taste and my stomach roils. But in its wake, a pleasant warmth spreads down my throat, taking the barest edge off the pain.

Once I get the chance to stop, I'll pour the rest on my wound. At this point, I doubt it will do much good—the arm probably has to go—but I'm too desperate not to try.

Close up, the city is even worse off than I initially thought. I have to swerve around piles of rubble, and at one point, turn around and take an alternate route altogether. The structures that rise on either side of me have been tagged, and bullet holes riddle many of them.

There's so much evidence of civilization, and yet I see not a single soul.

A sound like thunder rises up behind me. When I glance out my side view mirrors, I see a helicopter heading straight for me. It quickly overtakes the vehicle, before banking left and circling around.

"Fuck."

I jerk the wheel and pull the car off into a subterranean parking garage.

Across the street a building rises high into the air. Most of its windows have long since fallen away, but it appears sturdy enough for me to occupy until the chopper passes.

Shoving the liquor bottle into my back pocket, I stumble out of the car and head for the skyscraper across the street. The stairwell inside cants a little to the side. The whole building is starting its slow slide back into the earth.

I make it up ten flights before I stagger out onto a random floor. This is the last push my body will endure. I can feel it in my marrow.

The plate-glass windows that once covered the outer walls are shattered. A howling wind slides through what remains, kicking up dust and stirring my hair.

The blades of the chopper beat outside, and I can hear a chorus of engines closing in on our location.

Somehow, the king has found me.

CHAPTER 5

I PULL THE gun from the small of my back.

Heavy boots jog up the stairs. Despair sets in.

Sick, injured, but not free. Never free.

I back up as the king's men pour out of the stairwell. There's at least a dozen of them and they're covered from head to toe in gear. Their guns are bared, but almost immediately their barrels swivel around the room, looking for threats other than the one in front of them.

One of men parts through the group and removes his helmet. I have to lock my knees to keep from falling.

The king.

My tormentor and my husband.

I don't remember him, and yet a part of me aches with

such ferocity that I know he's imprinted in my bones. Or maybe it's just the look in his eyes. It's the first time I've seen compassion, and it railroads me.

There's also a good dose of horror in those eyes of his. They track each of my features. He can see my sickness and my wounds.

With a shaky hand, I point the gun at that face. I don't want to feel this way—like I belong to someone. I'd rather die than live a prisoner shuffled between two enemies.

Behind him, his men turn their weapons on me. The king holds up a hand and signals to his men to hold their fire.

"Put the gun down, Serenity."

I don't. I don't react at all. I'm incapable of reacting, frozen between my heart and my head.

He should die.

He must live.

He needs to pay.

He wants me safe.

"Put it down." I think he has an idea where my mind is because he's coaxing. "You're not going to shoot me."

I cock the gun.

His body tenses at the sound, but he's still edging forward. "You can't kill me. You know this. My men will take you out if you don't put the gun down and come with me."

"I can't." I don't know anything else besides this—fighting lost causes. I was always meant to go down with the ship, not to survive it.

"You can. My queen, you already have once before."

I waver, searching for a memory that isn't there.

My aim droops. A wave of dizziness passes over me and I stumble.

"Serenity?" Is it my imagination, or does the monster in front of me sound frightened?

I try to focus on the king, but my vision's clouding. I fight to stay in the moment, but my body is finally, finally giving out.

The King

SERENITY'S EYES ROLL back. Ignoring my men's warnings, I run the last distance between us and catch her as she falls, her gun clattering harmlessly to the floor.

This feral woman. I'd learned long ago that she was most ferocious once you peeled away her layers. Whatever happened to her over the last few days had done exactly that. She didn't know enemy from friend.

I pull off a glove and touch her cheek. She's burning up.

"Serenity." I shake her lightly. "Serenity!"

She moans but doesn't wake.

"Soldiers! I need a medic!"

Men rush to my side, and things happen quickly after that. A stretcher makes its way to our floor. They have to pry her out of my hands, and when they move her, she's limp, lifeless, this woman that burns so brightly.

Fear tastes like gunmetal and blood. How long it's been since I've feared for anything, save myself. I don't like it that the most important parts of me live inside a dying woman.

When we've boarded my jet, I follow the medics into the back cabin, where a hospital room and a Sleeper have been set up. I'd known that she would need medical attention, but I'd underestimated the extent of her injuries. Vastly so.

They cut away her clothes, and her head lolls to the side. One of the men working on her curses, drawing my attention. He removes the last of Serenity's bandages. I almost gag at the sight of the wound on her upper arm. It's swollen and festering. Another medic pushes me out, and I don't fight him.

I place a shaking fist to my mouth. No, fear doesn't sit well inside me. I'm the leader of the entire globe, and the Resistance dared to hurt *my* wife, their queen.

I head to the onboard phone and dial the head of my special weapons unit. "Move ahead with our original plans." By nightfall, that Resistance outpost will be obliterated. Everyone and everything that hasn't escaped by then will be captured, and I'll make sure they understand what happens to those that cross me.

Serenity

I BLINK MY eyes open and stare at the white molding decorating the ceiling above me.

I don't know where I am.

A hand squeezes mine. "You're awake."

My entire body reacts to that voice. I've only met this man twice, and already his presence overwhelms me.

I turn my head to face the king. He sits next to the bed I'm in, my hand clasped in both of his. His eyes look sad, regretful.

I try to sit up and look around. Already my body's tensing. I may be a woman without a past, but I haven't lost the memory of the past few days. This world eats the innocent for breakfast, and it does far worse to those like me.

The king gets up to sit on the edge of my bed. He's too close. Gently he places a hand on my chest and pushes me back down.

"Not so fast," he says.

I'm a cornered creature. It makes me want to lash out.

"Let me up," I demand.

"Serenity, you're safe."

He can read me. That's good to know.

Rather than letting me up, he leans down. All sorts of unforgiving angles have sharpened his features. His expression's only tempered by his eyes, which are devouring me. When his mouth's a hairsbreadth away from mine, I realize what he's going to do. At the last second I turn my face away. His lips brush my cheek.

The king pulls away enough for me to think through the haze of his presence. Does he not know that I lost my memory? I assumed my previous captors told him, but in hindsight, they had plenty of reasons to keep this a secret.

"Is my wife suddenly shy?"

My cheeks flame.

One of his fingers trail my blush. "She *is*. How very

titillating." He leans back in, his breath warm against my throat. "Let's see how long it'll take for me to make you forget your embarrassment."

He presses a kiss to my neck.

I can't hold it in any longer.

"I don't remember you." I stare at the velvet chair the king sat in not a minute ago, but I'm not really seeing it. I swivel my head to face him. "I don't remember you."

Above me, the king's fallen ominously silent. I feel the weight of it bearing down on me. Nothing this man does is subtle. Not even his silence.

"What do you mean?" he says carefully.

"My memory is gone."

The King

MARCO.

The Resistance made it appear that he'd died at their hands, but Serenity's words paint a new picture.

Marco carried the memory suppressant on him at all times in place of a cyanide capsule. When he and Serenity were cornered, he must've used it on her. He could've still died at the Resistance's hands, but if he'd had time to give her the serum, he probably had time to die, either by his own hand or knowingly by another's.

Faithful until the very end.

The crushing weight of his absence tightens my lungs. I force my grief down. I've had plenty of time to mourn him while the Sleeper pieced Serenity back together. I won't let it ruin this day.

I stare at my wife, flummoxed by this turn of events and more than just a little unnerved that she lost her memory and I hadn't noticed.

She remembers nothing.

All those reasons she hated me so viciously—gone. I could avoid her ire altogether. I could charm her as I had the many women who passed through my bed before her. It's tempting. But as I fall into her guarded, wary eyes, I find I want the old Serenity back.

I married my hardened, angry queen because her spirit was the twin of mine. Without her past, all her rough edges will be blunted; she'd only be a shadow of herself.

I touch her cheek. "Would you like your memory back?"

"You can do that?"

My thumb strokes her skin. I'm practically vibrating with the need to take action. The weeks spent waiting for her to recover have tested my patience. Knowing it'll be a while longer until my Serenity returns is almost too much.

"I can."

"Then yes," she says, "I want my memories back."

Serenity

I DON'T LIKE doctors. Soon enough I'll find out precisely why.

The king still hasn't let me up from the bed. He has, however, stopped trying to kiss me. I'm horrified that mixed in with my relief is regret. His touch awakens all sorts of slumbering emotions.

I'm supposed to hate him, and yet he's the first person I've encountered who treats me like I'm something precious. It's heady, feeling cherished, and it's making me question everything I've been told about him.

I do, however, believe he's a bastard—otherwise, he wouldn't be holding me down while the doctor comes at me with a needle.

"Let me go," I growl, trying to push him and the other guard they called in off of me.

"I'm seriously questioning your memory loss," he mutters under his breath. Louder, he says, "It's just a needle."

I don't care if it's just a needle. I'm tired of people asserting their will on me.

The king nods to the doctor. The man in the white coat captures my arm and steadies it. Before I can pull it away from him, the needle slips under my skin, and he empties the antidote into my veins.

It's over before I can react. The king lets up as the doctor moves away. I glare at him as I rub the crook of my elbow.

Belatedly, I realize I'm rubbing my arm with my injured one. Only, it no longer hurts.

I've been too distracted by the king to notice what else about me is different. I roll back the sleeve of my shirt, expecting ... something.

What I don't expect is smooth skin.

It's gone—the wound, the infection, the scar that should mark it. My skin prickles. Not only has the king saved my arm from amputation, he's removed all evidence that there ever was an injury to begin with.

It reminds me eerily of my memory wipe, replacing the ugly and scarred with something new and unsullied.

"It's gone." I run a finger over it. When I look up at the king, I can tell he's drinking in my wonder. "How?"

"The East's medicine is better than the West's. You've been inside the Sleeper for a long time."

"'The Sleeper'?"

The doctor's lingering at the foot of my bed, and now he clears his throat. "Your memories won't return all at once," he says. "The bulk of them will come to you in three hours or so, but it'll take up to several days for the drug to fully reverse the effects of the memory suppressant."

"Is that all?" the king asks.

"Yes, Your Majesty." The doctor bows to the king, and then he and the guard take their leave.

It's just the two of us again.

My eyes meet the king's.

"Want to see the rest of our home?" he asks.

My heart skips. From prisoner to queen. I may be trapped in a whole different way here, but I much prefer the king's presence to that of Lieutenant Begbie's. We'll see if it'll remain that way once I get my memories back.

I nod to the king. Hopefully a tour of this place will break up the strange tension crackling between us.

He extends a hand to me. I don't bother taking it, not so soon after he held me down. I'm not above pettiness.

This, oddly enough, makes the king's eyes twinkle. "Some things, Serenity, not even memory can touch."

CHAPTER 6

Serenity

NOTHING'S HAPPENING.

Granted, it's only been thirty minutes, but I've taken to stalking through what appears to be an honest-to-goodness palace. The king's sly smiles only serve to make my foul mood even fouler.

The man beside me, for his part, has been cordial and chivalrous and completely and utterly fake. It makes me want to rake my hands through his hair and shake him until the calculation in his eyes drips onto his tongue and out his mouth. He's acting like I'm a ticking time bomb and he's waiting for me to explode.

I hate it just as much as I hate each subsequent room I enter. I don't like the gold filigree that adorns just about everything, or the intricate designs carved into the very woodwork of this place. I don't like the white, white walls and the polished floors. The delicate art and the crystal chandeliers.

The sheer opulence of it is an insult to the land beyond the walls.

"They were right about you, weren't they?" I ask, rotating to the king. When I catch sight of him, déjà vu ripples through me, but I can't place it—yet.

He's already studying me, like I'm some fascinating creature he wishes to collect.

"Right about what?" He lays his hand on the small of my back, trying to steer me out of his drawing room—or is it his tea room? They all have absurd names and more absurd purposes.

"Your cruelty." I shrug off his touch, striding ahead of him.

The ploy doesn't work. He's much taller, his legs much longer, and in a few short paces he's cut me off.

The king looms over me, and he takes a step forward.

I stand my ground, though it means brushing against him.

"Have you not already figured that out for yourself? You've always been able to see right through me," he says, his voice low. The pitch is both secretive and threatening, and I can't stop the goosebumps that spread down my arms.

He's the boogeyman, and he's come to claim me all over again.

With that thought, I catch a memory. Just a snippet,

really.

"Serenity?"

My hand was already on the door. I turned back to face an older man with hair the color of dusty wheat.

The wrinkles around his eyes and mouth deepened. "As an emissary, if an accord is ever to be reached between us and the Eastern Empire, you will likely be a key player in it."

I swallowed and nodded. I now carried a heavy responsibility.

"Do you know what that means?"

I waited for him to finish.

His gaze lingered on me a long time before he finally answered his own question. "One day you'll meet the king."

I blink, and the object of my memory is in front of me again.

The king tilts his head. "You just had your first memory, didn't you?"

I nod. The man from my past—the man I spoke with—he's at the edge of my mind and the tip of my tongue. I'm positive I know him, but his identity still eludes me.

"What did you remember?" He picks up a lock of my hair and rubs it as he asks.

He wants to touch me. He's been fairly obvious about this, but I sense his impatience increasing.

"Nothing that I can make sense of."

Those dark eyes probe mine. "That'll change soon enough." *And then you'll be mine.* I swear I hear the promise, though he never voices it.

The king backs off, but that stubborn hand of his presses into the small of my back again. There's no use fighting him on this; he's going to keep doing it, and I'm going to keep losing.

In the halls, men and women pass by, and they're just as ridiculous as the rest of this place. The people here wear fabrics with fine names I doubt, even if I could remember, I'd know.

Their outfits are intricate things that come in colors brighter than I knew existed, and each one is paired with decorative medals and sabers or ropes of jewels wrapped around necks and wrists. Their hair's too coiffed, their teeth too white, their skin too stretched, their bodies too soft.

It all looks so luxurious and impossibly fake.

I don't belong here.

The king must see my lingering attention on the people who side-eye me. He leans in, his lips brushing the shell of my ear. "None of them are as beautiful as you, *nire bihotza.*"

I scowl at him. "I don't care about your standards of beauty."

If anything, it annoys me. These men and women bask in the opulence of it. But how many lives has this lifestyle cost?

The king's gaze tracks my movements, and I wonder if I'm one of the lives it's claimed.

I suspect I am.

In the brief silence between us, a dizzying number of questions bloom. It's amazing how many a girl with only a few days of memory can have. I want to know more about who the king is, who I am, who my enemies are, why wrong seems right and right seems wrong. Most of all, I want to know how I've been bent and twisted into this person that seems to hate and be hated so fiercely by everyone, save the king.

"Why did you marry me?" I ask as we leave the king's grand ballroom. I won't even touch on the ridiculousness of a room dedicated to nothing but dancing.

"Ssssh. I'll answer your questions soon enough. Let me enjoy the last few minutes before you hate me again."

I know his words are meant to grate, but I doubt he realizes how ominous I find them. What would it take for a woman like me to hate him?

"When I was a prisoner, they told me you killed my family," I say.

"They told you that?"

"They told me many things. Is it true?"

His features are guarded. "You'll know soon enough."

And I do.

WE'RE IN THE palace gardens when it hits.

I stumble, reaching out for the king—Montes. After the bits and pieces I received inside the palace, I assumed the rest of my memories would subtly surface. I didn't imagine *this*.

This is a barrage of enemy fire. It rips through me suddenly and violently.

Montes's arms lock around my torso as I gasp, my messy golden hair dangling around me.

Every memory feels like an epiphany, and I can't possibly describe the euphoria that comes with each. Life is a series of experiences that stack, one on top of the other.

I see my mother and my father—the man from my first recalled memory now has an identity! I see bikes with training wheels. Suburbia. My parents hold my hands and, on the count of three, they swing me. There are candles and birthdays and mentions of war breaking out in Europe.

There are chalk drawings and games of tag with the kids on my street—some I've known for ages, some who are part of the recent influx of immigrants. Nail polish and days out with my mother while my father buries himself in work. My childhood crush that lives down the street.

The act of remembering is magic; I get to live a little of my life all over again.

And then ...

And then, somewhere along the way, they turn.

For every ray of light each happy memory casts, there is a much darker shadow.

I moan as I hear phantom explosions. I see blood spray. This dark past is sucking me under.

I step out of the king's embrace and hold my head. "No, no, no."

One bad memory follows the last. My mom's broken neck, soldiers with glassy eyes. The first four men I killed—my friends watch me with wary eyes after that. A bomb that takes over the sky and hides the sun. My city, my home, my childhood crush and everyone else is obliterated in a single blast.

Then, radiation, everywhere. In the food, the water,

our bodies. Civilizations swiftly fell into depravity when the last pillar of humanity gave out.

My father's body cradled in my arms.

I feel the loss all over again. Fresh. New. As though in this moment I lose my mother, my father, my land, my freedom all at once.

Through it all is a single face, the answer to all my anger and anguish.

Montes Lazuli.

The king did this. I blink back tears. He did this and now I'm his. Bound to the root of the evil I tried so hard to stop. It's almost unfathomable. There is no fairness in the world. There is no kindness.

A sick feeling twists my gut. I've laid with the king. I've let him into my body. Worse, I've let him into my heart.

I only have a moment to register that I'm going to be sick before I begin to heave. But there's nothing left in my empty stomach to purge. The queasiness doesn't abate.

"Serenity!" Montes's voice cuts through, and it's so concerned. I jerk myself away from the monster.

More memories force their way through and I press my palms into my eyes. I scream as bloody, broken bodies flood my mind. And behind it all, the kind's white, white smile. I want to smash it in and not stop until those teeth rip up my knuckles and fall out of his mouth. I let out a sob because I *like* the very smile I also detest.

It's the face behind every nightmare I've ever had, and the face that awakened my heart. It's ripping, bleeding. This shouldn't be the way of things, hating and loving something at the same time.

But it's not enough for my mind to end there. I feel the squeeze of my heart as a memory of the king holding me sneaks its way in. Another of his fearful expression when he learned of my cancer. The unguarded face he wore when nothing separated us. And through it all I see his eyes, filled with a bottomless reservoir of emotions reserved for me.

The heartless king has found his heart after all. It rests beneath my ribcage. God save me, he swapped mine for his when I wasn't looking. And now we're stuck—me with the weight of his death count, him with the guilt of my suffering.

Flesh and bone aren't meant to contain all this. The mind shouldn't stay sane when the world's fallen to chaos, and love shouldn't be able to grow in the wastelands of our consciences.

But, God save us all, it does.

It does.

CHAPTER 7

Serenity

IT'S OVER. FOR now.

But it isn't, because I have to live with a past I might've been better off forgetting. My memories are horrifying. I'm a woman remade—but into this *thing*.

I'd asked myself what kind of person married the king. Now I know. Now, I know.

I straighten, drawing in a ragged breath, my hand just above my stomach.

The world around me sharpens. The green hedges that rise up all around us, the cyan sky beyond, the marble statue of a woman holding her loose robes against her body.

"Serenity."

I focus on the voice. Montes stands in front of me, his

brows pinched together. For once he doesn't appear over-confident. He reaches out for me, but lets his hand drop.

What feral expression must I be wearing to scare him off?

"What do you remember?" he asks.

"That I hate you." A hate so deep and vast that it's blackened my soul. Even now I fight the urge to lunge at him and make good my age-old vendetta.

"Ah, yes," he says, sliding his hands into his slacks, unaware of how close I am to snapping. "I'm well acquainted with your hate." He's not even fazed.

We've done this before. Traded words like we've traded wounds. That puts me at a disadvantage because I have more memories to unearth, and he knows how to handle me.

I don't like to be handled.

Montes doesn't remove his hands from his pockets, but he does extend the crook of his arm towards me, like I'm some kind of lady.

I dropped that ruse the moment my father died in my arms.

I'm about to reject him when I notice our audience. People have planted themselves everywhere—at windows, on benches, strolling by. They act as though they're not transfixed by us.

I have a duty to uphold. I married the king to save my land. My hate is a vulnerability, one the Resistance preyed upon when they took me. I can't let these people see it. The king and I have many, many battles ahead of us, and our relationship is the least of them.

The world's still in turmoil and the king—the ruler of it all—has used fear to win his subjects over. I know quite a bit about fear. It pulls people into line, but it also draws in the predators. The moment he shows weakness, they'll attack.

I can't let that happen, even now when I'd like to see him suffer. So I take his arm and let him lead me away like I'm a frail, dainty thing. All the while, I flash hard looks at those that catch my eye.

For I, too, am something to fear.

"Do I finally have my Serenity back?" the king asks, leaning his head towards mine.

"I am not yours."

"You are."

"No."

He stops us in front of a bubbling fountain, our audience still pretending not to watch.

His hand glides out of his pocket and captures my arm, reeling me in. "Yes, you are," he breathes. He brushes a lock of hair from my face. "Hello, Serenity."

"Let me go." I give his hold the barest of tugs, aware of the eyes on us.

"I'm glad to have you back." He smiles at me, and it's almost too much. "I missed you and your anger."

I narrow my eyes on him. "I never left."

"You did, and now you're back, and I want a kiss."

I look at him like he's mad—he *is* mad. I'm still trying to get over the fact that I have to kiss him at all, and now he wants me to freely give him affection amongst an audience?

60

Up until now, I've been careful dolling out my affection. That won't change today.

He must see that I'm not going to give in because before I have a chance to respond, his lips descend on mine and he takes matters into his own hands.

THIS IS SOMETHING else that the king does—he seizes what's not freely given. You could say it's a strength of his.

And now it's a kiss.

None of my memories could've prepared me for the sensation of being enveloped by the king. I taste him and breathe him in through my nose. How I'd forgotten his scent. It's unnamable, but I enjoy it nearly as much as the glide of his lips. Lips that took something that wasn't his.

I bite his lower lip. That only serves to ratchet up his hunger. His hands secure me closer to him, and he unleashes more passion, his tongue sliding over mine.

Montes's hands knead into my skin, coaxing me to give in further. If he had it his way, he'd probably strip me bare, ravish me here in the gardens, and then order everyone who saw us killed.

Like I said, he's good at instilling fear.

Someone whistles, and then I hear clapping. I break away from him at the sound, and he flashes me a triumphant grin.

The crowd continues to cheer, praising the king for what? His vigor? The ease with which he commands everyone, even his wife? That he's human enough to enjoy a kiss?

My money's on that last one.

Montes tucks me under his arm, and with a parting wave to the crowd, leads me back inside his palace.

We're still not alone here, but I've burned up the last of my patience. There's appearing weak to the outside world and then there's appearing weak to yourself.

I push his arm off of me and stride away. I've only taken a few steps when I realize this is yet another palace of his that I don't recognize. I know that I still have some memories left to remember, but I'm pretty sure I've never been here before, regardless.

"Where, exactly, are you planning on going?" Montes asks. I can hear the smirk in his voice.

"It doesn't matter so long as it's away from you." I can't do this with Montes right now. Not with all those memories so fresh. Even now they crowd my mind. The dead want vindication, and I can't deliver it.

"You have to kill him, Serenity." It's just an echo of a memory, but the voice and the vehemence of the words has me placing a shaky hand on a side table.

"You work for the king; you can't say things like that anymore," I whispered.

"No one man should have that much power," Will said.

"And what happens once he's dead, huh?" I asked. *"They'll kill me too."*

I finally remember Will, General Kline's son. We'd been friends, but something happened ... something I still haven't recalled. Now having had a taste of my memories, I dread that one.

The last remnant of memory echoes through me.

62

Perhaps I will be the WUN's Trojan horse. Perhaps I will kill the king.

I rotate to face Montes. I'd planned on killing him. Me, the dying girl, thought she could execute the immortal king.

"I wanted to see you die," I murmur. I don't know why I say it.

Montes flicks a glance at the people that linger in this area of the palace. "Leave us."

The servants and an aging couple vacate the room. The guards hesitate.

"Unless you'd like to be relieved of your duties," the king says, "I'd suggest you do as I say—and tell the men we are not to be disturbed under any circumstances."

Reluctantly, the guards leave. I see them eye me as they do so.

Once the room's emptied out, the king returns his attention to me. "You were saying?"

Not for the first time, I'm taken aback by this man. If his goal was to unsettle me, he's accomplished that.

"You've already forgotten? And here I thought I was the one with the memory loss."

"You wanted to watch me die," he says.

"Yes." Admitting this is high treason. Should he feel so inclined, the king could have me killed. It doesn't stop me from continuing on. "I wanted to be the one who killed you."

"And would you?"

My skin's crawling. I remember the horror of my situation as though it befell me yesterday. "*Yes.*"

Montes strides forward much faster than I back up. I hate it that I can't help but flee this man. Maybe once all my memories return, I will wear them like armor so that he cannot get under my skin. But right now my emotions are raw, and I feel everything—my intense hatred for him, my budding feelings.

He corners me against the wall, and then there's no escaping him.

"You can't kill me," he says, and in this moment he looks every bit as unnatural as he claims to be.

"Can't I though?" I say, peering up at him. "You bleed the same as every other man."

He slides a leg between mine. "This isn't about my immortality. It never was. See," he tips my chin up, "I don't think you *would* kill me. I think you like me too much."

"Ask me that again when I'm armed, Montes."

"That won't change anything, lonely girl." He rubs my lower lip with his thumb. I swat his hand away, and he smiles.

"I'm all you have left," he says. "Your family is gone. The last of your people gave you up."

My hand strikes him before I even think twice about it. The slap snaps his head to the side. Already I can see the beginnings of my handprint forming.

It's not enough.

"*You* are the reason my family is gone," I say. "You are the reason I'm here. You forced everyone's hand and I will never, ever let you forget it."

He rubs his jaw and his cheek. "And you think that bothers me?"

His mouth lies, but his eyes don't. I'm starting to think that some of the things he's done do in fact weigh on his conscience.

The king leans in close. "If you wanted to scare me off, you went about it the wrong way." His breath brushes against my cheek and chin. "I love your anger and your hate, and I have many regrets, but marrying you is not one of them."

I'm glaring at him. I try to move, but his body pins mine to the wall. His lips skim my jaw, heading for my mouth. I turn my head away from him.

He places a kiss at the corner of my lips. "And if you think your reluctance will stop me, then you've read me wrong."

I have read him wrong, but not in the way he thinks. My mind needs him to be wholly evil, and he's not, and my spirit does not have the iron will that it should to keep him at bay. Even now, I react to his nearness. I want more of him, and that shames me. It is one thing to enjoy the mechanics of sex, another to enjoy this—our power plays, our magnetism.

He steps away. "I have something for you."

I straighten. "I don't want anything from you, Montes."

"Not true. You want many things from me; my body, my power—"

"Your head."

"Between your thighs," he finishes.

A flush crawls up my neck. It would help not to get embarrassed about this.

"On a stake," I amend.

He clucks his tongue. "I thought you said you didn't want anything from me."

I'm at a momentary loss for words, and that's precisely when he strikes. He takes my hand and drags me out of the room.

I would fight him, but a million different memories crowd my mind. I haven't had time to process the multitude of them, but now I do.

The hours leading up to my memory loss, the Resistance attacked the king's coastal palace. We'd been cornered, I'd been close to escape, but I never made it out. Marco, the king's right-hand man and my nemesis, and I had been left to face the enemies with the last of the king's soldiers.

With my free hand I rub the skin over my heart. That's when I lost my memory. The king hadn't administered the serum, Marco had—right before he blew his brains out.

I suddenly have context to attach to all the memories I acquired from that point on. The Resistance took me to one of their outposts, held me as they would any important prisoner of war, and tried to leverage me to their advantage.

General Kline ... he'd been a part of it. Now knowing what I do, I can't decide how to feel about seeing him. He was my commander, and had my life not unfolded the way it had, he might've one day been my father-in-law. I respected him, and I was close to him. That makes the role he played during my capture that much worse. And yet, I'm not without blame either. I did something to his son, and he still managed to be civil with me.

Then there was that final day of my imprisonment. Had the king not firebombed the outpost, I would've died.

"How did you find me?" I ask Montes as he walks us down the hall. The guards posted along the corridor eye me warily as we pass. I have a reputation among their ranks. I remember slaughtering them after my father died.

Montes doesn't turn around when he replies, "The Resistance isn't the only one with spies."

"You bombed the place," I accuse.

All those bodies, all that carnage ...

"And?"

"Were you trying to save me or kill me?" It's real rich of me to be critiquing his efforts right after I admitted I wanted to execute him.

But I never pretended to be a saint.

Montes stops and swivels to face me. "You were five floors belowground, and when my contact came to retrieve you, you put a bullet in his thigh. By the time my back up came to free you, you were gone.

"Death, Serenity, is the last thing I want from you."

Montes resumes walking, tugging me after him. He leads me to an office much grander than anything I ever saw in the bunker.

I enter the cavernous room. There's a wall of books to my left and a giant oak desk towards the back of it.

"Why did you take me here?" I ask, stepping away from him.

Now that I've got my memories back, the last thing I want to do is continue to tour the king's palace. Once you've seen one palace, you've seen them all.

Montes saunters in after me. "You'll figure it out for yourself soon enough."

I give him a dark look. The king and his games ...

I meander towards the desk. When I reach it, my fingers trail over the wood surface. There are several photographs resting on it. I lift one of them up. It's a wedding photo of me and Montes. Not one of the official ones. Those I particularly relish—I'm glaring in most of them.

This is one of us outside at the reception. I'm smiling at something outside of the photo and Montes is beaming down at me. You would've almost thought we were happy in that moment.

I was terrified.

I set it down only to lift another. As soon as my eyes fall on the image, I drop it like it burns me. The heavy metal frame hits the carpet with a dull thud.

"Where did you get that?" I ask, my eyes locked on the photo. I don't want to look at it, it *hurts* to look at it, but for the life of me I can't tear my gaze away.

"Where do you think?"

Staring back up at me is a younger version of myself. In the picture I'm giving my father a side hug. He used to keep this photo in his office.

I can't breathe. I'm not sure I can keep that photo here. Seeing his face makes my soul ache in terrible ways.

I miss him, but that's not nearly a strong enough word to describe life without him. He was the sun; how do you go on living when something that huge gets extinguished?

And now to have him sit there day in and day out and watch this mockery of my life unfold. I don't know if I can stand that.

Montes picks the frame up from the floor and returns it to my desk. He doesn't say anything. He lost a father tragically too.

Resting next to the photographs is my mother's necklace. I pick it up, a slight tremor running through my hands.

The gold pendant catches the light. Montes left me the few items that have any value to me. I don't have many things to call my own, but what I do, I cherish.

"And my father's gun?" I ask.

"I'll give it back to you the moment I trust you not to shoot me with it," Montes says.

"So you *do* think I'll shoot you," I say, studying the necklace dangling from my hand.

"You're a woman that loves a good dare. I'm not gambling my life on your ability to prove me wrong."

He takes the necklace from me and clasps it around my neck. I run my fingers over the delicate chain. My eyes drift around the room.

It dawns on me. "This office is mine."

"It is—my queen needs a place to carry out world affairs."

He's given me an office before, not one that was outfitted with my personal affects. Not like this one. I don't know what I'm feeling, but it makes me uneasy.

"Why did you do all this for me?" I ask.

"This is such a small thing." He runs a hand over the veins of wood. His wily, conniving side disappears altogether. "You are my wife. I want to make you ... happy."

The man who always takes is now giving. And he wants me to be happy. Here. With him.

I don't have the heart to tell him that will never happen.

CHAPTER 8

Serenity

MONTES SHRUGS OFF his suit jacket and throws it over my chair back before rolling up his sleeves. My eyes linger far too long on his tan, corded forearms. I'd forgotten that underneath all those layers of fine clothing was a fit man.

He then grabs a cardboard box sitting off to the side and heaves it onto the desk. Tossing aside the lid, he pulls out the first file and drops it in front of the chrome computer situated in the middle of my desk.

"Here are reprints of the files you were working on. Any notes you had with the originals are, unfortunately, lost," he says, sitting on the edge of the desk.

It's hard to focus on anything he's saying. He might be six feet and some change of a man, but his presence fills the entire room.

An unfamiliar part of me wants to step between those powerful legs of his and trail my fingers over the backs of his hands.

I could do it—I know he would welcome it—but I fight the impulse. He still feels alien to me.

I'll have to lay with him tonight.

An odd combination of anxiety and anticipation flares through me.

The king watches me with those penetrating eyes of his, and I swear they can see into my mind.

I try to stay as far away from him as I can when I open the folder in front of the computer.

"Ah, yes, these reports," I say, remembering them. I'd been reading through the files when the Resistance laid siege to the king's palace. The reports had been largely skewed for the king's purposes. I'm too ruffled to point that out. "Thank you," I say instead.

"'Thank you'?" He reaches out and catches my wrist before I can step away, then reels me in.

I end up between his thighs after all.

His other hand steadies my chin. "What's going on in my vicious little wife's mind?"

I try to jerk away, but he holds me in place.

"Montes, let me go."

"Not until you tell me what you were just thinking about."

I'm so close to kneeing him in the crotch.

However, neither of us gets the chance to see our actions through.

Not before another memory hits.

All I saw was crimson blood and all I heard were Will's screams. The outer walls must've been thick to silence such agonized cries. The king's wrath was just as frightening as I'd always feared.

I squeeze Montes's thighs as a memory rolls through me. I'm being swept up in its tide.

"I'll do whatever you want, Montes, just please, stop torturing him." It was Will, after all. I might hate what he'd become, but torture ... I didn't wish that on my worst enemy.

I was halfway down the hall when I heard a bang. My body jumped at the sound, and a tear leaked out.

Gone. Will was gone.

Back in the present, I choke on a gasp.

"You killed Will." After torturing him nonetheless. Death, at that point, had been a mercy.

I try to pull away again, and again Montes refuses to release me.

"Let me the fuck go."

He ignores my command and instead forces me to look at that pleasing face of his. "Yes, I did have my men kill him," he says, "and I'd make the same decision over and over again. In case you still don't remember, your friend Will had his men shoot you," the king says. That vein in his temple pulses. "He threatened you with torture.

"Anyone who thinks to torture you, Serenity, will be made an example of, and I don't give a damn how well you know them."

I stop struggling against him, though none of my ire is gone. "Well, I do."

He sighs. "Out of all the slights against you, that's the one you punish me with?"

He catches my fist before I can land the blow, and now he holds both my hands prisoner.

I try to knee him, but the angle is all wrong. The last of his mirth leaves his face. Using the grip he has on my hands, he yanks me onto the desk next to him and rolls over me. The file scatters and the computer monitor topples over as he pins my torso down.

That vein of his still throbs, and several loose strands of his dark hair brush my cheeks. He smiles down at me, but it's not kind. "You try that again," he breathes, "and you won't like the results."

But I have rage to match his. "It'd be worth it," I say.

"For you, I imagine it might." Slowly, the anger drains from his face. He doesn't let me go, however.

Instead, he moves both my hands into one of his, and he uses the other to reaches into his pocket. Pulling out a phone, he types something onto the screen.

A moment later, the guard enters the room. I'm still pinned to the desk, and Montes appears to be five seconds away from having his way with me, yet the guard doesn't bat an eyelash.

I renew my struggles against the king.

Montes readjusts his hold, his eyes trained on his man. "Please tell the staff to see to the earlier dinner arrangements we discussed."

The guard inclines his head and bows. As his footsteps retreat from the room, the king returns his attention to me. All at once he releases my hands and straightens.

I work my jaw as I push myself up to my forearms. The urge to hit him is still riding me hard.

"You will dine with me." *You will surrender to me.*

His mouth and his eyes say two very different things.

"No." I'm not interested in either.

I stand and brush myself off. I'm wearing a dress someone else clothed me in. This entire day has been one unpleasant experience after the last.

He steps in close and tips my chin up.

"Yes, you will, even if it means having my guards drag you to dinner. Fight all you want, it won't change my mind."

Even if I didn't already have a vendetta against this man, I would develop one quickly enough.

"I'll drop you off at our room and give you time to rest and get ready," he continues.

I step away from him. "Don't bother. I'll find it myself."

I DON'T HEAD back to our room because fuck him. Instead I spend the next several hours figuring out the basic layout of the palace. When I was with Montes I didn't want a tour of the place, and I still don't, but there is use in knowing how a machine like the palace works.

This one is U-shaped with east and west wings. Montes already showed me most of the central building and the west wing. Those appear largely to serve formal functions.

The east wing, on the other hand, contains the king's official business. I pass several doors fitted with placards of the king's highest-ranking advisors. Another conference room, and a room that bears a sickening resemblance to the map rooms of the king's other palaces. I leave before I can look at any of the crossed out faces too closely. The last thing I want to see is my father's face among them.

I head back outside. A maze of hedges rise up on either side of a central pathway. Beyond them are a series of structures.

I squint up at the sky. Pinks and golds have replaced the earlier blue. I won't have time to explore all of this place, not before the king drags me off to dinner. And I'm sure he will indeed drag me to it if I resist. Montes doesn't make idle threats. Like me, he stands by his words, no matter how perverse they are.

I take in the many buildings that sit off in the distance. Towards the far corner of the palace grounds, I notice a series of long, squat structures. The soldiers' barracks, if I had to guess. I have enough time to visit them, I think, before the king calls on me. So I head there next, ignoring the two guards that follow several feet behind me.

When I arrive, I can tell I guessed right. Several soldiers loiter between buildings, some laughing with each other. Of course, that all ends when they see me. Quickly, they stand at attention, bowing as I make my way through the barracks. I sense a good dose of that earlier wariness here. It's just a feeling—perhaps the soldiers' eyes are a tad too hard, their spines a bit too straight—but I know that I'm not entirely welcome. It doesn't stop me, however, from moving through the buildings.

Mess hall, sleeping quarters, and to my utter delight, several training rooms. This, I belatedly realize, is what drew me out here. Amongst all the soft, painted faces, I feel hopelessly different. But this place that lacks adornment and smells like sweat, this I understand.

I run my hand over a metal dumbbell stacked against the wall, the grips worn down with use. I decide then and there that I won't become what I detest. I'll come here to train, and I'll earn the guards' respect or I won't, but I will not lose the soldier in me.

From behind me, one of the guards now approaches. "Your Majesty, the king's called for dinner."

CHAPTER 9

Serenity

WHEN I MEET Montes back inside the palace, he doesn't lead me to the dining room like I thought he might. Instead we head outside once more and cross the garden. The sun's already set and the sky is deep blue. I feel summer in the breeze, and it stirs such intense longing in me. The last time I felt like this, I still had my mother.

As we move beyond the hedges, it becomes clear the king is leading me to another one of the buildings sitting at the far end of the grounds. It's made of copper, marble, and most of all, glass. Hundreds of panes make up the dome alone. I've never seen a structure like this.

Montes holds my hand against the crook of his arm. I think he knows that if he lets go, I'll pull away immediately. But the gesture's strangely intimate

"Are you still angry?" he asks.

"When it comes to you, I'm always angry."

"Mmm, you must not have recalled all your memories yet. For instance, the last time I laid between those pretty thighs of yours, you were far from angry."

A blush spreads up my neck at the memory I do, in fact, recall. "Do you always get enjoyment being lewd?"

"My queen, *that* is not lewd. Lewd would be telling you how your tight little pu—"

"*Montes.*" My cheeks are flaming now, and I can't tell if I'm more embarrassed by his words or the fact that I still react like this. Both he and I are aware it's a weakness of mine.

He glances down at me, his eyes luminous as they catch the light of a nearby lamp. "That's not lewd, Serenity. That is just what it means to be your husband. And yes, I get enjoyment from making you blush. It's so very ... unlike you."

He squeezes my hand. And as I feel his fingers envelop mine, I'm reminded again that with him, intimacy isn't just a handful of memories. It's something that'll happen again, and sooner rather than later, if the intense look in his eyes is any indication.

"What are you thinking about?" he asks.

He must see all my nerves, all my anxieties, but I won't hand them to him on a platter by voicing the words.

I don't tear my eyes from his when I say, "I'm thinking that you'd give the devil a run for his money. In fact, he's probably worried that you'll set your sights on his territory next."

The corner of Monte's mouth lifts. "A good idea, Serenity. Perhaps I could consult you on hell's layout? I hear you're familiar with it."

God, I hate this man.

I turn my attention away from him, back to the structure he's leading me towards. We enter the building, and I realize exactly what it is.

A greenhouse.

My lingering irritation evaporates as my eyes sweep across the interior. I've never seen so many different plants so close together. Their leaves are waxy and their colors—I didn't realize so many different shades of green existed. But it's not just green. Pinks and yellows, reds and oranges, whites and purples and every color in between, each plant stranger and lovelier than the last.

Without thinking I begin moving through the clusters of them, inadvertently tugging the king along with me. I can feel his gaze on my face, drinking up my reaction. I pull away from him to pet a leaf.

It's a captive here, living in its own gilded cage.

Just like me.

Releasing it, I lift my gaze and take in the rest of the greenhouse. The glass panes are misted over, and the humidity is curling my hair. Hundreds of plants line the building. The size and beauty of this place is staggering.

After living in a gloomy, subterranean bunker for the last five years, the idea of a room filled with light and plants is almost incomprehensible.

So, naturally, the king has one of these places on his

property.

"And my queen's frowning again."

"This is just another room with a ridiculous purpose."

He actually looks pleased, and I can't fathom why.

He takes my hand and leads me down an aisle. Then he begins pointing. "*Papaver somniferum*—the opium poppy. Extracts of the plant can be used as high grade pain relievers, amongst other things. *Camellia sinensis*—the dried leaves of that one make tea. *Coffea arabica*—the plant that's saved you from killing everyone before eight a.m."

"Not everyone. Just you," I correct.

He smirks and points to another plant. "*Cannabis sativa*—helps with appetite, sleep, anxiety, lowers nausea. A wonder drug, really.

"Many of these plants are already being used medicinally," he continues, "and outside of my greenhouses, they are hard to find. Many more of them are being researched and genetically modified, again for science."

And now I understand the king's smug expression. I assumed he didn't care about saving the world his war had broken. I hadn't imagined that maybe some of the laboratory testing he'd been working on was to benefit the people he'd so abused.

He steers me down the aisle we're on and we enter another room of the greenhouse. High above us I see the stars through the domed glass roof I'd caught a glimpse of outside.

The plants here cling to the edges of the room. In the middle of it all is a table set for two that's illuminated by candlelight.

I clutch the chain of my mother's necklace. I've never been romanced, outside of one other candlelit dinner also hosted by the king. And that last time, to my great embarrassment, it worked.

It probably will again.

Montes herds me forward, his dark eyes twinkling. It's even harder to not be drawn in by him when the room's dim glow draws attention to all the pleasing angles of his face.

He likes this, I realize. Indulging me in his lavish lifestyle. He hasn't yet figured out that it's a double-edged sword. I am a child of war and famine. I don't know how to indulge, and I don't want it.

He must see me backpedaling because he increases the pressure he places on my lower back. Reluctantly I let him steer me to the table. I approach it the way I would anything else that's too good to be true.

The plates and cutlery rest atop indigo and gold linens embroidered with the king's initials. I glance down at my rings. The colors match.

"Blue and gold—they're your colors," I say. I'm only now putting together the symbolism that's been woven into the king's rule.

"And yours as well, my queen that loves the stars and the deep night," he says, shrugging off his jacket and taking a seat across from me.

Just like earlier today, he undoes his cufflinks and rolls his shirt up past his elbows. And now I'm back to staring at his forearms.

This is carefully crafted seduction, and I'm defenseless

against it.

"What do you want from me?" I ask, forcing my gaze up. His face isn't a better option.

I can't bear this. I was raised on duty and honor, and I can't find any in my situation. I'm trapped in a role where I'm everyone's traitor—even my own.

He gives me a penetrating look. "Everything."

"You know that's impossible."

"Is this another one your facts?" Montes asks, leaning forward.

Before I can answer, I hear the door to the greenhouse open. A long beat of silence stretches on while two servants enter, one bearing a bottle of wine, the other a tray with two plates on it.

"Here, I'll take that from you," the king says, grabbing the neck of the wine bottle from the server while the other one sets the plates in front of us.

Once the food has been laid out, both servers bow and exit the room.

Montes pours us each a glass of wine from the uncorked bottle he holds. "Let's play a little game," he says, handing my glass to me. "I'll ask you a question and you'll either tell me the answer, or you'll drink."

I narrow my eyes at him but take my drink from his outstretched hand. The last time I played this game, I slept through the next day's negotiations, and when I woke, I was sicker than a dog. A downside. I also kept the king from sleeping with me. An upside.

"I'll play, but only if you answer my questions as well."

His mouth curves up. "Of course. That's only fair."

As if he knows a thing about fairness.

He leans back in his seat, the flame of the candles danc-ing in his eyes. I might as well be seated with the devil; Montes is handsome enough and wicked enough for the job.

"You told me once that hate isn't the only thing you feel for me," he says. "What else is it that you feel?"

He starts with that? *That?*

I take a drink of my wine. Montes smiles, and I realize too late that my reaction was an answer in and of itself.

"Were you planning on killing my father and me before we arrived in Geneva?" I ask.

If he gets to ask hard questions, then so do I.

Montes's sighs. "This is supposed to be fun."

"It's not my fault you're a bastard," I say. "Now answer my question."

The vein in his temple begins to pound. "Tread lightly, my queen," he says softly.

We stare each other down, and I think we both realize we've met our match.

Finally, he says, "Death is always on the table when it comes to my negotiations. You know that."

He *had* planned to kill us.

"Did you order my father killed?"

"Ah-ah," he says, his voice jovial, but his eyes are hard. "Already forgetting the rules."

I glower at him.

"Why did you marry me?" he asks.

I go still. "It was me or my country."

"That was the only reason?"

"It's my turn." My voice is icy. I'm seconds away from overturning the table—or lunging across it and attacking the king.

"Did you order my father killed?" I repeat.

"No, Serenity, I didn't."

I swirl my wine glass, agitated. What had I hoped for him to say—that he had?

"Was saving your country the only reason you married me?" he asks.

Did he really expect any answer but yes?

"I vomited when I learned I'd have to marry you," I say. "Do you really want to rehash this all out?"

"No. What did the Resistance do to you while they held you prisoner?"

He tricked me out of a turn.

I grip the stem of my glass tightly and force myself to muse on his question. The man across from me is not a soldier. He has no true concept of torture and humiliation. But he is my husband, and he is the megalomaniac that has bent the world to his will.

I grab my glass and drink. With him, violence begets violence.

I tilt my head back and look at the stars that I can barely see through the domed ceiling above. I want to say I watch them because they are beautiful, but I can't lie to myself about this. I'm avoiding the king's reaction to what I'm about to ask.

I pull myself together. I'm not a wimp, and if I have the courage to ask the question, then I should also have the courage to face the king as I do so.

Leveling my gaze on him, I ask, "What do you feel for me?"

Surprise flickers through his features before he collects himself. Once he does, I wish I could draw the words back into my mouth.

Montes gives me a slow, smoldering smile, one that I feel low in my belly. He lifts his glass and takes a drink.

Neither of us has touched our food yet, and at that the moment, hunger is the furthest thing from my mind.

He sets his glass down, his gaze dropping to the base of my throat. "How old were you when you lost her?" He nods to my mother's necklace.

I wrap my hand around it, and already I'm shaking my head. No, he doesn't get to know about her. His war killed her, along with a million other mothers. She's beyond his reach now, and I won't give him what's left of her.

The wine I swallow down barely makes it past the lump in my throat.

It's my turn, and all the words I can think of have turned bitter on my tongue. "Tell me, what is the price of my life, Montes?"

Montes has been swirling his glass, but now he stops. "What are you really asking?"

"That," I say. "I'm asking that. What is the price of my life?"

I'm setting myself up for failure, and I want him to fail me. I want him to disappoint me with his answer because I don't hate him with all my heart, but I desperately wish I did.

He takes a sip of his drink.

That's what I thought.

Maybe my life is worth one country to him. Maybe it's worth less. Whatever the cost, he knows it would burn me worse than his silence.

I push back my chair and stand. "Some epic love you are," I mutter. My words carry no vitriol. Perhaps that is what makes him flinch.

"You love me?" He says.

And he latches onto that. I shake my head. "I don't blame you for it, you know. Thirty years is a long time to spend collecting countries like toys." Long enough to lose your conscience.

He stands. "Serenity."

I ignore him as I stride away, and there is something satisfying about unveiling the monster behind all the pretty prose.

"*Serenity!*"

I can hear his shoes click against the marble floor.

"You're wrong," he says when I don't stop. "You want to know why I didn't answer the question? Because I don't know the answer, and that terrifies me. But I do know this: what we have is epic. Why do you think our enemies want to separate us so badly?"

Now I halt.

"We were enemies before this all began," I say.

"I was never your enemy, Serenity. The world saw that when they watched the peace talks, and they saw it again when they watched our wedding. That is why the Resistance is trying to come between us."

I swivel to face him. Even this far away, he swallows up

space. If anyone were to be a world leader, it would be him. He's mesmerizing, and not just for his looks. Maybe it's all those hidden years of his that take up space in this room because they can't be worn on his face. Whatever it is, it only makes him more of an enigma.

"You married me to secure your power," I say.

He laughs at that and takes a step forward. "Is that what you've convinced yourself of? That my primary reason for marrying you was to secure my power?"

The hairs on my arm lift at what he isn't saying.

"You and I both know I could've crushed the WUN under my boot if I so chose. They are more of a pain because I secured them peacefully."

The scariest things are those that you don't understand. That was what always frightened me about the king—I couldn't fathom his motives. I thought I was beginning to understand him for a while there, but I wasn't.

He saunters towards me slowly. "I'm afraid that when it comes to strategy, my queen, I've outmaneuvered you."

Adrenaline courses through me as my body gets battle ready. "Why would you marry me if not for power?" There's no more diving into a glass of wine for either of us.

I'm the ugly truth and he's a pretty lie, and we are always, always circling each other. I think that he's right. What passes between us is every bit as epic as I'd always feared.

He closes the last of the distance and reaches up to cup my jaw.

I tilt my head away from him. "Don't."

"Can't I touch my wife?"

It's so unlike him to ask.

There's nothing left for me to hang onto when he's like this. My hate's too ephemeral, my heart too hopeful.

I close my eyes and nod.

A second later the smooth skin of his fingers brush my cheeks, my mouth. They leave, and then his lips are caressing mine.

He tastes like a taboo. He's mine.

"It was better when I simply hated you," I murmur against him. My head and my heart are at war, and the fallout's ripping me in two.

"I know," he says, his lips still pressed to mine. "That won't stop me from trying to win you over, but I know."

I open my eyes. The king's dark, unfathomable ones stare back at me. My pulse quickens a little more. I'm not supposed to want to know what he's thinking or be pulled in by the same allure that's won over countries and officials.

But I do and I am. His life frightens me, but he's also a kindred spirit. His darkness complements my own.

"Sit back down," he murmurs against my lips.

I let him lead me back; I have nowhere else to go. He takes his own seat and reaches for his cutlery.

I lift my own fork and spear a pasta noodle. They used to serve us spaghetti in the bunker, but as soon as the flavor hits my taste buds, I realize this is a different beast entirely. If what I was used to was water then this would be wine.

Montes watches me the entire time.

I swallow. "Stop that."

"Then stop making that expression when you eat."

"What expression?" I ask.

"Like you're being sweetly fucked."

I shouldn't have asked. And I definitely need more alcohol for this conversation. Montes refills my glass right before I reach for it.

"I'm surprised by you," I say, eyeing my topped-off drink.

His eyes noticeably brighten. "Oh, really?"

This man and his ego.

"Feeding wine to the woman with stomach cancer." Last time I overdrank, I vomited blood up.

The luster in his gaze dies out a little. "The Sleeper's controlling the cancer."

That's good enough for me. I take a healthy drink.

"But I still have it." I place the glass back down.

"You do. But you won't for long."

I really want to kick my legs up on the table and settle into my chair. Instead, I take another bite of the pasta. It's heavenly.

Damnit, I think I *am* making a face while I eat it.

"We haven't discovered a cure yet," he continues, "but my researchers are close."

I take another drink of my wine. "I wouldn't hold my breath if I were you." Sure, there are experts galore, but Montes has only been funding those that furthered his war.

"What are you saying?" That vein begins pulsing again.

"I don't think you can save me."

Montes lets my words sink in, and for a split second he looks so reasonable. Then the bubble pops.

He stands swiftly, shaking the table as he does so. I stare up at him as he rounds it, his eyes sparking with emotion.

We're fire and gunpowder. Something's about to explode, and I lit the match.

He kicks my chair out and leans in, resting his hand along the back of it. "I can save you, and I *will*."

I meet his gaze. God save me, the man means it.

I swallow. "Montes, it's always going to be this way." I feel like a soothsayer as I speak. "Whether it's the cancer or the Resistance, something's going to get me."

My number's already been drawn. It's simply a matter of time. Montes is the only one besides me that's fighting it at all.

"Haven't you heard?" he says. "Death doesn't come to this house."

CHAPTER 10

Serenity

IT'S LATE BY the time we return to the palace. Before I can think twice about it, I take off my shoes. I can't remember the last time I walked barefoot outside, and I shouldn't be taken by something as simple as my naked feet touching the ground, but I am. In times of peace, people probably don't have to think about wearing shoes, but I've always had to. You never know when you're going to have to run.

It's a little thing, this freedom, but I enjoy it. I steer us off the stone path to feel the sensation of grass between my toes. I have to bite the inside of my cheek to keep from smiling as I feel the spongy, moist earth beneath my feet and the itchy prick of the lawn. Right now I don't care that a dozen lights are still on in the palace windows, or that we're in view of several guards. Nothing can come between me and this small pleasure.

Montes must notice my fascination with the textures of the earth because he maneuvers us towards an area where the soil is free of grass and plant life. Neither of us acknowledges that I'm interested in walking through the mud and dirt.

He subtly steers me to another section of the palace grounds. Sharp pebbles bite into the pads of my feet. I curse, and suddenly, Montes's hand is trembling in mine.

When I glance over at him, he's laughing.

I push him. "You did that on purpose."

Now he's not bothering to curb his laughter. "I did."

"That's what I get for trusting you." The usual venom is gone from my words. I find I enjoy Montes's teasing at the moment.

"C'mon," he says. "I promise no more nasty surprises."

He leads me to a hose. Like many things here, this mundane piece of equipment is something of a novelty. I've seen and, on a couple occasions, used hoses before, and the WUN still had some running water when I left it, but no one waters their lawns anymore.

Montes turns it on and angles the spray at my toes.

"Lift your foot." I do so. He grabs my ankle and rinses the dirt off. I have to brace myself against his shoulder to keep my balance. It's oddly intimate. He lets go of my right foot and beckons for the other.

I study his features as he rinses me off. He's caring for me, I realize. This is what friends do, what family and lovers do. I must indeed be a strange, strange girl to covet

93

these moments with the king more than the fancy dinners he arranges.

He releases my foot, and then we're moving again.

The king's palaces have always looked ominous to me, and tonight's no different. Beneath the stars, we have no ranking, no responsibilities, no civilization, but inside this building that all changes.

We cross the threshold, and I bid goodbye to the few threads of freedom I found outside. I let myself lose count of all the twists and turns that take us to Montes's room.

Our room, I correct as we step inside.

I hover near the door. A big four-poster bed looms in front of me. I have to get in it with the king. I sober up instantly.

Most of my memory has returned. I know what we do in beds like this one, but I still feel like a stranger in my own body. And after our dinner in the greenhouse and our walk through the gardens, I'm feeling strangely vulnerable.

The slick sounds of material sliding off jolts me. I glance over at Montes just as he removes his last article of clothing. His deeply tan body is fully on display, and I'm having trouble fighting my own impulses. It takes most of my energy just to pretend he's not every bit as lovely as he knows he is.

He pads over to me. His hands brush my hair off my shoulders. "Scared?"

How have I ended up here? With no family save for Montes, the very person that took them all away from me.

"Of you? No."

94

It's my conflicted emotions that scare me. They're sucking me under, and I'm afraid that once they do, I won't like the woman they fashion me into.

"Then come to bed."

It's not a request, it's a dare, and he punctuates it by pulling loose the tie around my dress. The fabric parts with a little encouragement from the king, and then my outfit slides off.

Montes circles me, his hand trailing across my flesh. With a flick of his wrist he undoes my bra. His fingers move to my panties, and he hooks them around the thin bands of material and yanks them down before returning once more to face me.

I blink, startled, as we stand naked across from one another.

Montes's eyes dip down and then he's backing up towards the bed. "Come, Serenity."

I hesitate, but even this is a lost cause. He's my husband. This is a part of the package.

Following him to bed, I slip beneath the sheets and keep my back to Montes. My muscles tense. I'm not going to fall asleep anytime soon.

An arm snakes around my waist and Montes pulls me against his chest. I can feel every naked inch of him pressed along my back.

He breathes in my hair, nuzzling the shell of my ear. "I will never let you go, and I will never let you die. You will be mine, always."

HANDS GLIDE OVER my legs. Am I in a dream or out of one? I can't tell.

I crack my eyes open. Early morning light filters into the room, and my lips crack into a smile. As long as I live, the sight of it will never grow old.

Montes's lips brush against mine, stealing my smile. The kiss is quick, gentle, and his mouth's gone before I can react at all.

He moves down my body, his hair tickling the skin of my chest as he drops lower.

I push myself up onto my elbows. "What are you doing?"

Montes skims a kiss along my ribcage, his rough cheek scraping my flesh. "Waking my wife up."

This isn't terribly out of character for him, but I'm still not used to it.

He presses my torso back to the mattress. His hand stays against my sternum until I stop resisting. His other slides lower. And lower.

I catch his wrist.

I'm so, so terribly conflicted, mostly because I enjoy doing this with the king.

"Let go, Serenity," he says, gazing down at me. His eyes are too dark, his skin too tan, his teeth too white. His features are unnatural, just like the rest of him.

"You first," I say.

Ever so slowly, he lifts his hand from my skin and holds it up in surrender. I don't trust him to play by any sort of rules when it comes to being physical.

A knock on the door interrupts us.

He sighs. "Grab a robe."

"Why?" I ask, but I'm already pushing myself out of bed and heading towards what looks to be a closet. The sheer quantity of clothing inside it has me reeling back. I'm not seeing a robe. This really would be easier if someone thinned out the clothes in here by a factor of ten.

I grab the first item I do see and don it. Too late I realize I've slipped on one of Montes's button-downs, and now the door's opening.

The king flashes me a heated look at my outfit. I want to knock the expression off his face. For his part, he's managed to slide on a pair of lounge pants.

A group of women enter the room, and—oh God. No, please, no.

They're carrying canvas bags in colors ranging from pink to black. I've seen those bags before. This doesn't bode well.

"What's going on?" I take a step back.

"Press conference in … " he strides over to a dresser and picks up a watch resting on it, "three hours."

"You're telling me this now?"

"Someone has to keep you on your toes." He flashes me a grin, like this is all good fun.

As soon as I reestablish myself here, I'm getting my own schedule.

The women bustle over to me, and my earlier fears are confirmed. They're here to primp me up.

"I can do this myself." I speak to the room in general, but it's Montes who answers.

"I didn't ask if you could."

They usher me over to a chair and get to work, touching my face, running their hands through my hair, brandishing sets of jewelry for me to try on.

The only things I tend to accessorize are my weapons.

Montes pulls up a chair next to me.

"Oh, staying this time are you?" I try to turn my head to him, but that earns me a firm tug on my scalp and a gentle admonishment from the hairstylist hovering over me.

I give myself fifteen minutes before the last of my patience runs out and I turn violent.

"I need to prep you on your speech." I can hear mirth in his voice. My trigger finger itches.

"What speech? Wait, *my* speech?" Just when I thought all of the morning's nasty surprises were over.

"The video of you returning to the WUN has been leaked. The world's seen the footage of you." The footage of me drenched with my enemy's blood.

And my father's.

"They also know that the Resistance captured you—albeit, briefly. The terrorist organization released video and a statement on the event, and I spoke about it shortly after you were taken."

For a girl who's lived underground for the last five years, there's an awful lot of media attention on me—and most of it bad.

"What do you want me to say?" I ask. I'm legitimately curious how the king handles affairs like this.

"What would you say if you were still an emissary for the WUN?"

"I'd tell them that you were the devil."

Above me I hear at least one woman suck in a breath.

"That's not what I meant," the king says.

"I know." And I do. "You want me to debrief them on my experience?"

"You don't actually have to worry. We have a speech already written for you. All you're going to do is read from the teleprompter."

"You're seriously trusting me with a microphone and your subjects?" I badly want to look over at Montes just to read his face.

"*Our* subjects. You've been practicing for this for the better part of your life, Serenity. This isn't just my world; it's your world and it's their world. Do right by it."

DO RIGHT.

Montes's words linger with me even as we slide into the car that will take us to the press conference.

What is right?

I don't know anymore.

I glance over at the king, who's flipping through a stack of papers one of his aides gave him.

He is so sure of everything, and I am sure of nothing. I can't tell which is the worse fate—to question everything, to be paralyzed by indecision, or to question nothing and move through the world blind to any other way of existing save for your own.

My thoughts are whisked from me as we leave the palace grounds. This is the first time since the king retrieved me that I see the world outside.

I place my hand against the window. Fields of weeds and wild grass float by. Wherever we are, it's far from any broken city. A morning mist clings to the ground, but with each passing minute it dissipates a little more.

"Where are we?"

I don't expect Montes to answer. He didn't last time. So I'm surprised when he does.

"We're in what used to be known as England."

I remember England from the history books. It was one of the first countries to fall. By the time my father and I flew to Geneva for the peace talks, the Northern Isles were one of King Montes Lazuli's most secure regions. The Resistance didn't have a great foothold there, which might be one of the reasons why the king and I are currently here.

It strikes me all over again how intent Montes is on keeping me safe. It's been this way since he learned of my cancer. The thought leaves my throat dry.

I grab a water bottle nestled in the center console of the car and take a drink of it before going back to staring out the window.

Nearly an hour goes by in that car. Sometimes we pass through villages that look completely unaffected by the king's war, and twice we pass through bigger towns that show only the barest hints of repair—scaffolding along the sides of some buildings and a temporary wall erected around a block. This might just be general maintenance. It's been so long since I've seen how normal cities function that I can't be sure.

When we reach the city, everything gleams. If there was

once war here, the evidence has been painted and rebuilt away. People here stand by the side of the road, waving as we go by. They actually appear ... excited to see the king's procession of vehicles.

That's a first.

The car slows to a stop in front of what appears to be an enormous coliseum. We're shuffled past the waiting throngs of people, down a series of halls, and out to an outdoor stage.

"This is all you now," the king says. He peels away from me while the organizers direct me from the wings of the stage towards the podium.

I almost stagger back when I catch a glimpse of the crowd. There are thousands of them. The seats are all full. It's a far cry from the last speech I gave.

Covered in blood, my body shaking. My father was dead and I had to inform the WUN.

The crowd roars as they catch sight of me.

These aren't the same people who waited for me to disembark all that time ago. These people are foreigners with entirely separate histories. This new world of mine has been theirs for far longer. What could they possibly want from me? What would I want from me?

A leader. A real one. The world doesn't trust Montes.

They continue to cheer as I approach the dais. Their applause is a terrible, terrible sound because it's a lie. I've killed their comrades, their sons and daughters, their friends and neighbors.

I draw in a shuddering breath at the podium, and it echoes from the speakers. Montes stands only a handful of feet away, back in the shadows hidden off to the side of the stage, but we might as well be separated by oceans.

My eyes find the teleprompter. Just as quickly, they leave it. If I'm going to give a speech, the words will be my own.

I clear my throat. "I'm honored that you've cheered for me, given that most of you have seen the footage of me stepping onto former WUN soil."

Any remaining noise dies out at that, and I can see PR people gesturing wildly to cut off my mike.

I curl my hands over the edge of the podium and bow my head. The pain is right there. All I have to do is give it a little attention and I'll fall apart. Luckily for me, I have no interest in indulging it. I've spent the better part of a decade too busy surviving to afford the luxury of living inside my sadness. I won't start today.

"Several months ago, you were my enemy and my husband, the king, was the one man I most wanted to see dead."

More wild gesturing comes from the wings of the stage, but Montes must be refusing their requests because no one comes to drag me off.

"I was born in Washington D.C., the daughter of an American congressman. When I was ten, I watched my mother die. The aerial attack came from the sky. A few years later, a nuclear blast wiped out my city. Aside from my father, everyone I'd known and loved was gone in an instant."

My words are met with utter silence.

"I'm telling you this because many of you have similar stories. They might be older, but they're no less painful."

The ominous silence turns to murmuring. People are listening, some nodding.

"I may have married the king, but I am not him. I am one of you. I hurt like you, I love like you, and I can die like you."

The words flow out of me. I don't know if anything I'm saying finds its mark, but this is the best I have to offer.

"I've seen what war does to a place. It brings out the worst in us. But the war is over. It's time for us to not simply survive, but to thrive ..."

The crowd's talking and shifting. People point to the erected screens and I follow their gazes.

I see myself, my face angled slightly away from the camera. Dripping from my nose is a line of blood. I reach up and touch it, staring at my fingers.

The noise of the crowd rises. People are shouting, and they're repeating one word over and over—

Plague.

CHAPTER 11

Serenity

"IT'S GOING TO be okay."

Five words every soldier fears.

You can rephrase them, elaborate on them, parse them down, but the meaning is always the same: you're fucked.

It doesn't help that the royal physician—Dr. Goldstein, the man who administered the antidote to my memory loss—says this while wearing a hazmat suit. He's already swabbed my cheek and taken a sample of my blood for testing, and now he's cleansing my arm for a shot.

What no one's mentioning is that the king's pills should've prevented me from catching plague in the first place. Or that the plague has run its course in this region of the world.

"What are the odds that the shot will work?" Montes asks from where he holds me down alongside his guards. I've obviously been a little too transparent with my hate for doctors.

I don't fight them too hard, however. The king and his men have quarantined themselves with me inside this room in the palace, and judging from the bits and pieces I've gathered, they could be at risk.

Even the king.

It's unlikely, considering that prior exposure to the virus means their bodies should have the immunities needed to fight it, but it's not impossible.

The doctor's shaking his head. "Decent, though I'd need to see her bloodwork first."

He slips the needle under my skin, and now I do jerk my limbs.

"She can take a bullet, but not a shot," the king murmurs. I think he's trying to lighten the mood. He shouldn't bother. I know the odds. Despite what the king said last night, Death and I are old friends, and he's decided to pay me a visit.

TWO HOURS LATER it's clear the shot hasn't worked. I'm drenched in sweat, yet I have the chills. No wonder this plague killed so many. It has a swift onset and it escalates quickly.

My head pounds, my brain feeling far too swollen for the cavity it rests in. For once, there's no nausea, just an ache that's burrowed itself into my bones.

Montes sits at my side. "You're okay," he says, taking my hand.

My teeth chatter. "Stop saying that."

His lips tilt into a smile, and he brushes the hair back from my face. "This wasn't how I imagined getting you on your back."

"You're such an asshole," I say, but my lips twitch at his words. He understands that I don't want pity. I'll drink up his strength.

Unlike the others, he hasn't bothered donning even a mask. My eyes prick. Illness unwinds the last of my defenses. The immortal king risks his own health to be by my side. I'm too sick to wonder about this, but not too sick to be moved by it.

Montes wipes away a tear that leaks out the corner of my eye, staring at it wondrously. "She cries."

"Put on a mask, Montes." I can't think about the fact that I'm actually concerned about his wellbeing.

"I'll be fine."

I want to place my hands over his lips to stop him from speaking, but that might just increase his chances of catching whatever I have.

"Please."

A knock on the door interrupts us. A moment later the doctor, who had left to run my bloodwork, returns, clad once more in a hazmat suit.

One look at his face and I know whatever he has to say won't be good.

"Montes," he says, not meeting my eyes, "a moment please?"

DR. GOLDSTEIN PULLS me to the edge of the room.

"I sent Serenity's bloodwork to the lab," he says when I approach him. He looks tired, which is not the expression I want to see on his face.

"The lab confirmed that the queen does in fact have the plague. However," the doctor looks more than a little concerned, "this strain ... it's new."

"It's *new*?"

How does a new strain of plague show up out of thin air and choose my wife as its first victim?

"Where did it originate from?"

"One of your laboratories—the one stationed in Paris."

It takes me a moment to register his words. I'm expecting him to say a general region like the Balkan Peninsula, not a specific location, and definitely not one of my labs.

"From what I was able to gather, it matches a strain of plague your researchers have been testing."

The news is a shock to my system.

"They're in the initial stages of creating an inoculation for this strain," Goldstein continues, "but an inoculation won't do Serenity any good now that she's already caught it. We've already given her the antidote for the old virus."

"What good is an old antidote if this is not the same illness?" My voice is rising. I pinch the bridge of my nose and pace. "And how the hell did this get leaked?"

Heads are going to fucking roll. Now I just need to figure out whose those will be.

"Your Majesty, we have no idea. No one at the research station in Paris has reported a contamination, but that could be a failure in oversi—"

"Don't feed me that bullshit."

This was a deliberate attack. Someone went into one of my laboratories and harvested a super virus to kill my queen with.

I run a hand down my face. I'll torture all those technicians one by one until I have my answers, and then I will hunt down whoever did this and I will kill them slowly. A point must be made: those who dare to turn my weapons against me and my own will die, along with many innocents.

"What's the kill rate?" I ask.

"Pardon?" Dr. Goldstein says.

"The kill rate. How lethal is this strain?"

"Your Majesty—"

"Just give me the goddamn number, Goldstein."

He shakes his head. "I don't know. Your researchers in Paris didn't know, but they thought it was somewhere around," he takes a breath, "eighty percent."

Eighty percent.

Eighty percent.

I've turned away from him before even realizing I've done so. I rub my mouth at the horror of it all. Four out of every five victims die.

I glance over at Serenity just as she lets out a wet, rattling cough.

"What happens at this point?" I ask, returning my attention to Dr. Goldstein. "Do we move her into the Sleeper?"

Goldstein shakes his head. "The Sleeper specializes in trauma, not illness. It won't work for this, just like it won't cure Serenity of cancer.

"Your Majesty," he continues, his voice already apologetic, "this is out of our hands. If the queen is to live, she'll have to beat this on her own."

SERENITY'S CONDITION WORSENS. By the evening, she's strapped to several different monitors, and I tense at every beep.

No one else in the room contracts the plague. It's not too surprising given that on this end of the hemisphere, people have either survived the plague once, or been inoculated against it. Goldstein speculates that this mutated strain is much less transmutable, meaning that while lethal, it won't readily spread. This only strengthens the argument that someone deliberately infected my wife.

And Serenity, who's never encountered the plague before, has no defenses against it. The pills that should've protected her from this pathogen, the pills that prevent me from aging, she hasn't taken since the bombing on the palace, which was a month ago. Any she took before then have long since been purged from her system.

I watch her toss and turn in the hospital bed.

I brought one of the victims of my war into my house, and she's brought the world's blights in with her.

I run my hand over hers. Scars mar her knuckles; it's the same hand that wears my rings. Love and war—they battle it out across her skin. I thread my fingers between hers and bring them to my mouth.

Serenity doesn't react to the touch, but I do. My hand trembles, and I can't be sure whether fear or fury are responsible for the palsy.

Even as I sit here, my researchers are being interrogated and punished.

It's not enough to slack my need for vengeance. Not nearly.

Serenity lets out a moan and tugs against my grip. Only then do I realize I've been squeezing her hand so tightly my knuckles have whitened.

That night in Geneva, when I first held her under the stars, I told her all the ways she was unexceptional—how she wasn't the prettiest, or the smartest, or the funniest person I'd encountered. I didn't bother to tell her that she was the most ferocious woman I'd ever met, or the most tragic. I didn't tell her that whatever combination of pain and hardship she'd endured, it enthralled me completely.

She's not dying. She can't. Serenity's final act is not succumbing to fever in a hospital bed.

Serenity will live—she must. I rely upon it, and humanity relies upon it. Otherwise, I won't rest until the world burns.

CHAPTER 12

Serenity

THEY SAY IT took me five days to beat this thing.

They say that it was the most lethal strain of plague they'd yet seen. They tell me that four out of every five people die from it. That my compromised immune system saved me from death by a virus that primarily kills the healthy.

They say that someone planted the virus on or near me.

They say it was the Resistance.

I believe everything but the last.

"Trust me when I tell you that if the Resistance knew about your super virus, they would've taken advantage of it long ago," I say to the king's council.

I'm pacing inside one of the palace's conference rooms

as Montes and his advisors go over the attack.

"It's been months since you were part of the Resistance," one of his men says—a former West African ruler. "How would you know that?"

The king's lounging back in his chair, his calculating eyes moving between me and the advisor. He's been quiet, and that's probably for the best. Usually when he talks someone ends up with a bullet between their eyes.

"You were the one that suggested that Resistance members are planted everywhere," the man continues. "Now we're missing a driver and an official car; one matching its description has been found near a suspected Resistance stronghold.

"Correlation is not the same as causation," I say.

The man guffaws, and I thin my eyes. The derision these men have for me is almost palpable. I know what they see: a young, pretty girl from a backwards nation who wishes to talk to them as equals. They can barely stand it. And while I enjoy their silent seething, I'm never going to make inroads with these men if they don't respect my opinion.

I place my hands on the table and stare him down, letting the civility bleed from my expression. I'm no delicate flower. I've seen more of war's atrocities first hand than most—if not all—of these men have.

"It's reasoning like that that's set the world back decades and dropped the global lifespan from the high sixties to the mid-thirties," I say.

He stares back at me with flinty eyes. "It's reasoning like yours, my queen, that's nearly gotten you killed multiple times."

"*Efe.*" Montes rises from his chair, his expression ominous. The threat is clear—an insult to me is an insult to him.

"They're both right." This comes from Alexander Gorev—or Alexei, as he prefers. I know him better as the Beast of the East. Everyone in the WUN's heard tales of the former general's penchant for torture and rape. He's the man who replaced Marco's seat. Now he's trying to be everyone's best friend to make up for the fact that he's new to this council. I'm having trouble not stealing one of the guards' guns and putting a bullet in his belly, right where I know death will come only after an agonizing ten minutes.

My gaze flicks to him, and whatever he was going to say dies on his lips. He must sense how close to death he is. Him I will kill eventually.

I don't understand why Montes has chosen this group of despots as his advisors, but I now understand why he uses fear to get them to cooperate. It's the only mechanism that they react to.

"I didn't come here to discuss my mortality," I say.

"Mmm, but I did." Montes's voice coils around us all. He'd barely let me out of bed this morning, despite being cleared for activity by Dr. Goldstein. Only my expert opinion on the Resistance and his own thirst for vengeance swayed him.

"We've been working on this for a week," he continues, "and we've made no progress. Who do I have to kill to make things happen?"

If only the psycho were joking.

His men pale. Already the whispers I've heard suggest that the king's killed off several people he suspected of facilitating my assassination.

"Perhaps we could start with you, Efe."

The man's eyes widen, but before he has a chance to plead with the king, Montes's eyes move to Alexei. "Or you."

I swear the Beast stops breathing. He hasn't become accustomed to the king's threats.

"Hmmm, no," Montes continues, "I believe the blame must lie with all of you. You have another day. Bring me something tomorrow, or I'll find myself new advisors."

People nod and murmur, some shuffle papers. Just another day in the life of a demagogue's advisor.

Someone clears his throat. "We should discuss the former WUN."

My hackles rise at the mention of my homeland. These men are predators ready to tear into their newest kill.

My eyes land on the speaker. Ronaldo. He was the one that orchestrated the nuclear blasts that wiped my country apart, the one whose life I saved in one of these last meetings.

"No." The word is out before I can censor myself.

Montes swivels in his chair, an eyebrow raised.

"I will be dealing with the WUN," I say. Not Ronaldo, who played a key role in destroying it. Not any of these other men that hold no love for the scarred land I once called home.

Montes's advisors look aghast. Their gazes move from

me to the king and back.

"Your Majesty?" It's Walrus Man from our wedding who pipes up, the man with the bulging eyes and belly. I don't remember his name and I don't particularly care.

The king focuses all that disturbing intensity of his onto the advisor. "Yes?"

Walrus glances to either side of him, his face beginning to redden when no one else speaks up. Had he thought to dispute me? Was it his hope that breaking the silence would herald in more complaints from his colleagues? No one else seems interested in disputing the king's wife, despite the fact that many of them appear angry.

Such loyal comrades, these men.

"Nothing," Walrus says.

Weak, weak man.

"Good." Montes's eyes twinkle when they meet mine. He keeps me around because I'm still amusing to him. "Your queen's spoken," he says to the room. "All dealings with the western hemisphere will go through her from this day forward."

There's a collective exhale as twelve men hand over their balls to a woman. I can't help the satisfied smile that stretches across my face. I made a promise to myself that I'd help my homeland.

Today I've begun to in earnest.

"YOU DEFIED ME," the king says after the meeting.

The last of his men have left, and by the time we leave the conference room, there's no sign in the hallways that over a dozen of the world's wickedest men had convened here ten minutes ago.

"Taking control away from those men is not defiance."

The king's hand falls to the back of my neck, his fingers caressing the pulse points on either side of it. It's oddly sensual, but it's also an innate threat. Power flows from the king; for all my posturing I'm just his puppet.

He pulls the side of my head to his lips. "It is if I say it is," he said, his breath tickling my ear.

Even his words are some combination of sensuality and threat. My mouth usually gets me into trouble, I decide for once to muzzle it.

"How are you feeling?" Montes asks. He still holds my neck hostage, and he's using the grip to keep me even closer.

"Healthy."

Healthy is the last thing I'm feeling. The king doesn't know that half my bathroom breaks consist of me hugging the toilet rather than sitting on it, or that blood continues to speckle the evidence of my sickness. Up until today I've been on forced bedrest. I'm not about to blow my first taste of freedom.

"I was hoping you'd say so. Tonight we're hosting a very important dinner party; if you're feeling better, you'll be there by my side."

I've been cornered by a master manipulator. It's either attend the stuffy dinner party or languish in bed.

"This is revenge for speaking up today, isn't it?"

This twisted man.

"No, Serenity," the king says. He removes his thumb

from my pulse point to stroke it down the back of my neck. "That, I will collect on later."

THE DINNER PARTY we walk into is identical to the ones I went to during the peace talks with the king. The only things missing are the camera crews and my father.

I swallow down the lump in my throat. Had I felt objectified then? It's nothing compared to now. The room's collective gaze fixes on me. I can feel their eyes studying my hair, my makeup, my jewelry, and my outfit. If only they knew that when I walked into my room several hours earlier, someone else had laid it all out for me. The woman they see is a stranger. Maybe one day I'll get just as used to wearing dresses as I do fatigues, but not today.

"Relax your features, my queen," Montes says, his voice pitched low for only me to hear, "you look ready to massacre the room."

"Don't tempt me."

Out of the corner of my eye, I catch a glimpse of Montes's smile.

Ahead of me, thirty odd people lounge in whatever this room is—a sitting room? A standing room? Does it even matter? Most of these rooms look identical to my untrained eyes.

The people here are just as interchangeable, and I have to study their features closely to distinguish them. What I find surprises me.

Some of the younger women wear their hair loosely curled. Just like mine.

Another sports a jewel just below the corner of her eye. It's on the same side as my scar. Several women wear pale yellow dresses. Another wears a gold dress eerily similar to the one I wore at my engagement announcement.

They're emulating me.

I work my jaw. I hate it. What's worse, I'm fueling this.

I don't think I can be civil tonight. Not here, not with these people.

I have to remind myself of all the lessons my father taught me. Not everything needs to be a confrontation.

Shortly after they catch sight of us, Montes's guests begin to approach. Many of the men are his advisors, but not all of them. The bejeweled, bright-eyed women join them, smiles fixed on their faces.

I'm glaring at all of them while Montes charms the group.

"Montes, can I steal your wife away?" This comes from the woman with the jewel at the corner of her eye.

"I'm right here," I say. "You can ask me."

She reels back slightly. "Of course, Your Majesty. Would you care to meet the wives of the king's advisors?"

I would care very much. But this is the world of politics and diplomacy, a world my father schooled me on. Study your enemies.

"It would be a pleasure." The words come out clipped. It's my one lie of the night. I'm tapping out after this.

The king flashes me a look. He knows exactly how deceptive I'm being at the moment.

I'm dragged away from the king towards the far left side of the room, where most of the women are grouped.

"I'm Helen," the woman says as she leads me. "I met you briefly at the wedding, but there were so many people."

She's apologizing for me, like I need or want an out for not remembering her name.

I stare at the rubies that drip from her ears. So this is how the rich bleed—elegantly.

"We're so excited to see the king finally settling down. We thought that he would never," she says as we join the group.

"Your Majesty," the women echo, dipping their heads.

"This is Beatrice, Anouk, Isabel, Katarina, ..." Helen introduces. I forget each name the moment my eyes move on to the next. Some are old; most are young.

They can't all be the advisors' wives. The way some of them are looking at me ... if I had to guess, I'd say that the king's mixed business and pleasure plenty of times in the past.

Jealousy lances through me before I can stop it. To think that any of them might've also experienced the king as I have ...

The thought is followed by a good dose of self-loathing. For me to be jealous of the affections of the king—it's unconscionable.

I square my jaw, forcing my emotions down. I swear the group notices my anger. They shift a little restlessly. I'm a predator among prey.

Someone breaks the silence that follows the introductions.

"Beautiful dress, and—" she gasps, "are those heels from

Vesuvio's summer collection?"

I glance down at my toes. Vesuvio?

"They are!" she exclaims. "I adore his entire summer collection. I would *kill* for a pair."

My jaw tightens. "Would you?" I say, looking back up.

The woman falls silent, and the rest of the group tensely watches the exchange, some clutching their jewel-encrusted necklaces. They must sense how offensive I find it to even jest about killing over *pretty* shoes.

Finally, someone breaks the silence and asks the woman next to me about some recent trip she took. As the group gets swept up in the newest conversation, I withdraw further inside myself.

These women are nothing like the ones I'm used to. They care about the length of their skirts and the color of their face paint and the weave of their clothes. They have no idea what goes on outside these walls.

The women I lived with sharpened knives and oiled guns. I saw one fight through a bullet wound to the stomach, even though it eventually killed her. Another performed CPR on an unresponsive boy lying in the streets we patrolled while we were being attacked by local gangs. They were some of the hardest women I ever met, but they would die for you.

And they'd never give a shit what you wore.

Remembering is all it takes.

I leave right in the middle of the conversation. At my back I hear a chorus of soft-spoken protests. I ignore them. Some people you can't change, and the effort of trying would be wasted.

My eyes sweep the room as I walk. The genders are divided. Men to one side of the room, ladies to the other. The women gossip and preen like all those exotic birds that died off first when war struck. They're just like them—pretty and soft and so unenduring. The men swirl amber liquid, their faces ruddy. They look so damn proud of themselves. I want to shout at them that anyone can destroy a city.

And, amongst them all, there's Montes. I never glance his way, but I feel his eyes on me the entire way out.

As SOON AS I leave the room, the king's guards fall into step behind me. I come close to threatening them, but even if I promised them death, they still wouldn't leave me. Say what you will about Montes, he has some loyal guards.

I storm through the palace, heading for the gardens. I feel a great deal of disgust. This is what the new world order does while its citizens starve. I can't be a part of it.

Once I push open the palace doors and the cool evening air hits my skin, I give into the impulse riding me since I entered that dinner party. I kick my shoes off and wipe my lipstick away with the back of my hand. I pull out the few pins in my hair and shake my locks loose. I pass through the gardens and bypass the giant hedge maze.

I break the delicate clasp of first my bracelet and then my necklace, and let them fall to the ground. Only then do I feel like myself again. I'm still in my dress, and my hands itch to tear into the fabric, but I hold myself back.

I walk across the palace grounds until the back fence comes into view. I head straight for it, my mind replaying the last time I ran towards one of the king's fences. Odd how something as bland as a wall can conjure such memories.

My chest tightens. All my friends are ghosts, and all my memories are dust in the wind. Out here, beneath the stars, I can't help but remember that I am hopelessly, achingly alone.

I stare up at the wrought iron fence. It took losing all that I held dear for me to learn a valuable lesson: only when everything is gone are you truly free.

CHAPTER 13

The King

SERENITY CARVED A path of destruction in her wake. She's the untamable wilderness. Of course she can't palette civilized company.

The women are speaking frantically to one another, their eyes darting in my direction. They're worried about my anger, but I don't blame them for being sheep and my wife a wolf.

I'm done sharing my queen anyway. I don't want these politicians or their wives to have any part of her, and I don't want her to give herself away to anyone but me. So after some parting exchanges, I head after her, moving towards the back of the property where my soldiers indicate she went.

Serenity leaves me a trail of expensive breadcrumbs to follow. A satin shoe here, a diamond bracelet there. I follow them to the edge of the palace grounds. She's several feet away from the wrought iron fence that circles the grounds, and she's staring up at it like she's considering the best way to scale it.

"And here I was hoping that you might consider shedding your dress along with the jewelry."

She doesn't flinch at my voice, nor does she turn around.

"How do you live with yourself?" she asks, touching one of the wrought iron bars.

For one instant I fear that if I ever let her go, she'd disappear into the land, never to return. God, she'd want that. And I probably just caught her as she was tasting the possibility on her tongue.

I've been vacillating between anger and arousal since she stormed out of the palace. I settle on anger.

"You make a fool out of me and now you insult me?"

Finally she turns. Her wild eyes search mine, and it doesn't matter that she's broken in all the right places and whole in all the wrong ones. Or that out here with her bare feet and windblown hair, I catch a hint of the woman she should've been. That soul of hers, tempered by the hottest of forges, has been and will always be mine.

And it is probably the evilest thought I've ever had, but I'd ruin the world all over again just to be brought back to this very moment.

"You set yourself up for failure the second you decided to pursue me," she says. "I'm never going to be one of them." She gestures to the palace.

"No, you're not." And I'm glad for it.

"Then why bother making me try?"

"Serenity," I chastise. "I'd think you more than anyone would know the answer to that."

Her dress flaps in the breeze as she waits for me to explain myself.

"Ruling," I say, "isn't always about getting to be who you want to be. It's about sacrifices."

"And what sacrifices have you made? Bombing innocents? Taking a hostage wife?"

Usually I like the chase, but not like this, not when she's deriding me while eyeing my perimeter walls like she's considering escape.

"I am still your king, and you will *not* speak to me that way." My voice resonates in the evening air.

"Then kill me already, or let me go." She has the audacity to look exasperated.

Don't yell at her.

Don't threaten her.

Don't rip off her dress and fuck her.

I should just walk away. I have before when I wanted to shake her. She doesn't realize she's not the only one being tormented here. Instead I take her hand.

She tries to jerk away, but when I don't release her, she relaxes.

She steps in closer, and I only realize what she's about to do the moment before her fist slams into my face. Those scarred knuckles of hers that I admired only days ago now smash into my skin and teeth.

I stumble back at the impact, and she uses the distraction to throw me against the fence. Her hand goes to my neck.

"I am not something you can control, Montes," she says, and the way the shadows play on her face make her appear downright sinister. "I'll do many things for you—"

I raise an eyebrow, though I doubt she can see it out here.

"—but don't try to make me become one of you."

Had I thought I was angry or aroused before? It doesn't hold a candle to the way my blood now heats at her presumptions. She thinks she has me in more ways than one.

I swipe her feet out from under her. I may not have the combat experience she does, but I've had plenty of military training. A moment later, it's me that has her pinned. My legs straddle her torso, and I capture her hands in one of my own, pulling them high over her head.

She glares at me as I press my other hand gently to her throat, noticing the way her hair spills across the lawn. For a woman who has little time for appearances, she takes awfully good care of those golden locks.

"My queen," I say, "you're seriously misguided if you think you have any agency outside of what I give you. I will *allow* you some measure of control over our empire, and in return you will attend every dinner party I host. I'll chain you to my side if I have to."

She's moving beneath me, trying to pry my hold from her. It's only serving to display every pleasing angle of hers.

"Now," I say, "about those many things you'll do for me ..."

"Give me a knife and I'll show you."

I let out a husky laugh and move one of my legs to the inside of her thighs. "Still uncomfortable with sex, I see. I'm taking that as a challenge."

I remove my hand from her throat to grasp her freed leg. Her skirts pool around her waist. She looks indecent, and on Serenity, indecent is a good look.

She's no longer trying to free herself from my grip, and her chest's rising and falling faster and faster. From what I can make out of her expression, I'm thinking she has no idea what to make of intimacy in all its forms.

A spark of protectiveness flares in me. Despite everything this world's thrown at her, Serenity still maintains a shred of innocence when it comes to things between a man and a woman. That's going to disappear eventually—marriage will force her hand—but I'm not too keen on rushing her in this.

I'm a wicked man. I've never made bones about that. So I don't readily recognize myself when I get off of Serenity and extend a hand towards her. I'm not sure I like this side of me, either.

Slowly she sits up. I can feel her gaze on me. We've been here before. She doesn't take my hand, but she does stand.

She turns her head to the blazing lights of the palace. "We should probably go back."

I stick my hands in my pockets and study her. This is her peace offering. She'll go back inside what she sees as a bastion of depravity.

"Alright," I say.

And together we return to the castle.

Serenity

SOMETHING'S HAPPENING BETWEEN me and the king. It's been happening for a while, but it's not slowing down.

I stretch my legs out in the tub. I can still feel the phantom fingers of the king as they moved up my calf last night. The sensation reminded me of another time he ran his hands up my legs, only then I'd been trying to seduce him. Both times, he'd backed off.

Both times, I'd felt conflicted by his reluctance.

I hear the rustle of sheets in the adjoining bedroom, pulling me back to the present.

The king's awake.

Heat courses through me, and I hate myself a little that he can make me feel this way at all. And that while I might be in the bath, my mind is with the king.

It takes him all of thirty seconds to make his way to the door.

I startle as it opens, water splashing against the walls of the tub. I cover myself with my arms.

"What are you doing in here?" I demand.

I hadn't locked the door because I had thought Montes would give me privacy here of all places.

I obviously thought wrong.

He's naked and sleep-ruffled, and in this moment, I can't possibly reconcile him with the evil dictator I've hated so passionately.

"There's my wife." Even his voice is rough and uncultivated in the morning. It's just one more small intimacy that I get with the king.

His molten eyes move from me to the water. "Now I know who's been using up the palace's water supply."

"Are you going to let me take my bath?"

"That's not a bath," he says, "that's a puddle." He bends down, uncaring that I'm clearly uncomfortable, and sticks his hand in the water. "And it's tepid." Montes turns on the hot water spigot.

"What are you doing?" I ask, alarmed.

"Taking a bath," he says, stepping in. "My wife thinks it's good to conserve water. I'm supporting the cause." By joining me. This man is slippery.

"You can uncover yourself," he adds. "Your nudity doesn't offend me."

My gaze slits.

He settles against the opposite side of the tub, stretching his legs out until they brush mine, and he drapes his arms along the rim. It's a good thing the basin is large enough to comfortably fit two people. Even so, he's still crowding me.

Is this what married couples do? Step on each other's toes until the notion of privacy is entirely done away with? I can't escape this man.

I uncover myself and lean back against the tub, all too aware of our nakedness.

Montes settles that heavy gaze of his on me, and he wears his acquisitive look. This isn't just a bath if he has it his way.

He picks up my foot and begins to rub it.

"Montes—" I try to jerk my foot from his grip.

"I'm helping you relax, *nire bihotza*."

"I will kick you."

He sets my foot back down and returns to staring at me.

"I have a question for you," I say.

He raises his eyebrows. "She has an interest in her husband? Who would've thought?"

"'She' is sitting across from you and 'she' would appreciate it if you stopped referring to her in the third person."

His mouth curves into a smirk. "No death threats for me this morning? I'm disappointed."

"If you don't stop referring to me in the third person, I'll drown you in this puddle—as you so eloquently put it."

"There's my girl."

"I'm not your girl."

He leans back in the tub. "Don't you have a question for me?"

I work my jaw, annoyed he's caught me in a web of my own making. "Why are there no women in your government?"

"There are."

"You know what I mean."

"You mean my inner circle of advisors and officers? There were once women. They ended up being too soft for the job."

"That's your reasoning? Fuck you, Montes, and all your sexist ideals."

"They're not ideals. The women couldn't stomach it."

And the one woman that—according to him—apparently can has stomach cancer. I'm not going to peer at that one too closely.

"Had you ever considered the fact that maybe what you saw as weakness was instead compassion?"

"What, are you a champion now for women's rights?" he says. "Odd since you seem to clash with most of them."

In fact, I got along quite well with the women I lived with. It's just the ones here that I can't stand.

"I clash with most people. That has nothing to do with it."

He pushes away from his end of the bathtub and moves towards mine. He's eating up the final space between us, and there's nowhere for me to go.

Montes looms over me, his glistening torso close enough to touch. That dark hair of his hangs near his eyes as he looks down at me. Just when I think he's going to make a move, he reaches up and shuts off the water.

It goes to show you how captivated by this man I am that I don't notice until now that the water level is past my shoulder.

Montes is hovering over me, his knees on either side of mine. The crook of his index finger dampens my chin as he tilts my face up. "We can hire more women. Is that all you wanted to talk about?"

"No—"

He cuts me off with a kiss, his hand moving from my chin to my cheek. His other one finds my hip and grips it tightly.

It hits me then. He wants me, badly; he's practically quaking with the need. I can taste it in his kiss, I can feel it in the pressure of his grip.

The entire time since my memories returned, Montes hasn't pushed sex on me. He takes many things, but not this. It's the barest glimmer of a conscience.

And here I was disappointed in him for it. I need to shed this shyness.

So I give in.

I let myself slide my fingers through his mussed hair and kiss away the droplets of water that drip onto our lips. Our mouths open and I taste this taboo that's forced his way into my world.

He's poison and radiation and he's seeping into my bloodstream, tainting me from the inside out. I'll never be free of him.

And God, he tastes just like me.

Montes moves between my legs and I help him angle my pelvis up to meet his. If he hadn't known before that I was willing, now he does.

The last of his restraint falls away.

I gasp into his mouth as he fills me. This is our world, this starved, desolate place. Both of us want things we don't know how to attain. So we seek solace in each other.

Our eyes lock as Montes draws away and pistons back into me. His hands are on my breasts and in my hair. I get the impression that he wants to be everywhere all at once. It's not enough to taste me and move inside me.

My hands glide down his backside, leaving watery trails in their wake, and I pull him closer. My hair floats about us, curling about Montes like it never had a problem with him in the first place.

Finally his restless hands find my face, and they cup it. We stare at each other while he moves in and out of me. My heart pounds as I fall into his eyes. We stay like that until the king's hot water turns tepid once more.

And for once the two of us make love instead of war.

CHAPTER 14

Serenity

ALL PRODUCTIVE GOVERNMENTS have schedules and patterns. Reliable systems put in place to chart out the ruling of a country—or, in this case, the world. The king's is no different. So despite the early morning festivities, we both get ready for work.

We dress—me in black jeans and boots, the closest thing to combat gear I now own—and the king in a pressed suit.

Since the bath, we've both been keenly aware of each other. I don't think either of us is prone to softer emotions, but what happened less than an hour ago hasn't happened before.

We've had sex, yes, but we've never fallen into each other the way we just did. It wasn't supposed to be like this.

Marriage—and sex—I'd agreed to. But not love.

I hadn't even thought I'd be vulnerable to falling for the king. I'd only ever meant to bide my time until I could thrust a dagger into his heart or a bullet into his brain.

But now I know that won't happen. Not now that I've seen the sharks he works alongside. Not now that I've grown to care for him.

"Ready?" he asks, extending his arm towards me.

I ignore his arm and reach for the door. Where I'm from, after all, chivalry is long dead.

"Happy to see that I put you in good spirits this morning," Montes says as he follows me out.

He doesn't know the half of it. My heart's still beating too fast, and every time I close my eyes I see the way he looked at me as he moved inside me. Like more than just sex passed between us. I hate that he's convinced me that there's another side to him. I hate that I want to drop back and take his hand, or hold his face in place while I memorize those irises that scared me for so long.

My own urges make me feel dirty. It's one thing to be taken by a monster, and quite another to be taken with him.

"You vastly overestimate your skills, Montes," I say. "I'm beginning to understand why you settled on world domination before marriage."

"My queen *did* enjoy herself," Montes says. He sounds so smug. "Perhaps a little too much?"

I run my tongue over my teeth. It would do me no good to respond to him. But it burns to not rise to his bait.

The palace is already bustling with people. Save for the

guards, all the men are in suits, and the few women I do see wear heels and skirts. I'm the only one wearing anything sensible. It's just another reminder that these people were once my enemy, and they were so untouchable that safety never dictated what they wore. They never had to worry about fleeing the palace at a moment's notice.

This den of iniquity is now my home, and at the moment I'd love nothing more than to burn it to the ground, just to let these people feel a shadow of what I have my entire life.

Ahead of us, the servant carrying tea is the only one, as far as I can tell, who's wearing shoes she can run in. Not even the others that mill the halls wear the same sensible black shoes she does.

Perhaps it's that small detail that has me giving her a second look. A linen cloth is thrown over her forearm, and the base of the silver teapot she carries rests on it.

She's only feet away from me, her eyes downcast. She's not looking where she's going, and even as I try to sidestep her, she manages to bump into me.

I feel the pressure of the knife sliding into me well before I feel the pain. That's all it takes for my training to kick in.

Working on reflex alone, I grab the woman's wrist and yank it behind her back. She cries out as I sweep her feet out from under her and follow her to the ground.

Jesus. Now I feel the pain. It only makes me more aggressive. I grind my knee into her back and pull her wrists more tightly together. My blood slips down the hilt of the dagger protruding from me and drips onto her.

"Nice try," I whisper in her ear.

"*Guards!*" Montes yells.

The people in the hallway stand frozen as guards run to our side, a few gasp as they catch sight of me. Here in their world, nothing bad happens.

The guards gently push me away as they take over restraining the woman.

I rise to my feet slowly, careful not to cut more of myself. Montes helps me up the rest of the way.

"We need a medic!" he shouts.

He's staring at the line of blood blooming across my abdomen, his face shell-shocked.

Two attempts on my life within a single week. Someone wants me dead. "You really should give me back my gun."

It's only once I'm standing that I realize the woman inflicted more than just a flesh wound. My hands move to my stomach as I sway.

"Serenity?" Montes's eyes are wider than usual. He turns to the guards not dispensing with the hit woman. "We need a doctor! Now!"

I place a hand on him to steady myself and stare down at the woman who's now being jerked to her feet by several of his men. That was bold of her, trying to kill me in the king's headquarters. She had to know she'd get caught. That she would be killed.

Montes holds my sides like he wants to draw me into him, but he's afraid of jostling me. His eyes follow mine to my attacker.

"Make her talk by whatever means necessary," he says. "Then make an example of her."

The woman hasn't said a word this entire time, and really what is there to say? She catches my eye as the guards drag her away. There's nothing there. No remorse, no anger, no fear. That's something else I've learned from war. Sometimes, violence isn't personal. Sometimes it's cold and passionless. And sometimes, you'll never know a person's motives.

As she's taken away, several sets of feet sprint down the hall. A handful of medics move towards us, pushing a stretcher between them.

Now I'm half considering removing this knife from my belly and attacking my attacker for making me face more doctors.

Once the medical crew reaches us, they make quick work of laying me onto the stretcher. I reach for Montes's hand and grip it in my own bloody one.

"Stay with me," I whisper.

His nostrils flare as he breathes through his nose. That perfect suit of his is now rumpled. "I'm not going anywhere."

I've heard that love was messy, but ours is downright bloody. It turns men into monsters, and monsters into men.

I don't care that soldiers, medics, staff, and politicians are watching. I bring his bloody hand to my lips and kiss his knuckles. And the entire time they wheel me away, I hold my monster tightly to me.

The King

THEY PUT HER in the Sleeper again.

She fought it. Again.

Her pain almost broke me.

Again.

I've never bloodied my own hands, but I'm honestly giving it thought at the moment. Someone's targeting my wife, someone wants her dead.

The Resistance had been the likeliest suspect. Serenity herself warned me that they had eyes everywhere. But Serenity's attacker never fully broke under interrogation, which in and of itself means that she wasn't just some crazed vigilante. What she did say was that someone paid her off. That's not how the Resistance does their dirty work.

But if not them, then who?

I sit outside Serenity's Sleeper, my elbows braced on my thighs and my hands shoved through my hair. I've taken to coming here between my meetings. This time, the doctor joins me.

"You had some information for me?" I say to Dr. Goldstein, staring at the Sleeper as it hums away.

"Yes."

My heart's thundering, though I don't let on that it is. I'm afraid, I'm desperately afraid of what this man is going to tell me about Serenity. Special news from Goldstein is almost always unwelcome.

"What is it?"

"Her injury's fully healed. The Sleeper is removing the malignant tissue it has detected. It should be done in another two hours, then she'll be out."

I already know this.

"If nothing is done for her ... the cancer will eventually overtake her system. It's only a matter of time. If you want her to live, not just for the next year, but for as long as you intend to, then I'd advise you to consider leaving Serenity in there for ... a longer stretch of time."

He wants me to leave her in there like some sort of vegetable until we find a cure for her cancer. Marco advised the same thing while he was still alive. And if we were talking about anyone other than Serenity, I might. But now that my oldest friend's gone, my wife is my closest companion, and she's swiftly becoming something more.

She could be in there for years, imprisoned in a box. A coffin, really. All that ferocity of hers forced to lay dormant. For Goldstein to even suggest that has my blood pressure rising.

I rub my knuckles. "No." I feel selfish, even as I say it. "We'll continue with treatment as we have been. Is that all?"

He lingers. "That ... wasn't what I came here to talk to you about."

My cheeks suck in. "Then get it out already." If he gives me one more piece of bad news ...

"Your Majesty, when I was looking at the imaging of the queen's cancer, the machine captured something else as well." He takes a breath. "Congratulations, my king, the queen is pregnant."

CHAPTER 15

The King

THE NEWS DOESN'T immediately take. I stare at the tiled floor as the doctor's words sink in.

Serenity is ... pregnant?

With my child?

My gaze moves up slowly to the doctor. "She is?"

He nods.

She's carrying my child.

Serenity's carrying our child.

I draw in a lungful of air.

Now it takes.

Fierce joy surges through my system, followed on its heels by possessive, masculine pride. I can't stop my reaction. Now my heart's pounding for an entirely different reason.

A child.

We hadn't planned on this. I wasn't trying to get her pregnant, despite my eventual plans for an heir. I'd never considered kids, and now I don't know what to do with this strange elation I feel. If I'd have known I'd have this reaction, I'd have pushed the issue sooner.

I want to grab my wife and hold her. My eyes move to the Sleeper. Instead she's unconscious, hurt once again.

She and our child.

A burst of anger punches through my joy. Someone needs to die, and Serenity and I need to leave the palace. It's clear that if we remain, this will continue to happen. It grates me to flee my own home, but I'll do it for her and the baby.

I'm going to be a father.

Had I once worried that no one who knows me will love me? Already my wife's long-standing hatred is toppling. And my child—I rub my mouth. I'll make damn sure they love me.

"How far along is she?" I ask.

"Just shy of eight weeks—Your Majesty, I need to caution you, the child might not survive. Women like Serenity who have been exposed to high levels of radiation often have fertility issues. And if the child does survive, it might have problems of its own."

These words, too, don't immediately sink in. But when they do—and they eventually do—they slaughter me.

This is karma, giving me everything I want only to steal it away.

I'm shaking my head. I won't believe it.

Usually I'm a reasonable man. But reasonableness has nothing to do with this. Not now that I have a future to look forward to and something to hope for.

"The Sleeper can fix this." Serenity is a survivor. Maybe our child will be as well.

"The Sleeper, as we've previously discussed, has limits."

"Then fucking *enhance* it! Goddamnit, I will not sit here and listen to you tell me all the ways this won't work." I rise to my feet and get in Goldstein's face. "You're the royal physician. Consider your life now tied to my child's." I mean every word.

He blanches.

Good. Perhaps the threat will be enough to prompt him into usefulness.

Once he recovers, the doctor bows his head. "As you wish, Your Majesty."

"Leave—and tell no one of this." If my enemies knew of the pregnancy, they'd redouble their efforts to kill Serenity.

Goldstein exits the room, leaving me with my sick, pregnant wife.

I stare at the Sleeper, my excitement offset by Goldstein'swarnings. I place a hand on the machine.

Deadly, savage woman.

Now that I'm alone with her, I realize Serenity won't react to the news like I have. I don't know quite how she'll take it, but I doubt joy will top her list. I remember her barely masked revulsion on our wedding day when the subject came up. It burns me raw to remember. She still hates me; I haven't won her over enough for her to forget the bad blood between us. And when she finds out she's pregnant with my child ... it will set off all sorts of her triggers.

I'm a wise enough man to know telling her will earn me her famous wrath. I might not survive an angry, hormonal Serenity. Better she figure it out on her own.

I smile at the prospect of a pregnant Serenity stomping around.

I've only gotten the barest taste of this future, but already I know I want no other.

Serenity

WHEN I WAKE up, it's in the king's bed.

I push myself up and rest my back against the headboard.

How did I get here?

I have to jog my memory to recall the knife wound.

The Sleeper. Of course.

Now I wear a dress someone else slid onto my body while I slept. I try not to think about that too hard. Same goes for the underwear I see when I lift the hem of the dress up. There really isn't anyone who I'd want to see me naked.

I continue to raise the material until I see the smooth expanse of my stomach. I touch the skin that had been split open last time I'd seen it. Nothing remains of that wound, not even a scar.

How many days did I lose this time?

I pull my dress back down and lean my head against the headboard. A glint of metal catches my eye, and I turn to the bedside table.

A row of bullets are lined up along the polished wood. Next to them are a giftwrapped box and a card with my name scrawled across the front. I reach for the card.

I thought you'd prefer this to flowers.

I run my thumb over the king's handwriting.

A reluctant smile spreads across my face. I do prefer bullets to flowers.

I pick one of them up and study it.

My smile falls away. This ammunition is familiar.

I turn my attention to the gift wrapped box. When I lift it onto my lap the weight, too, is familiar.

I tear away at the ribbons and paper that cover it. I'm breathing faster than I should be. And then, when I open the lid of the box, I stop breathing altogether.

Inside, resting on tissue paper, is a gift I have already been given once before. I pick up the piece of cold, hard metal. It fits in my hand like it was born there.

The gun had originally been a gift from my father, and ever since he'd given it to me, it had been the most constant of comrades.

Montes had held onto it this entire time. I can't stop the anger that rises at the thought. He'd taken away one of the few possessions I'd coveted.

But he had given it back. With bullets.

What a trusting, stupid man.

I'm LOADING BULLETS into the chamber of my father's gun when Montes storms in. His eyes capture mine, and he stalks towards me.

My anger is no match for the emotion pouring off him.

He doesn't bother removing the gun from my hand before he cups my face the same way he had the last time we'd been intimate. The same intensity burns through him now as it did then.

He takes my mouth savagely. When the kiss doesn't let up after a few seconds, I set aside the gun to better return it.

I can tell without asking that Montes's emotions simmer just beneath his skin. Usually I doubt his motives and intentions, but there is no confusion here: I'm no passing fancy of his.

He threads his fingers through my hair and his tongue invades my mouth.

It's not enough.

I can practically hear the thought running on repeat in his head. The man who owns the world has finally found something he can never have enough of, and he's trying to figure out a way to remedy that.

He breaks off the kiss and leans his forehead against mine. "How do you feel?"

"You gave me back my father's gun." Even as I speak, I reach for it.

"Thinking of using it on me?" His eyes are full of mirth,

and any anger I was planning on directing his way now dissipates. He enjoys the vicious side of me; it's hard to threaten someone when they relish it.

I turn my attention from the king to the weapon. I flip it over and over in my hand. I miss my war-torn country and my father. I miss knowing right from wrong and friends from enemies. I miss knowing my place in the world.

I can feel the king watching me. The bed dips as he sits at my side. "Your gun had me thinking."

That train of thought can't end well.

His fingertips touch the scar on my face. "I have a serious question for you: Now that you're the unofficial representative of the western hemisphere, how would you feel about returning to the WUN?"

NOT TWO DAYS later Montes and I are on the plane heading to the last land to fall to the king.

Up here, the sky is bluer than I've ever seen it, and the clouds are whiter than even the king's smile. It hurts my chest that a day can be this beautiful.

We're not headed to the continent formerly known as North America. It's an odd mix of relief and disappointment to not be returning to the place I called home. It's all I've ever known, but there's nothing there left for me.

Instead, we're heading to the land on the other side of the equator. The king's having trouble pulling together the fractured nations of Southern WUN, and now, as the self-appointed representative of the western hemisphere, I'm to help him fashion some sort of cohesive government. I smile to myself as I stare out the window. What he wants to do is damn near impossible, and it may be petty of me, but I look forward to seeing the king struggle.

I steal a glance at Montes, who sits across from me, his legs pressed against my own. He's pinching his lower lip as he scrolls through a document on his tablet. Without warning, Montes looks up and our eyes meet. I squeeze my chair's armrests.

A wry smile spreads across his face. "Still plotting my death?"

I frown. I don't want this casual familiarity with him, no matter that it's inevitable.

Absently I touch my holstered gun. "You shouldn't remind me. The prospect is too tempting."

"So you *weren't* plotting my death while you were staring at me? Hmmm, I wonder what my queen was thinking." He leaves the thought hanging there.

More bait for me to rise to.

"This is where all your delusions of grandeur come from," I say.

"They're not delusions, Serenity, if they come true."

He has a point.

"Who are we meeting with first?" I ask, purposefully changing the subject.

We land in Morro de São Paulo, a city along the continent's eastern coast, in another several hours. The discussions don't begin until tomorrow, but I want to be ready. Not only is this a chance to establish my own abilities, I know many of these people either directly or indirectly from my time with the WUN.

"Luca Estes," Montes says.

I groan. "Don't tell me you're giving him a government seat."

"Not just a government seat, *the* government seat. He'll spearhead the South American region of my rule. You have an issue with this?"

"Yes." A huge one. "He's a sellout."

My eyes flick over the luxurious cabin we sit in. Greed, in the end, got to Estes. It's as corrosive to the soul as outright violence. After all, if not for greed, there would be no King Lazuli.

I click my tongue. "He's not a good person to have working for you. Before he was a politician, he was a thug. He only came to power once he killed enough people."

Something you two have in common.

"I dare you to find me a single person in office that hasn't gotten his or her hands dirty—including you."

I can't say anything to that. Our world is one of hard choices and bloodshed.

"After you detonated the nukes across the WUN," I say, "Estes began destabilizing many of the neighboring regions."

When I was just the daughter of an emissary, Estes had been one of the thorns in the WUN's side. He often pulled aggressive maneuvers on his allies rather than trying to come together and provide a united front against the Eastern Empire.

"That's because he was working for me the entire time."

Montes's words aren't surprising, but they are disheart-

149

ening.

"So you would have a sellout—a traitor to his comrades—holding the seat of Southern WUN."

"South America," Montes corrects.

"What would you have me do?" he asks, leaning forward.

He really wants my advice, this man who's taken over the world.

"You have better experience with bad men than I do." He convenes with a whole room of them on a daily basis. "Perhaps you can handle Estes. But I'd listen to what the people here want."

"My reports indicate he's a favorite amongst the people."

I know all about Montes's reports. They'd serve more use as kindling than as information.

"Fear and love wear similar faces," I say.

"Not on you."

This is hedging too close to subjects I don't want to talk about. "You've never seen love on my face," I say, staring him down.

"I thought you and I were beyond the lies." He holds my gaze.

My fingers dig into my arm rests. I'm itching to unholster my gun, but not because I'm angry. Heaven help me, it's because Montes might be right and I can't bear that he of all people lured something as soft as love out of me.

Montes lifts a cup of coffee to his lips. After he sets it down, he says, "I will take what you say into account. For now, let's keep our friends close and our enemies closer."

"I already am, Montes." And that really is the problem.

CHAPTER 16

Serenity

THE WORLD WE descend into is rapturous. There's no other word to describe it. From the sky, the world is a blanket of lush green. I know this place was hit hard by the king, but it's hard to appreciate the destruction from my vantage point.

The king's eyes are trained on mine as we step out of the plane. I've come across photos of jungles and the tropics, and long ago, before the war, my parents had taken me on vacations, but faded memories and two-dimensional images are nothing compared to this.

The air is a hot breath against my face; the humidity sticks to my skin. Beyond the tarmac, shrubs and trees press in, their stalks and leaves swaying in the light breeze.

I can smell brine in the air. It's like war and corruption never touched this place. I know that's not true, but nature paints a pretty picture.

A small contingent waits for us. I scan the group for Estes or anyone else I might recognize, but these are just more of the king's aides and soldiers stationed here to guard us. They shuffle us into a sleek black car, and then as quickly as we arrive, we leave.

The damage to this place becomes apparent on our drive. It's not so much the broken buildings that tell the story of war. No, it's more subtle and insidious than that. It's the vines that grow between the skeletal remains of houses, the side streets that have been all but smothered by the plants.

Goosebumps prickle along my skin. Mother Nature is the apex predator here.

We crest a hill, and I see the deep blue ocean spread out before us. The king's managed to find one of the few places on the western hemisphere whose beauty is unsullied by war.

But it's like overripe fruit. To the eyes, everything's fine, but there's a sickness that's settled just beneath the surface.

It's no surprise when the car pulls up in front of a seaside mansion. What is surprising is the place's seclusion. We have no neighbors, and I already know we will be hosting no meetings here. It's not the kind of home that demands an audience, it's the kind made for secret rendezvous—or so I assume. I have no other point of reference save for my imagination.

"This seems a little underwhelming for your taste," I say, stepping out of the car.

He gets up behind me, and his lips press against my ear. "I'm not doing this for me."

I don't bother keeping the skepticism from my voice. "You thought I would appreciate the seaside getaway?"

"I thought you'd appreciate not having to worry about assassination attempts—and banal conversations with politicians and their wives."

I study Montes as he passes me. *Thoughtful* is not a word I would use to describe him—nor is *caring*—and yet both seem to motivate him when it comes to me.

"You and I both know we'll still have to participate in banal conversations, seaside getaway or no," I say, following him inside. Politics really only gets exciting when people are stirring up trouble. Otherwise the legislation can put you to sleep.

"Yes, but this way I won't have to constantly worry about you shooting those that piss you off."

"Do their lives really matter that much to you?" I ask.

He pauses in the living room. This may be no palace, but each lavish detail—from the painted tile to the carved mantle to the marbled archways—indicates just how expensive this place is.

"Not in the least. But I prefer to burn bridges on my terms, not yours."

I shake my head and wander through the kitchen. I head over to the stovetop and flick a burner on, watching the flames bloom in a ring. Instant fire. Does the king have any idea just how precious this one thing is? Turf wars have been started over less.

Stirring utensils hang along the wall. Jars of oils and seasonings sit on display in fancy glass containers. The line between food and art is blurry here.

For years now, meals are a morbid occasion for me. Everyone must eat to live, but when the food and water are in short supply and what's left is riddled with radiation, it feels a bit like Russian roulette. Will today's meal be the one that poisons your system? It's the reminder that while we stave off death for the day, we're always beckoning it closer.

But here in this place, food appears to be a joyous occasion. One that celebrates life and gluttony. I envy the lifestyle even as I reject it.

I head over to a faucet and turn it on. Clear water pours from it.

"The radiation ... ?"

"Reverse osmosis filters it out. It's simple enough technology."

I run my fingers under the stream. "Not if you don't have running water to begin with."

I turn off the faucet. If this house is supposed to be inviting, it has the opposite effect on me. I don't belong amongst plush carpets and polished surfaces and crystal goblets made for delicate drinks that are to be sipped.

I belong around gunmetal and smoke, around the weak and the violent, the broken and battered.

But not here, not here.

I head up the stairs to the second story. An expansive bedroom takes up most of the space. A wall of glass doors line one wall, facing the water. They're already propped open, and a cool sea breeze blows through the room. I head out to the balcony beyond them.

Places like this make you yearn for things you can't put your finger on. I always imagined myself too hardened for something like whimsy, but even I feel a deep stirring in my heart.

I can't take it. Hope is a dangerous thing when you're in the business of loss. Better to expect the worst.

In this world, that's often what you receive.

THE NEXT MORNING, I wake to fingertips on my back.

They trail down my spine and I arch beneath them. I sigh, stretching out my body. I feel a kiss at my temple, then another where my jaw meets my neck.

This is Montes's wake up call, and each morning it happens, I enjoy it a little more. Unfortunately.

I flip onto my back and he continues to trail kisses down my throat, between my breasts, all the way to my stomach. There he stops. His hands move over the skin there, like he's cradling it. I've gained weight, not enough to lose my waist, but enough to fill me out.

He must notice.

I begin to move, about to slip out from under him, but he holds me in place.

"You're beautiful," he says, his gaze trailing up the length of me to meet my eyes. I can tell from his expression how much he means this. And he's looking at me like it should mean something to me as well.

"I already told you what I think of beauty," I say, fighting my own impulse to touch him. It's a losing battle, and I end up running my fingers over his jaw.

"Yes, you have very little regard for it." His hands are still on the swell of my stomach. "It doesn't change that you are."

His grip tightens on me. "You're also brave, fierce, reasonable, and despite all your violence, you have a good heart."

I trace his lips. "Compliments won't save you from my gun," I say. It's not a threat, not like my others which are said in anger. I don't know when that shift happened, when this easy camaraderie became a part of our relationship.

"Serenity, I'm serious."

I know he is, and he's forcing me to be as well. I don't want that.

I cover his mouth with my fingertips. "Don't," I say.

He removes my hand from his lips. "Don't what? Make you face this?"

"Caring for me doesn't change anything," I say.

Did my voice sound a tad distressed?

"It changes *everything*," he says.

I push my way out of bed and angrily begin dressing. He follows me.

"Serenity."

I try to ignore him. I can't. He's everywhere. On my skin, in my mind, inside my heart. I wear his ring, share his name and his empire.

He turns me. "Serenity."

"*Stop.*" I'm shaking.

"*No.*" His voice resonates.

We stare each other down.

"I don't care what you think of me," he says. "I don't care that you think I'm evil. We're both guilty of horrific things. Why do you think I wanted you in the first place? Death in a dress. That's what you were when you descended down those stairs in Geneva. I knew you'd either redeem me or you'd kill me."

"You and I both know there's only one way this ends," I say.

Six feet under.

He shakes his head. "No, Serenity. You want to believe that, but you and I both know this doesn't end in death."

He's apparently the keeper of wisdom, on top of everything else.

"Then how does it end?"

"In love. And life."

CHAPTER 17

Serenity

I'M IN A foul mood when we arrive at some swanky hotel for the morning's first meetings. For one thing, the king cornered me into facing emotions I'd rather ignore.

For another, the people who packed my bags sent me away with a suitcase full of dresses. They look similar in style and cut to the gowns I wore during the peace talks. I hate them all. It's just my luck that I now have a style, one I didn't choose, and it's getting perpetuated.

To top it all off, we're going to a morning soiree before our first meeting so that the traitors of the southern WUN can rub elbows with the king and his newest acquisition—me.

Montes's hand falls to my back. His other waves to the

audience gathered on either side of the roped-off aisle made for us. They scream when they see us, like we're celebrities.

The beads of my dress shiver as I walk down the pathway. I feel the brush of Velcro and metal as my leg rubs against my thigh holster. This was my compromise—I'd wear these ridiculous outfits and attend the king's stupid gatherings so long as I could carry my gun. It doesn't inspire much faith when political leaders walk into meetings armed, but considering that I'm now the queen of the not-so-free world, exceptions are made.

As soon as we enter the building, it's to more applause.

"Who did you pay off to make them all clap?" I ask.

"Mmm, no one, my queen. Here before you are the people who respect power and money above all else."

I stare out at the room. We might as well be back at the king's palace. The crowd's coloring may be slightly different, but they wear the same expensive clothing. These people, however, I take note of. They are the ones who ended up siding with the king before, during, or immediately after the WUN fell.

The room watches us while I watch them. I'd imagine they don't much care for me. Or worse, they think we're alike—westerners that turned their backs on their former allegiances.

I would sooner die than willingly become a traitor. The king and the general forced my hand on this matter.

The conference hall is more a resort than anything else. I can see the ocean out the back windows, and between us and it lounge chairs and umbrellas line the sand.

Waiters carrying delicate silver trays move throughout the room, offering hors d'oeuvres to guests. It's strange to not see them descending upon the food like their very lives depend on it. That's the kind of reaction I'm used to in the WUN.

A man steps into my line of sight, bowing low to the king before taking my hand and kissing it. "Your Majesties, it's an honor."

The hairs at the nape of my neck rise at that voice. I sat in on a lot of calls my father had with that smooth baritone. I snatch my hand away as he straightens.

Luca Estes wears middle age well. His salt and pepper hair is trimmed close to his head, as is his goatee, and he sports the same lean build that many active military members do.

His dark eyes glitter as he takes me in. "It's been too long since we last spoke."

My skin crawls, and I stop my hand from groping towards my holster.

"I saw the peace talks," he continues, "apologies for not joining. I hadn't realized until then just how much you've grown up, Serenity," he says, his accent barely there.

He rests a hand on my shoulder and turns to the king. "I've known your wife since she was a child."

That is stretching the truth quite a bit. He's known my father since I was a child; he's only known me since I began to train for my role as emissary.

I flash Luca a dark look. "Yes, we're practically family."
You sellout.

My father had all sorts of advice for dealing with political figures you didn't like. I was never very good at following any of it, and now, married to my archenemy and
facing down another, I'm having a hard time controlling
my emotions.

Montes studies Estes, his mask firmly in place. "I hadn't
realized how close you and my wife were."

Tread carefully.

Montes's subtle threat sends a thrill through me. I find
I don't mind them when they're lobbed at other bad men.

Estes turns to me, a smile plastered on his face. I can
see just a touch of panic in the corners of his eyes. We're
all having two conversations at the moment—one spoken,
the other implied. He's only now realizing how treacher-
ous knowing the traitor queen can be.

"Yes," he pats Montes's shoulder; the fatherly gesture
is made all the more ridiculous by the fact that he has
to reach up to do so, "well, congratulations on stealing
Serenity's heart."

"He didn't steal my heart, Luca," I interject. "He just
stole me."

That temporarily silences the corrupt politician.

"She's kidding," Montes says, giving me a look.

I raise an eyebrow. He knows I'm not going to muzzle
my mouth.

Estes barks out a laugh. The whole thing is wooden and
awkward, because the three of us know just how wicked
both men are, and it's not something you're supposed to
bring up.

So naturally, I'm going to bring it up.

162

"All those conversations, Serenity," Estes continues, "and I had no idea how quick tongued you were."

"She can do many things with that tongue of hers," Montes says.

That's it.

I'm reaching for my gun when the king grabs my wrist.

"Let me the fuck go," I hiss.

"She hasn't had her coffee yet," Montes explains calmly.

I'm seeing red.

"Apologies, you both must be hungry." Luca waves down a waiter.

"Whatever you give me is ending up on your shirt," I say while Estes is distracted.

Montes leans into my ear. "You keep this up and we won't make it through the first hour of meetings before I have you pressed up against one of these walls."

I think he's threatening me until I see the heat in his eyes. It's still a warning, but this one's of a wholly different nature.

His arousal only pisses me off more, as does my response to it. He told me once that I'd be good at angry sex. I think he's right.

"This is all just a game to you, isn't it?" I say.

"Of course." His face is only inches from mine. "But you already knew that."

I straighten and speak low enough so that only he hears. "One day you're going to underestimate the wrong person, and then your pretty empire is going to come crashing down."

"I'M STILL DEBATING shooting you," I say an hour later.

"I know," Montes says next to me. "My pants have been tight all morning because of it."

"You are a sick, sick man."

We're back to greeting people, just like we had at our wedding. The line of men and women eager to meet the king winds through the room and out one of the exits. This is not how I imagined changing the world—giving the privileged my time in a few empty lines of greetings.

"Perhaps I should just pull down your pants," I say after the next round of guests leave our side.

That gets Montes's attention.

"That way it'll be easier to bend you over and let everyone here kiss your ass."

King Lazuli stares at me for several seconds, then he lets loose a deep laugh, the sound carrying throughout the room.

He reels me in for a kiss. "Life is infinitely more interesting with you in it."

It takes another hour to meet with everyone, and then we're being shuffled down the hall to a conference room.

The entire time at least two cameras stay trained on us. They hover like flies, orbiting us, drawing in as close as they dare, then backing off before I get a chance to break their lenses. I've come close.

"They're fascinated with you," the king says as we walk. His silken voice raises my gooseflesh. "They've always been."

I give a cameraman a hard look, and he quickly retreats.

Montes is right, but he's also wrong. They're not fascinated with me so much as they are our relationship. I'm the blood-soaked soldier that defended the WUN, and he's the bloodthirsty king that captured my land. We're enemies that became lovers. Two terrible people that rule the world together.

Montes's hand skims down my back, and it's a far more intimate gesture than it has any right to be. He's undressing me with his fingers and his eyes, and even after all we've seen and done together, I still feel like a bug caught in a spider's web.

Estes is already in the conference room when we enter, along with a handful of other faces I recognize from my time spent as an emissary. Several of them my father communicated with directly or indirectly. Back then they'd worked for the WUN—when they weren't challenging and usurping each other's territories. Now, only months after the war ended, they're here fawning over the king.

For once I would like to meet with leaders who weren't completely unfit for the job.

They eye me as I enter the room. Like Estes, they're trying to figure out whether knowing me benefits them or not.

I decide to help them out.

I stop at the table and take them in. "Corruption looks good on you all."

I render the room speechless—for a moment. Then, all at once, half a dozen people are speaking in Spanish, Portuguese and English.

Ah, southern WUN. They were always very vocal when they disagreed. It's nice to see they're consistent about at least something.

Montes cuts through the noise. "We're not here to talk about prior alliances. The war has ended. South America now needs some stability; let's focus our attentions on that."

Only the king has the balls to make me look like a bad guy and him the martyr.

I take a seat at the table, hyperaware of the tension I've stirred up.

Their anger revitalizes me. People are easier to read when they take their masks off.

The chair next to me scrapes back, and the king sits heavily down. He picks up the papers his aides have set in front of his seat and spends a good minute flipping through them while everyone else waits.

Finally he sets them back down. "Thank you all for being here. I figure we might as well just dive right in: what are the main issues standing in the way of a unified South America?"

And thus begins the first hour of meetings.

"YOU HAVE MANAGED, yet again, to get an entire room of people to hate you in record time," the king says as he closes our front door behind us. We're back from the conference after four nearly unbearable hours. The only people the South American representatives hate worse than me are each other. Everyone wants a piece of the pie that Montes is giving to Estes.

That was the main theme of the meetings—who was

going to get what. The only time anyone brought up the region's general health and welfare was when they wanted to use it as a talking point for why they deserved something or why someone else didn't.

I almost pistol-whipped the lot of them.

If that wasn't bad enough, I have to see them again this evening at another one of those needless dinner parties.

I pass through the foyer, kicking off my shoes. This damn dress is a cage. It's too tight around my stomach and thighs, and if someone attacked, I couldn't run in it. I need it off.

"It's probably the first genuine emotion they've displayed since we arrived," I say, groping for my zipper.

Montes comes up behind me and drags the zipper down. Material peels away from my skin, and now those hands of his are coaxing the rest of the fabric off me.

"Perhaps if they weren't turncoats," I continue, "I'd be a little nicer—"

Montes pushes me up against the wall. He captures my hands in his own, "You know what I think upsets you?" he asks, his nose skimming my jaw as he breathes me in. "I think you see yourself in them, and you hate it." He pitches his voice low, and it drips with all sorts of dark intentions.

They and I are nothing alike. But Montes's words dig under my skin. Am I not for all outer appearances a traitor just like them? Perhaps, like me, they were cornered into this. And perhaps, like me, they too have lost themselves somewhere along the way.

The king captures my lips, his hand sliding up my thigh.

I feel the remnants of my lipstick smear as our mouths move against each other.

He doesn't bother undressing. He simply unbuckles his belt, unzips his pants, and pushes aside my lingerie.

With one hard thrust, he's inside of me.

I gasp at the sensation. It's just on this side of pain, and that's when I love sex best. I could never indulge in something wholly sweet with the king. Not without at least a little grappling.

He lets my wrists go to grip my hips, kissing my neck as he does so. I feel his hot breath fan down the column of my throat. His pace increases, and each rock of his hips causes my back to pound against the wall.

I cradle him in my arms and arch my neck back. What I can't possibly understand is why anyone wastes time with war when they could be doing this instead.

Montes pulls us away from the wall. We don't break apart as he carries me to our room. We fall in a tangle of limbs on the mattress. The pins holding my hair in place are coming loose, and as I tug on the king's dark locks, his fancy gel disintegrates beneath my fingertips. Civilization is giving way to our primal savagery.

He thrusts into me, and dear God, I'm willing to admit that right about now, I love the king. It's fucked up, and if ever there was proof of my twisted nature, this would be it.

I don't give a damn.

I slide my feet along the back of the king's legs.

"Tell me you love me," the king says next to my ear.

His thoughts are clearly moving in the same direction as mine.

I grip his hair tighter and tilt his ear to my mouth. "No."

He moves harder against me, the friction causing a moan to slip out. I'm far beyond caring that the king's torn down most of my walls and my modesty along with them.

"Say it," he breathes.

I don't.

As a result, he stops.

We're both panting like animals, and when he stares down at me, I see sweat beaded along his brow.

"Say it," he repeats.

Staring at him, our bodies joined and our limbs entangled, I almost do.

He moves against me, just a little. Enough to remind me that he controls the strings.

I shake my head. "I'm not giving that to you."

He flashes me his wickedest grin. "Has my queen forgotten who she's married?" he whispers, his nose dipping down to nuzzle my hair.

He cups a breast through the fabric of my dress. "I'll get you to say those words just as I have everything else."

I'm too far gone to give into his witty rapport. "Just shut up and fuck me."

And he does, but not before he says his final piece. "I will, Serenity. And when I do, you'll mean them, too."

CHAPTER 18

Serenity

AN AFFECTIONATE KING. It should be impossible, but it isn't.

He hasn't stopped touching me in some way since we were intimate. And now that we're at Estes's estate for a dinner party, he's being affectionate in public.

To be honest, I'm not entirely opposed to it. The ball-buster in me wants to slap his hands away, but each touch regrettably also draws up memories of heavy breathing and slick skin, and when I meet his eyes, they're heated, as though he's ready to repeat the afternoon's activities at any given minute.

Like the one I wore earlier, this dress is far too constricting. That's the only reason why I can't catch my breath.

My eyes move around Este's extravagant home, and they

latch on to each piece of wealth the man's accumulated. To think this was all acquired while his people starved—while *we* starved.

I see the guards posted at the four corners of the room. There are more outside, and even more stationed in the watchtowers that border the entrance to the estate. Everything here has been acquired through bloodshed and lies.

This will all come to an end. I vow it then and there.

A waiter passes by carrying a tray of various drinks. I snatch one of the champagne flutes. Just as my fingers wrap around the stem, Montes intercepts it.

I give him a disbelieving look.

"You really shouldn't be drinking this with your cancer," he says.

He can't be serious.

"Give the alcohol back to me," I demand.

"No."

"I thought it didn't matter to you whether I drank or not."

"I lied," he says. "It does. Now," Montes looks around, "Let's find you some sparkling cider."

I breathe through my nose. "Give me the fucking drink." The promise of alcohol was all that was keeping me from open mutiny.

He smiles at me and downs it.

People are watching, cameras are rolling. Our explosive interactions are on display. I can't just brawl it out like I might've back in the bunker. Here it's all about posturing.

I breathe in and out of my nose, and settle on glaring at him. "I hope you don't expect me to be nice tonight."

"You? Nice? I wouldn't dream of it."

Bastard.

I leave him as soon as the first group of politicians approaches. My violent tendencies are bubbling to the surface, and if I don't take them out on Montes, I'll surely take them out on the fuckers in this room.

I feel the king's eyes burning into my back as I walk away from him. He doesn't like parting from me. I'd written this particular detail off as an aspect of his controlling nature—and it is—but it's gotten worse as the attempts on my life have increased.

The most powerful man in the world has a single weakness, and that's me. And I'm not above using it against him.

"*La reina del mundo.* It's an impressive title." Luca Estes steps up to my side, a glass of amber liquid in his hand.

"Mmm," I manage, watching the room as the evening toils on. A warm breeze blows in from the open windows at my back.

At the moment, I'm mourning the fact that I left Montes to fend for myself among these people. Had I swallowed a bit of my pride, I might not have to bear Luca's company alone. Estes is one of those men that doesn't have a good side. He's corrupt, violent, greedy, lecherous. The only question is which side of him I'll see tonight.

"From what I hear, your father was against the match."

Apparently he's chosen asshole. At least he's no longer trying to be nice.

"My father's dead." I take a sip of my drink. I need something stronger than the glass of water in my hand.

"Yes, my condolences," he says, leaning in. I can smell the strong spirits on his breath.

"Fuck your condolences, Estes." I don't bother looking at him. "I know you didn't like him."

"I like him better than your new husband."

Now I glance over at South America's premier dictator. "That's because my father couldn't control you." Montes can.

He grunts in agreement and takes a swallow of his drink. When he glances over at me again he levels his gaze at my cleavage.

"Last time I saw you, you wore a shapeless uniform. This is a much better look on you."

Now he's being a *lecherous* asshole.

"You and I both know the last time you saw me, it was the leaked footage of my return to the WUN. I believe I was wearing a dress then."

"There was a dress under all that blood? Forgive me for not noticing."

I don't say anything.

The king throws a glance in our direction, which Estes notices. "He keeps you on a pretty short leash, doesn't he? If I didn't know better I'd say that he was obsessed." He swirls his drink, the ice cubes clinking against the glass. "Tell me, does the infatuation go both ways?" He looks over at me. "I suppose it wouldn't, considering what he did to your family—and your country."

Even before Estes approached me, I knew what kind of

man he was. So his words shouldn't get a rise out of me, but they do. It's taking every last ounce of restraint not to smash my glass across his face.

"I've been wondering what sort of bed play comes out of that union ..." he muses.

Enough.

"In case you needed the reminder, I am '*la reina del mundo*', and I won't hesitate to use my position to remove you from power if I feel the desire. I am not half as decent as my father, so keep your sick perversions to yourself, Luca, and don't fucking cross me."

I stalk away from him. People give me wide berth, and I'm sure it has something to do with the harsh set of my face. The cameras begin panning in on me. I set my drink down on a sideboard and make a beeline for Montes. He's in the middle of a flock of admirers. They too give me wide berth the moment I cut into their circle.

Montes watches me, a dark gleam in his eyes. He always did like my flare for the dramatic.

I wrap my arm around the back of his head before I kiss him. I'm angry, and I'm sure he can feel it in the harsh movements of my lips. This is no passionate kiss. All my usual rage and violence is wrapped into it.

"I'm done," I say against his mouth. I've had enough fake smiles and false endearments for one evening. I should have had enough of the king as well, but instead, he feels like my one ally in a sea of enemies. It's an illusion, but I can't reason it away.

My father was right when he said appearances are everything. Let the world believe the king and I are some odd love match. Better that than the messy truth—that I hate him every bit as much as I care for him.

When I break away from the kiss, I take the king's hand. He's all too willing to follow me away from the quickly dissolving circle of admirers. But not five seconds later, he tugs my hand and reels me back into him until my chest is pressed against his.

He gazes down at me with amusement. "My vicious little queen," he says low enough so that only I can hear him, "you should know by now not to test me in public." His voice becomes husky. "And you should definitely know by now how to give your husband a real kiss."

I warn him with my eyes that I'm in no mood, but it does nothing to stop him from bending me backwards and taking my mouth with his own. In this position, nearly parallel to the ground, I'm at his mercy.

Wolf whistles and claps come from the crowd.

This is ridiculous.

I bite his tongue even as I grip his arms. He smiles against the pain. The psycho actually enjoys it when I get mean. He drags the kiss out longer than necessary, just to further push my breaking patience. Finally, with flourish, he pulls me back to my feet.

The crowd's still cheering.

Montes waves and steers me out. The last glimpse I catch is of Estes. He lifts his glass in salute. And then the front door closes behind us and all the pretty people are gone.

Our shoes click down the steps of Estes's estate.

"What did Estes say to you to put that expression on

your face?" he asks as we descend the stairs.

"The truth." Isn't that what hurts us so much?

"My queen doesn't run from the truth. She leaves only after she's threatened someone. So what did he say?"

I push away from the king. "What does it matter to you? My business is my own."

The king makes a noise low in his throat. I can hear him at my back. "Your business is anything but your own. It's mine, and it's our empire's."

Our car pulls up to the curb.

"I don't know how many times I have to say it," I say, "but you don't get to have everything, Montes. That includes knowledge."

He grabs my arm and spins me so that I face him, and then he backs me up until he has me braced against the car. There are people out here. Not many—mostly just valets and guards, since the camera crews stayed behind—but we have onlookers all the same.

So much for appearances.

"You are very, very wrong." I think this is the same tone he takes right before he ends someone's life. His lips are a hairsbreadth from my own. "I do get to have all of you, whenever I want." He grips my thigh, and it's incredibly suggestive. "Even your conversations. Even your thoughts."

Estes was right. Montes is nothing short of obsessed.

The king kisses me, and even that feels possessive, like he's taking my lust along with everything else.

He hauls me away from the car and opens the door for me. "Everything you are is mine, and no threats of yours will ever change that."

CHAPTER 19

Serenity

I WAKE UP in the middle of the night, clammy with sweat. If I close my eyes, I can still see the last moments of the dream—the blood, the shattered bones, the death throes of the mortally wounded.

I run a hand down my face. I'm used to nightmares; I have too many bad memories for my mind to prey upon. Tonight's just reminded me of the abyss I've traveled down since war broke out.

The king stirs, and his arm goes around my stomach. He drags me against his chest, his fingers stroking my damp skin.

"It's okay, my queen," he murmurs against my hair. I'm not even sure he's awake. "You're safe now."

Safety's not what I crave, and no one can rescue me from my life. I wait until I'm sure Montes is asleep before I slip out of bed.

My demons ride me hard. I change as quietly as I can, and I pad out of the room and onto the balcony.

I swing one foot over the ledge, then the other. Once I'm standing on the outside of the balcony, my arms wrap around the railing behind me. I gaze out at the dark sea. The surf crashes, calling to me.

All at once, I let go of the railing.

I feel weightless for an instant, and then my feet meet grass. I clench my teeth as the impact sends a stabbing pain through my knees and abdomen.

I head towards the ocean, and the lawn gives away to sand. I scoop up a handful of it and let it run through my fingers. The lamps out here are few and far between, and the nearly full moon casts the edge of the garden in shades of blue. The king's many guards patrol this place, but they've either made themselves scarce for the evening, or they blend in well. Either way, I can almost pretend that I'm alone.

Now that I have some small measure of privacy, I can finally settle my thoughts on things I'd rather keep from the king. I place a hand over my stomach. I'm dying, and not even Montes can stop it. I still vomit blood, my stomach still aches sharply. Whatever the Sleeper's abilities are, I'm not sure they're making things better for me.

I would've thought I'd be happy—it's finally an end to this sad life of mine. I'll return to the earth, just like everyone else I've loved.

But I'm not pleased about it.

"I'm sorry, Mom and Dad," I whisper to the stars above me, "but I'm not ready to come home yet."

I watch the sky. A cool evening breeze runs through my hair, beckoning me closer to the water. If I had it my way, I'd let the wind and the waves carry me far, far away.

I head over to the water and stick my toes in the sand.

"What are you doing out here this late?"

My spine stiffens at that voice, and I rotate.

Montes stands a few short feet away from me. He shouldn't look as handsome as he does. Moonlight pools against his features, illuminating half of them and casting the other half in shadow. He wears only loose lounge pants, and I have to force myself from fixating on his torso.

"Enjoying the view," I say, casting a brief look up at the stars.

"The one sleeping next to you wasn't good enough?"

All I want is to be left alone. Not even in the deepest recesses of night am I allowed this. "Not everything is about you, Montes," I say, weary.

"You can talk to me."

I almost laugh. I'm not sure this man could handle my past. But more than that, he gave me this past of mine. "I will never tell you my burdens."

He closes the distance between us. "You're lying again."

I search his face. "Why do you try so hard with me when you so obviously don't with anybody else?"

"Your heart has always been mine. I knew it from the moment I met you. I try because I cherish what is mine."

"I don't believe in love at first sight."

He laughs. "I'm not talking about *love*, Serenity."

"Then what are you talking about?"

He shakes his head. "Something else. Something poets know more about than I do."

I hate to concede anything to Montes, but I felt it, too. Maybe not the moment I met him—I had too much hate for that. But when I caught sight of him on the flat screen when I was the Resistance's prisoner, I still recognized him in a way that had nothing to do with memory.

"I will never forgive you," I say.

"I don't want forgiveness from you. I never did." His hand slides to mine.

My beautiful nightmare. That's what he is, what all of this is—the nightmare I can never wake from. And it doesn't frighten me any longer.

I take one look as the stars. "They're waiting for me. You know, they might be even more powerful than you."

"Who are you referring to?"

"The dead."

The king appears unnerved by my words. "I didn't know you were superstitious."

"I'm not." I sit down in the sand. The king joins me.

"Superstitions are nonsensical," I say, slinging my arms over my knees. "I've seen a person's soul leave their body. You can't *not* believe once you see proof like that."

"Is that what you've been dwelling on out here? All the people you've killed?"

"All the people *you've* killed."

The king leans back on his elbows and stretches his

body out. My eyes linger first on his chest, and then those long legs of his.

"Throwing blame around doesn't change the fact that they're dead," he says.

"Dead, yes. But gone? No, they're not gone." If anything they are more present than ever. The dead haunt my memories and my dreams; I'll never be free of them. That's the penance you pay when you take a life.

Montes glances over at me, and lounging back on his forearms, he's the poster boy for irreverence. "Let the past go," he says. "Be happy."

I stare up at the lonely stars. "I don't know how."

WE SIT NEXT to each other in the sand for who knows how long, and somewhere along the way Montes sits back up and his arm finds itself around me. I pretend I don't notice. Better that than to admit I might actually enjoy him holding me close.

"Now that you no longer live in the bunker, have the stars lost any of their allure?" Montes asks.

I shake my head and smile. "None. If anything, they've gotten more beautiful."

When I look over at him, he's already watching me. The intensity of that stare makes me acutely aware of myself. Sometimes, like right now, I believe that if the king could, he would drink me up and swallow me whole just to absorb every single bit of me into him.

It's disconcerting, to say the least.

I glance back up at the sky to shake my strange awareness. Amongst a sea of unfamiliar constellations, I see a dear one.

"Want to know a secret?" I ask.

"Of course," Montes says. "If it has anything to do with you, I'm interested."

I will give the king this: he never does anything half-assed. Especially not when it comes to pursuing his cold wife.

"I have a favorite constellation," I admit.

In the moonlight, I see him raise an eyebrow. "Which one?"

I lean into him, for once uncaring at our closeness, and point far above me. "Do you see that cluster of dim stars?"

"The Pleiades?" the king says.

I nod and wrap my arms around my legs. "My mother taught me about that constellation. The Seven Sisters. She said those were the wishing stars. That if you wanted something badly enough, you need only to wish upon them and it would come true."

Montes is flashing me a rueful grin. "And have you ever?"

I give him the side eye. "Once or twice."

"What did you wish for?"

The end of the war. The end of my sorrowful life. "Things I won't admit to another soul."

"Not even to me?"

Now I laugh. "*Especially* not to you."

He pushes me back into the sand and rolls over me. "Why not?"

We're gazing into each other's eyes, and now I see the

night sky in his irises, and I can only imagine what he sees in mine.

"Because you're my enemy, and you don't tell your enemy your secrets."

He captures my hands, like I knew he would, and presses them into the sand on either side of me. "But I'm also your husband, and you *do* tell your husband secrets," he says, threading his fingers through mine.

"You're going to have to force them out of me."

"Oh?" His interest is piqued. "Lucky me," he removes one of his hands from mine to slip it into my robe, "I know exactly the type of torture my wife likes best," he says, cupping a breast.

"Stop referring to me in the third person."

"Or what?" His lips are just an inch away from mine, and his voice is husky. "You'll *really* never tell me your secrets?" He thumbs my nipple as he taunts me.

Already my breath has quickened. "I sleep with my gun. You'd do well to remember that."

"And you know I'll take that gun away from you if I feel like you're abusing your power."

I guffaw. "Do you seriously want to get into a debate about the abuse of power?"

He laughs low in his throat. "I don't want a debate at all."

He takes my mouth then, his lips gliding against my own. I like to think myself a complicated, toughened person, but it never takes Montes long to pull me apart piece by piece.

I press my torso into his, and now he releases my hands

so that he can skim his along my skin.

Beyond us the tide has risen, and it licks at our toes. I can feel it dampening the edges of my robe, which—thanks largely to Montes—is no longer serving any sort of proprietary function. I'm splayed open to the king, something it doesn't take him long to figure out.

First his hand, then his head dip down between my thighs, and my fingers are grasping uselessly at sand. My legs open further, and the king groans, pausing his ministrations to grip my thighs.

"I enjoy it when we fight," he says, "but I enjoy it even more when you finally give in."

"Ssssh ..." I don't bother clarifying that I was trying to tell him to shut up, but I couldn't get past that first syllable.

I've come completely untethered. I thread my fingers through Montes's hair, getting sea salt and sand all over the king's dark locks. I mess it up further, which I'm unashamed to say is a favorite pastime of mine.

I don't know how he does it, but the man manages to shed his pants while keeping me preoccupied. But then his mouth leaves my core and his bare chest slides up my torso. I laugh as the sand I put in his hair sprinkles down on me.

He kisses my mouth, and I taste myself on his lips.

"Maybe I'll make a wish upon those Sisters," he says between kisses.

"Mmm, you don't get to claim the Sisters on top of everything else," I say, nipping his lower lip.

"That's not very egalitarian of you." That wicked grin

of his stretches against my lips.

"Wishes are for people who can't just buy what they want."

"Hasn't anyone told you, *nire bihotza?*" he says between kisses. "The best things can't be bought."

"What does that even mean?" I ask, fighting the impulse to move against him now that his weight has settled between my legs.

"'*Nire bihotza*'?"

I nod.

"Mmm, you'd like to know, wouldn't you?" He touches my scar. "Too bad it takes sharing your secrets to learn mine."

I huff. What he says is fair; it doesn't mean I like it.

"Now," he continues, "about that wish ..."

Back to this?

"Fine, make a wish, man-who-has-everything," I say.

He lifts my hips and slides into me, breaking away from my mouth to watch my reaction.

"I will: I wish that one day, you'll finally know happiness."

And, staring into his eyes, I fear that one day, I just might.

CHAPTER 20

Serenity

MONTES SLIPS OUT of bed the next morning only to return sometime later, bearing a tray with breakfast on it. His hair is mussed from sleep and sex, and he smells like man as he sets the tray on the bedside table and runs a hand through my locks.

"Morning, my queen."

I stretch and force myself to sit up.

"Morning," I mumble, stifling a yawn. It's as pleasant as I can be. After the prior evening's late-night foray, I feel like I've gotten steamrolled by a tank. The king, on the other hand, looks positively refreshed.

"You know how to cook?" I ask, my eyes falling on the tray. I know maids have come in—that or the bed magically remade itself yesterday—but aside from that, I haven't seen any staff on the premises.

"I'm a regular Renaissance man," Montes says, winking at me.

I furrow my brows at his carefree expression, and then at the spread of food. I can't take him when he's like this—selfless. Sweet. Or that, for a girl used to waking up early and standing in line for breakfast, having a decadent one prepared and delivered to me is a significant gesture.

He reaches out and smooths the skin about my eyes. "You don't have to be conflicted about this. It's just breakfast."

I breathe in deeply, catching a whiff of bacon. A wave of nausea rolls through me at the smell. I wait for it to pass.

When it doesn't, I throw off the covers and run for the bathroom. I barely make it in time. My stomach spasms over and over as I clutch the toilet. It's even worse this time around—the nausea, the sharp pains that stab my abdomen.

Behind me, Montes lays a warm hand on my back. He rubs me affectionately while his other hand gathers my hair. First breakfast and now this. What does this man want from me today? I've already handed over my heart and sold him most of my soul.

Once the nausea passes, I flush the toilet and wipe the perspiration from my forehead. I stand, shakily, and Montes is there, wrapping an arm around my waist and letting me lean on him.

He has no questions for me, nor does he air his concerns about my worsening condition. He doesn't even glance over at the bottle of pills I'm supposed to take every day. Perhaps he's finally accepting the hopelessness of the situation.

He walks me back to the bed, and I sit down on the edge of it.

My body's trembling from exertion. It'll pass in another ten minutes, but until then I feel every inch of my mortality. How fragile the human body is when it's riddled with sickness.

He hands me a glass of water.

I look from it to him. "What's going on, Montes?"

He sighs. "Does kindness always have to have a price on it?"

"When it comes from you? Always."

I eye him over the rim of the glass as I take a drink. "You taught me that, you know—to never trust people's motives." Had I not lived through the king's war, I'd never have grown up so jaded.

"I know," he admits. "All your worst qualities lead back to me. And those are the ones I love most."

I shake my head, a reluctant, rueful smile tugging at the corners of my lips.

His eyes twinkle at the sight. We're sharing a moment, I realize. And it's not one based on hate, or humor, or lust. There's a chance we might actually be good together if we manage to not kill each other first.

"If I had even half as much money as Diego's receiving, I'd actually be able to implement good ground control ..."

My boots squeak as I reposition them. I've taken to kicking my feet up on the conference table while the idiots around me fight over scraps.

"My holdings are twice as large as yours," Diego says. "Even with the money allocated to my territory, it won't be enough for ground control."

Day two of discussions has begun. We're only two hours in, but I'm just about done.

Next to me, the king sits back in his chair, running his thumb over his lower lip. That same hand held my hair back while I was sick.

The king never was like other people; I don't know why I keep allowing myself to be surprised by him.

A third person jumps into the debate. "My holdings are larger than either of yours, and our budget is one of the smallest here."

On the surface, every person here sounds reasonable. They have convenient explanations lined up for why they should be paid more. As though they're not going to use most of the money on personal expenses. Already the line item breakdown of many of these proposed budgets includes extravagances like extra planes, additions to homes, and hefty vacation plans.

"That's because no one lives in your territory," another says. "Mine is one of the smallest, but it's also the densest, and it's one of the most violent regions of South America. If we are going to implement ground troops, they should be concentrated in the city centers."

I've reached my limit.

"Alright," kicking my feet off the table, I stand, bracing

190

my hands against the table, "if I hear one more goddamn reason why any of you deserve more than what you already have, I swear to God I will kill you myself."

The room falls silent. "No one is getting ground troops. Martial law is over. You will all set up your own police forces with the budgets we've already given you. Anything else will have to come out of pocket. And after reviewing your generous compensation plans, it damn well better.

"My husband may be king, but he has left me in charge of South America's affairs. *You* are one of those affairs, and frankly, I don't like any of you. You want to keep your jobs and your titles? I want to see some proposals tomorrow for government programs that will help your people. And they better use up every penny of your budgets."

Montes is now pinching his lower lip, his other hand drumming against his seat rest. His expression is pure satisfaction.

"Now get the fuck out of my sight if you don't want to lose your jobs right this instant," I say.

I've never seen a room clear so quickly. The silence that follows their exit fills my ears.

"Your father trained you well."

I turn to Montes. "My father would've been mortified by the way I handled that," I say, weary as I take my seat.

"This is not your father's world, and those men and women will take all that you have to offer and more unless you stop them."

"Then why do you deal with them? You clearly have no qualms about getting rid of people. Why keep the worst ones around?"

"Haven't you heard? All the good, honest leaders have been killed off. Only the weak and wicked remain."

We run in circles. It's no use telling him that before he rose to power the world had done a decent enough job keeping the sociopaths away from office. But in war, it appears they've popped up like weeds. Not just here, either. Montes's entire inner circle is made up of them, men too afraid or too evil themselves to stand up to the king.

"You handled that well, Serenity." There's genuine pride in his voice and I gain insight into something I hadn't noticed before.

"You really do want me to help you rule."

"Of course," he says.

But there's nothing obvious about this. "Why would you share that with me?"

He steeples his hands beneath his chin. "Despite everything, I trust you with my power."

I raise my eyebrows. "You really shouldn't. I've already admitted I plan on killing you."

He leans towards me. "And I've already told you, I don't believe you'll ever do it."

We stare each other down. Another battle of wills. I look away first.

"Do you really think they'll pull something together by tomorrow?" he asks.

I drum my fingers on my arm rest. "They better. Maybe for once they'll stop throwing parties and put their mind and their money towards something that actually matters."

"And what will you do if they don't?"

I give the king a piercing look. "Exactly what you would do—I'll make good on my threat."

He stands. "And you wonder why I give you a portion of my power. You know how to rule." He extends a hand out to me. "Enough plotting for a day. Come, my queen."

Together we leave the hotel. People who see us bow like I'm not just some dying soldier from a conquered nation and the king our tyrant ruler.

I am Montes's captive queen. I may have agreed to this fate for the sake of my people, but I'm a prisoner nonetheless.

It's my heart and the king's that have betrayed us both.

Our car pulls up, but I hesitate to get inside. I may be a prisoner, but I'm a powerful one.

"Serenity?" Montes says when I don't make a move towards the vehicle.

"I want to see the people here," I say, my gaze flicking to the king.

Montes glances around like that's a trick question. "You have."

I know enough about this region to know I'm seeing what powerful people want me to see. "Take me to the nearest settlement. I want to see how the impoverished live."

Montes studies me. "I don't need to warn you about the radiation."

He's actually entertaining this request. And here I thought I'd have to fight him.

"You don't," I say. I know better than most exactly what exposure can do to a person's body.

He squints and works his lower jaw as he considers it.

Finally, he says, "Ten minutes. Make them count because that's all you get."

IT'S EVEN WORSE than I thought.

Our caravan of vehicles pulls up to the edge of a shantytown. The houses are nothing more than bits and pieces of cinderblock, tin, tattered cloth, plastic, and palm fronds. The whole thing looks like it could be swept away by the first big storm of the season.

People stop what they're doing and watch us. It's not every day that shiny, fancy cars bearing the king's insignia stop at your doorstep. In my opinion, a day like that would be terrifying beyond belief.

As soon as our engine is idling, I step out of the car, uncaring that I've left Montes behind or that the king's men haven't cleared the area. The latter shout at me to stop, but I don't. What are these people going to do to me that hasn't already been done before?

My boots sink into the mud as I head towards the edge of the village, and I'm thankful that I decided today to wear boots and pants instead of another frilly dress. The place is muddy and it smells like open sewage.

In my peripherals, I can see the king's guards begin to flank me, but they keep their distance, and I can almost pretend that it's just me walking down the main road.

I don't get very far. Dirty, mostly naked kids run up to greet me.

"*La reina! La reina!*" Some of them call.

Even out here they know of me.

Their exuberance pulls a smile from my lips. "*Hola–hola*," I say to each of them in turn.

Already I can see signs of malnourishment and ill health. Some have distended bellies, others discolored skin from radiation burns. I'm almost afraid to touch them for fear that I'll somehow hurt them.

"Someone take pictures of this," I call to the guards. I want to show those contentious politicians what really matters.

"*Tiene comida para nosotros?*" one asks.

"*Comida?*" Other kids echo.

"Do you speak the common tongue?" I ask. "*La lengua común?*"

"Yes!" I hear some kids shout enthusiastically.

Despite all they must've endured at the hands of their government, they're still happy to see me. The resilience of children.

"Do you have food for us?" asks a girl with stringy hair. Her eyes are far too aged.

Food. Water. I'm used to hearing these requests. They came up many times during my tour as a soldier. No one wants money. Currency means little in these areas when a single meal might be the difference between life and death.

"I will get you and your families some food," I promise. For once I feel like my position as queen allows me to do what I've always wanted to—to save lives instead of taking them.

She jumps up and down at my words and translates

for the kids that don't understand English. Little squeals erupt from the small crowd.

Behind me, I hear the car door close. I don't look back, but many of the children do. I can tell by their widening eyes who they see.

"It's okay," I reassure them, "he's not here to hurt anyone."

I can tell they don't believe me, and why should they? We've all been spooked by tales of the undying king.

"Manuel!" "Esteban!" "Maria!"

I look up. The adults, who have been lingering outside their houses, now call their kids back.

It strikes me as odd—they're obviously frightened of the king but not of me. I'd assumed that people hated me worse than Montes, but out here it appears they trust a former WUN citizen a great deal more than King Lazuli.

Some of the kids peel away. Others hesitate.

"Go," I say. "Tell your parents I'll be personally arranging for food and medical supplies to be delivered to your families."

I watch them run off as the king steps up to my side. "This is why I fought so hard for medical relief in the negotiations," I say to him.

"I can see that." His gaze roves over the shantytown, and I can't get a read on his expression. Right now, I would give a lot to know where his mind is.

The people head into their houses. I can see them still watching us through their windows, but no one else approaches.

The king's hand falls to the back of my neck. He massages it as he says, "Your ten minutes are up."

It's a weak way to end the visit, but I doubt anyone would be willing to talk to us at this point, regardless. Not now that the king is among them.

If Montes is disgusted or unsettled by what he's seen, he never shows it. We get in the car, and our caravan leaves the desolate encampment these people call home.

This is what my sacrifices are for—making sure settlements like that one get what they need to survive and, eventually, thrive.

I glance over at Montes on our way back. "Why did you let me do it?"

The king in his ivory tower; I'd imagine a visit like that is far down on his list of things to do.

Montes lounges against his seatback. He lifts a shoulder and lets it drop. "You'd find a way regardless, and the radiation levels aren't too dangerous there. But most importantly, I want to get laid later."

I narrow my eyes at him.

"I expect I will too," he adds.

"You are a terrible person."

"I *am* terrible, and yet when I'm buried inside you tonight, you'll have your doubts. And tomorrow when I send the food and water to the village, your carefully crafted hate will die."

I glare at him.

"I wonder what will happen once we burn down all of it? What will be left of my queen when her fury no longer fuels her?"

I don't say anything. I can't. Already he's uncovered a

197

very real concern of my own: how to hold onto hate when there's nothing left to feed it.

He leans forward. "I intend to find out."

CHAPTER 21

Serenity

SEVERAL HOURS LATER, after reading a stack of reports on the South American territories, I head into the bathroom to change for dinner.

Another day, another dinner party. This one will be hosted back at the hotel where we're holding the discussions.

I give the black lace dress hanging on the bathroom door the evil eye.

I unbutton my shirt in front of the mirror. As I slip it off, I notice—really notice—what a difference a few months of living with the king have made. My hips and waist are fuller and my stomach slopes gently out. I run a hand over it. The skin feels taut. I'm still not as soft as I would've imagined.

I could still be getting worse. The king believes in the Sleeper the same way some people believe in religion. I, on the other hand, only have misgivings about the machine. To me the only thing it does is remove scars and kill time.

I slide the dress on, along with a pair of heels. I run my fingers through the loose waves of my hair and paint my lips a dark red. I still haven't gotten used to the type of grooming the upper echelons of society expect.

My hands move from the makeup set out on the counter to the neat case of pills I've been packed with. I hold one up to the light. This little thing is what keeps the king permanently young, and it's partly what started his war.

I swallow it, despite my compulsive desire to flush it down the toilet. After all the killing and dying, it seems too precious to waste.

The king knocks on the door. Giving my reflection one final look, I leave.

He waits for me on the other side clad in a tux. Montes leans back as I walk out, his gaze approving. He opens his mouth.

"Don't say it," I say.

"Can't I give my wife a compliment?"

"I don't want the compliment you're about to give me."

Montes comes to my side as we head downstairs. "Has anyone ever told you that you are a strange girl?"

"Because I don't like being called pretty? You all can take your stereotypes and shove them where the sun don't shine."

"Mmm, I'd prefer to shove something else there."

I glance sharply at him.

He looks unrepentant.

His hand falls to the small of my back. "You look lovely. I don't care that you don't want to hear it. I'm going to tell you over and over again."

"You don't get it," I say to Montes as I fold myself into the car waiting for us outside. "I don't want to be valued for my looks. That belongs to your world."

He follows me in. "You now belong to that world."

I think Montes enjoys having the attention on us. Not because he's a narcissist—though he is—but because it gives him an excuse to exercise his chivalry on me. He knows I won't fight him while we're being filmed.

But I don't. I belong to neither the old world nor the new one. I'm no longer one of the impoverished, but I'll never be one of the rich.

I'm a woman with nothing to her name but a few memories and a few more dreams.

"ARE YOU GOING to deprive me of alcohol again tonight?" I ask as we step out of the car. Immediately camera crews close in on us. I squint against the flashing lights. The king's guards step in and keep the media at bay.

"Yes," the king says, guiding me forward.

So the king's serious about preventing me from drinking. That's unfortunate. Talking to these people sober is its own kind of torture. I'll just have to snatch a drink or two when the king's head is turned.

He keeps his body slightly in front of mine, and he angles himself protectively towards me, as if the cameramen might suddenly pull out guns and start shooting us all.

"Tell me again why this dinner is important?" I take in the jewels dripping from one woman's neck as we enter the hotel's lobby.

These people and their beauty.

"Despite what you might think, not all my victories are won on the battlefield. If you charm the right people, you can get just as far without the bloodshed."

"Oh, so now you're a pacifist?" A waiter passes by, and I make a grab for one of the glasses of wine.

Montes catches my wrist. "Threatening works well too," he says, his eyes glittering. "No drinking, Serenity. I mean it."

I yank my hand away.

It wasn't the best strategy to go for it right in front of him, but I'm being slowly stifled to death by him and his rules.

"Or else what, Montes? All I hear from you are empty threats."

He raises an eyebrow, the corner of his mouth lifting. I think he's crafting some unusually painful punishment for me.

"So good seeing you both this evening," an older couple interrupts us. "How are you enjoying your stay?"

This inanity begins again. I think I'd prefer the king's punishment to it.

The couple eventually leaves, but not a minute later another couple takes their place, and then another. And so the evening goes.

My eyes drift away from one portly man's account of his last big game hunt. They move aimlessly over the crowd. I notice Estes is chatting with some of the other political figureheads that were in session with me and the king today.

Scheming, scheming, scheming. These men are always scheming. Sometimes I miss the battlefield for this very reason. The enemy is pretty obvious when they're shooting at you, and you have permission to shoot them back. Here the lines between friend and enemy blur.

I drag my gaze away from Estes. I'm about to check back into the conversation when I catch sight of a ghost.

I have to be mistaken. There is no logical reason why General Kline should be here in South America. And yet I swear it's him across the room bearing a tray of hors d'oeuvres.

He wears the same attire as the rest of the waiters—a white shirt and suit jacket and a bow tie at his neck. He looks thinner than he has in the past, but maybe I'm just getting used to the curves of the people here.

His head swivels, and I blanche as, for a moment, our gazes lock.

It *is* him.

The last time I saw the general, I was in a cell, my memory wiped. That feels like a lifetime ago.

My breathing picks up, something the king notices.

"Serenity, are you alright?" He follows my line of sight, but General Kline has already disappeared back into the crowd.

"Fine. I just need some air," I say, distracted.

I leave Montes's side before he can respond, though I feel his eyes on me the whole time.

I head towards where I last saw the general. It's slow going because, surprisingly, people want to talk to me. I nod to them, exchange a few words here and there, and push my way through the crowd. The entire time my eyes sweep the room.

I catch sight of the back of the general's head as he enters the kitchens.

I pick up my pace, no longer attempting niceties. If I don't want the general to slip through my grasp, I'll have to move a little faster.

My palms slap against the doors to the kitchen as I barge in. Inside, steam fills the air, and the staff shouts out orders. Once they see me, they bow their heads and their shouts turn to murmurs of "Your Majesty."

I stride past them, down the narrow kitchen aisle, following the retreating form of General Kline.

"General!" I shout.

Rather than slowing, he begins to jog deeper into the kitchens.

Damnit, this is why combat boots are far superior to heels. I pick up my skirts and run after him, accidentally elbowing some of the kitchen staff in the process. I don't care that I've probably committed half a dozen faux pas, or that a multitude of people have heard and seen me pass through. My former leader, now a high up Resistance officer, is posing as a waiter at a party I'm attending. I'm not going to wait for shit to hit the fan.

The general leaves through one of the kitchen's back

doors. I can't see anything beyond it.

Adrenaline gathers in my veins, and I prepare myself for an ambush. Mistake number one was not telling the king that I saw the general. Mistake number two was pursuing him alone.

I don't much care, however, that I might be endangering my life. It's been up for forfeit a while now.

Reaching inside my skirts, I unholster my gun and click the safety off. I push through the back doors, my weapon ready, only to find myself in an empty staff parking lot.

"You always did have a fondness for that gun." The hard as nails voice wakes all sorts of memories of a time when I knew right from wrong and good from evil.

The general steps out of the shadows. "I see you got your memory back," he says.

How can he tell? Is it the gun? Or something I've said while cameras are rolling?

I lower the weapon. "Why are you here?"

He glances at the door I exited. We both hear muffled commotion coming from the kitchens.

The king will be coming for me soon.

General Kline returns his gaze to mine. "You need to leave South America—tonight if possible."

It's all I can do to bite back a "yes, sir." Old habits die hard.

"What've you heard?" I ask instead.

The general looks to my stomach. "Is it true?"

"Is what true?"

He opens his mouth, but he can't get the words out.

I furrow my brows. I've never known the general to be

short of words. Not even when he delivered the news of my impending marriage to the king.

"What?"

The general grunts, squinting past me. He shakes his head. "The Resistance hears a lot of things—some true, some nothing more than rumors."

I already know this.

"Estes isn't planning on letting either of you leave here alive," he says.

I raise my brows.

"There are those in the Resistance that support him and his efforts, and I've heard whispers that they're just waiting for his call to take you out. That could be any day now."

Montes and I are scheduled to be here for another five days. If what the general says is true, then the attack will happen by the week's end.

If being the key word here.

"Where and how?" I ask.

"The men are getting the location when they get Estes's call. It's going to be messy, from what I hear. They won't just bomb you—they want proof of the kills."

They want our bodies, he means. It's easy to convince the world someone's dead when you show them evidence of it.

I rub the trigger of my lowered weapon. "Why are you telling me this?"

He slides his hands into his pockets. "You're the world's best chance at survival."

"If you really believe that, then why join the Resistance?" The king had let him keep his position as general.

"I'm not a betting man."

And I was a dying girl. Once I died, he'd need a backup plan.

The two of us have a strange relationship. I blame him for the ring on my finger and he blames me for his son in a casket. And yet here we are, working together.

"Now that really doesn't explain why you're telling me this—or why you're in South America for that matter."

"I'm a top operative for the Resistance, Serenity. I'm never far from you or the king."

Operative is a nice euphemism for an assassin. I'm sure the Resistance is also using the general for strategy as well, but in the Resistance's ranks, operatives are the ones that take out important figures.

"Why haven't you killed me?" I open my arms; I'm still holding the gun in one of them, but it's no longer pointed at the general. "You have your chance—but you better make it quick."

I can hear the king's men in the kitchen.

"You stupid girl," he says taking me by the shoulders and pulling me into a tight hug. "I *love* you. That's why I'm telling you this, that's why I'm not shooting you." He backs away as the soldiers' footsteps begin moving towards the door. "You were always the daughter I never had. Now do me and your father proud and right the king's wrongs."

My throat closes. How can just a few words undo me?

His hands slip away and he turns from me. I watch his form fade into the darkness.

He's almost disappeared entirely when I remember.

"Wait!"

I can barely make him out. He's already blended back into the shadows, but I think he pauses.

"Will's dead." I say quietly, but the night carries my words to him.

I'm not sure whether I'm relieved that I can't see the general's expression, or desperate for it.

"He captured me in the hospital where I was being treated for my cancer," I continue. "His men shot me, patched me up, then proceeded to interrogate me." It's hauntingly similar to my experience with the general. I suppose this is how the Resistance does things.

"The king ransacked the warehouse we were in and took Will." This last part's still hard. "The king had him tortured."

General Kline's quiet, but I hear a thousand things in that silence. We're talking about Kline's beloved son, the man set to take over the general's job.

War takes many things from people, but unfortunately, pain is not one of them. In some quiet, dark corner, when no one's around, General Kline will break down.

"I stopped the torture," I say. "That's why they killed Will."

The general steps back into the light, and his eyes meet mine one last time. He nods, and for that instant, we understand each other completely. The two of us have lived through a nightmare; we've both seen our worst fears realized, and we've been forced to make decisions no human should have to. We've lived more, done more, and stained our souls more.

The general disappears into the night, and the last of my past walks away with him. It's both liberating and crushing, being freed of your last ties. Once more I am the lonely girl that has everything and nothing.

CHAPTER 22

Serenity

THE KING AND his men descend on me not a minute later.

"Serenity, what the hell are you doing out here?" the king says, jogging up to me.

Half of me wants to say, "Getting air." That was the excuse I parted with, after all. But I'm in no mood to taunt the king. Not when my body aches from wounds that leave no trace.

However, I can't tell him about the general, either. Not here at least. If the general's bending loyalties to save my life, then I can do the same.

"I thought I saw someone I knew ..."

It's the only explanation I can think of. I'm a fairly terrible liar, and the king has a built-in bullshit detector.

Montes cups my face, frowning. "If you think you see someone worth tracking, you tell me, you don't go chasing them yourself."

I run my tongue over my teeth. I've always been independent; I don't plan on stopping that now. And I certainly don't plan on trapping myself in the king's gilded cage so that he feels better.

He catches sight of my gun. Up until now he's been concerned, but not panicked over my departure from the party. I can see the moment he begins to take the situation seriously.

His hands slide down my cheeks to the base of my neck. "Who did you see?"

Shaking the king's grip off me, I slide the weapon back into its holster, uncaring that his soldiers are seeing a lot of leg in the process.

"A ghost from my past," I say as Montes steps in front of me, shielding even this exposure from his men.

It's too dark to be sure, but I believe that vein in Montes's temple is throbbing.

"Do I look like an idiot to you?" he says sharply. "Tell me who you saw, or my men will quarantine the area and start interrogating everyone. I promise you, you don't want that."

I've seen the king's interrogation techniques. They involve pliers.

"You are insane."

"No, but you are if you think to keep information from me."

There is no dealing with a man who's willing to hurt

innocents for my compliance.

Several people from the party are drifting outside, drawn by us. Now's not the time to share secrets.

"I'll tell you, but not here."

The King

SHE DOESN'T TELL me until we're back at our villa lying in bed. I think she only admits it then because I begin to stroke the soft skin of her stomach. She assumes it's an advance—not that I'm ever opposed to sex—but at the moment I only want to revel in the fact that she's carrying our child.

"General Kline was at the party," she says, staring at the ceiling. "That's who I saw, and who I ran after."

My hand stills. "You chased after the same man who held you hostage—who nearly let you die—only weeks ago?"

My earlier rage is returning with a vengeance. I don't know whether to be angrier at the general, who thinks he can come between me and my wife, or Serenity, who ran out to meet him with no regard to her life. She could've died, along with my child, for all her stupid heroism.

Worse, she covered for the man. That's why she's only telling me this now; she gave him time to get away.

I know my eyes are icy when they meet hers. "If you were anyone else—if I cared for you any less—I'd have you strung up by your thumbs and beaten."

She's right to think I'm full of empty threats. For all my violent promises, I wouldn't dare hurt her, and I'd turn my wrath on anyone who'd try.

"Am I supposed to be frightened?"

"Goddamnit, Serenity." I pull back and look at her. "I'm serious. I will put you on house arrest—I'll take away your gun, strip you of your duties, and keep you secluded to a single room if I have to."

She pushes me back into the mattress and leans over me. "Kline warned me that Estes is planning an ambush. The man you want to spearhead the leadership of this territory is going to try to kill us both at some point within the next week."

I stare up at her. My mind's primed for a fight; I expected her to lash out, not to divulge. If it were any other time, I'd turn Serenity's reaction over and over in my mind and find all the ways that she's changed since I first met her. All the ways she's begun to give into me.

Her words sink in. An attack. The former general sought my wife out to warn her of an attack.

My reaction is instant—*I will take out any who try.*

All that is evil in me rouses at the possibility.

However, plots to end my life are a dime a dozen. And considering where this warning came from, I have serious concerns over its validity.

There are a hundred and one reasons the Resistance would want us to leave this place early. The one that tops the list—sabotaging the discussions. Weeds like the Resistance thrive in the wild. There is no room for them in the civilized world. South America is still largely in chaos, but as soon as I place certain figureheads into—limited—power, the territory will come to heel.

"Is there any basis for this accusation?" I ask. I'm glad she confided in me, but a warning from the WUN's former-general-turned-Resistance-officer is not a reliable source.

"Does there need to be?" Her eyes are wild. She thinks *me* crazy for not taking this seriously.

Wrapping an arm around her waist, I roll us so that now she is the one laying prone on the bed, and I am the one hovering over her.

"Of course," I say. "Serenity, this is the same man who nearly let you die when the Resistance held you hostage. This is the same man whose son arranged for you to be shot. And this is the same man who willingly gave you to his enemy." I hold her in my arms, completely unashamed that *I* am that enemy. "How do you know he's not trying to force you into some plot of the Resistance's own making?"

"The same way you know I won't kill you," she says.

I don't bother to hide my surprise that she admitted this. I'm not the only one who doles out empty threats, but this one in particular she wraps around her like a safety blanket. To acknowledge that she'll never have her revenge ... this is another turn of events I have to mull over once the time is right.

However, the only reason she would admit this now is because she wants to be taken seriously.

I can give her that.

"Alright," I say, already groping along the nightstand for my phone. "I'll inform my men of the threat, and I'll arrange a morning flight for us."

214

And I do.

Perhaps that's why we never make it out as scheduled.

CHAPTER 23

Serenity

SOMETHING WAKES ME up. I can only hear a phantom echo of the sound, but it's enough to have me sliding out of bed and pulling on my gear. Habit propels me into action.

Montes wakes just as I'm lacing my boots over my pants.

"Serenity, what are you doing?"

I must seem insane, getting hurriedly dressed as I am for no apparent reason. Just another difference between soldiers and civilians. I've been programmed to expect an attack.

Before I respond, I hear it. It's just a distant, dull thump, like someone sinking a dart into a dart board, but silencers also make that noise. It's so subtle that I almost discount it.

Almost.

"Get dressed," I say. "Quickly. Something you can run in. And keep the lights off."

Montes doesn't argue. As he's pulling on his clothes, I grab my gun from beneath my pillow and shove all my spare bullets into my pockets.

I recognize the sound of a jet in the distance. That's what woke me up, I realize. Before I even recognized the purr of its engine, I heard enough of its whine to set me on edge.

I cock my head as I listen to it. It's getting closer.

Shit.

Heading to the nearest window, I peer out. Shadows still cloak most of the yard, but I can make out one of the king's soldiers. He's splayed out on his stomach, near the edge of the property, and as I watch, two dark forms grab his legs and drag him into the thick foliage.

"Montes, your men are getting slaughtered. I think the enemy is approaching from all sides. Call whoever you need to." *But I fear we are alone.*

He swears. He's just finishing lacing up his own shoes when he swipes his phone and places a call.

War's taught me to be paranoid. I'm maladaptive in the king's decadent castle, but out here, out here I know how to survive.

That familiar, rising excitement begins to flow through my veins. I think I am addicted to this sensation. My mortality never means so much as it does now, when it could be seconds away from snuffing out.

Life and death are violent lovers, and today they do bat-

217

tle.

Moving to the sliding glass door, I return to watching our surroundings. I can see figures below, but I'm afraid to shoot when it's still so dark out. It won't stay that way for long; the sun's rising, and if we can survive the next few minutes, I'll be able to tell friend from foe enough to shoot.

"Montes, grab a gun if you have one," I say.

He nods, distracted. He's already on the phone, but judging by his tone, assistance won't be coming in time.

He covers the receiver. "I wasn't able to get ahold of my head of security." Montes's top guard, who's stationed here with us, wouldn't miss a call for anything short of death.

I'm sure death is exactly what befell him.

I hear another thump, and I turn my attention back to the sliding glass door. Two soldiers creep towards the house bearing guns; another man lays sprawled across the grass, a dark pool of blood widening around him.

They're closing in, and we're running out of time.

Opening the sliding glass door, I slip out onto the balcony and study the two approaching men. They wear helmets and Kevlar, which means I'll have to hit their necks if I want a kill shot. And as soon as I shoot, they're going to know my exact location.

The jet I heard earlier is almost overhead. This isn't some routine flight path. This is an orchestrated assassination.

We're dead if I do nothing.

Breathing steadily in and out, I clear my mind and line

up my sights.

Aim. Fire. Aim. Fire.

The shots pierce the silence. Blood sprays as one of the bullets finds its mark; the other buries itself into the second man's vest.

Several things happen all at once. Montes shouts for me, enemy soldiers hiding in the dense shrubs bordering the property now run forward, and the king's men—what's left of them—scramble to meet an enemy that's snuck up on them.

I duck and run for the bedroom. Behind me I hear shots ping against the house's outer walls as that second soldier returns fire.

I've barely made it around our four-poster bed when a violent wind blows my hair, and the jet's purring engine shakes the house.

I spin just in time to face down the aircraft lowering itself to hover outside our balcony. I stare at it, and for a single second the melee quiets.

This is the moment I meet my maker.

"Serenity!"

Montes tackles me to the ground just as the glass sliding doors shatter, and the pilot opens fire on us. A barrage of bullets lights up the room. Furniture is shredded in seconds. Feathers and cloth dance in the air, and the wooden dresser splinters as the jet unloads its ammunition into the room. In seconds the walls are riddled with holes.

Montes shields me with his body the entire time. I breathe in the king's cologne as a familiar rush of adrenaline thrums through my veins.

We might live, but we'll probably die.

We stare at each other the entire time, and I think he might be trying to memorize my face.

He covered me; in that instant when he faced down death, he thought to protect me. I'd expected that from the men I fought alongside, but from the selfish, narcissistic king?

Not in a thousand years.

The firing cuts off all at once.

"Time to go," I say, even though I know he cannot hear me. I jerk my head towards the door, and Montes nods.

Staying flush with the ground, we crawl through debris towards the door. Dust, plaster, and the odd feather float down on us as we move.

"*Are you hit?*" I yell. The ringing in my ears is dying down, but it's still hard to hear.

He shakes his head. "*You?*"

I shake my head. A fucking jet. Estes called in a jet to take us out on top of his ground troops. This is sloppy. Dramatic, but sloppy. Estes must've learned of our plans to leave and rushed the attack.

Montes glances over at me. I see raw fear in them.

"What?" I say, reloading my gun and keeping an eye on the doorway out. I haven't heard anyone breach the building yet, but when they do, things will happen really fast.

His gaze moves to my stomach. He licks his lips, and his eyes return to mine. "There's something I need to tell you."

I wait for him to speak. Now is not a great time to have a heart-to-heart, but if he feels he needs to confess while our lives are on the line, I'm not going to stop him.

"You're pregnant, Serenity."

I stare at him, uncomprehending. I don't think I breathe for several seconds.

"What?" I finally say.

I'm aching to return my attention to the business at hand, but I can't look away from him.

"You're pregnant."

I recoil from him.

This conversation might be the one thing that can make me forget about the fight occurring right outside these walls.

I don't realize I'm shaking my head until the king says, "Yes, Serenity, you are."

Pregnant? With the king's child? Horror and disbelief war for dominance.

No. *No.*

Impossible.

He has to be wrong. How would he even know this?

"You're lying," I say.

Below us someone kicks at the front door. A second later, I hear a shot fired and the thump of a body hitting the outside wall.

"*Nire bihotza*, I'm not."

There is not enough air for me to catch my breath.

I still don't believe him. But each second that he stares back at me unflinchingly, I lose a little more confidence. We're about to die. He has no reason to lie.

I'm going to be sick. The king's child is inside of me. I've never thought of a baby as parasitic, but I do now.

I'm carrying a monster's child.

"How would you know whether I was ... ?" I can't even say the word.

"It came up when you were in the Sleeper."

That was over a week ago.

I grip my gun tighter, but I'm not angry—not yet. At the moment I'm ... *blindsided.*

I draw in a deep breath.

It doesn't matter. The situation, the deception, the horror of it all. None of this matters if we're dead.

I nod to the gun in Montes's hand. "Know how to use that?"

He looks affronted by the subject change. "Yes."

"Good. We're going to survive this so that I can kill you myself. Until then, I need your help." I nod to the window. "There are too many of them. I'll need you to shoot incoming soldiers."

His eyes follow mine. I can't read his expression, but I know where his mind lingers. I can't afford to think about what he's just confessed, and if he's to do his part, he can't think about it either.

Montes has never personally killed before. It's almost frightening that he's never gotten his hands dirty with death, mostly because that needs to change today if we're to live. Even the monster that is my husband has limits to his terror, and today I'm asking that he break one.

"Montes." I recapture his gaze. "This is target practice. Don't see people. See heads and chests. If they're wearing bulletproof vests and helmets, you'll need to aim for the neck, groin, or thighs. And be careful, once you fire the

222

first shot, they're going to know your position."

That's all I can give him. It doesn't get past me how messed up the situation is—I'm giving the man responsible for the third world war tips on how to kill.

The man responsible for knocking me up.

I force down a wave of nausea and get up to leave.

"Serenity—"

I slip out of the room before he can finish whatever he'd been about to say. As far as I'm concerned, the time for talking is over.

I head down the stairs, both hands on my weapon. I can hear the pad of several sets of boots. The enemy is still trying to be silent and stealthy, which means they will be keeping their bodies crouched as they approach. I adjust my aim, knowing they will also likely be wearing Kevlar and helmets. It makes them harder targets, but not impossible to get past.

I peer around the corner.

A shot goes off, and the plaster just above my head chips away. I pull back and lean against the wall, closing my eyes and drawing in a deep breath. From the glimpse I caught, there are at least a half a dozen of them and one of me.

They've come outfitted for war while I have just a handful of bullets. This will take some creativity on my part if I want to survive the next several minutes.

I exhale and an open my eyes. I may not be used to the ways of queenship and polite society, but I'm intimately acquainted with death.

I push away from the stairs and sprint towards a nearby

couch. As soon as I hear the first gunshot go off, I slide the last few feet behind the couch.

They're relentless. They must have a bottomless supply of ammunition to use it so carelessly.

Above me, Montes's gun goes off. He fires three separate shots.

I don't have time to wonder about what's happening outside these walls. The couch I hide behind is getting shot up with bullets; stuffing and scraps of material flutter into the air. I have to flatten myself along the floor to avoid getting nicked.

And then I hear a sound that makes my stomach bottom out.

A grenade clinks against the ground next to my head. My eyes lock onto it. I don't give myself time to think. I simply grab it and lob it back over the couch. The split second decision ranks as one of the stupidest, riskiest maneuvers I've made in battle.

And this time it pays off.

The grenade explodes seconds after I throw it. I hear shouts and the thud of large bodies as they hit the ground. The blast shoves the couch against me, and a wave of heat ripples through the room.

I peer over the back of the couch and level my gun at my opponents. Some are getting up off the ground, some aren't. I take advantage of their temporary disorientation and fire my gun. I aim for their necks.

Five out of the eight shots find their mark. And then my gun clicks empty.

Shit.

While my opponents are shouting and scrambling to regroup, I duck again behind the couch and tuck my father's gun into my waistband.

This is the moment where my chances of survival are the slimmest. I'm out of weapons and the enemy hasn't retreated.

In fact, more vehicles are approaching; I can hear their engines in the distance.

It hits me again: I'm pregnant. Whatever happens to me doesn't just affect my life anymore. It makes me hesitate when I shouldn't.

Behind me, several of the windows have been shot out. It's no honorable exit, but honor has nothing to do with this entire situation.

I begin to crawl towards them, keeping my body as low to the ground as I can.

Two successive shots pierce the air.

There's a moment, right after the shot is fired and before the pain sets in, where you actually don't know whether or not you're hit.

But then the moment passes and the pain doesn't come. I feel the ground vibrate as two bodies collapse.

I cast a glance over my shoulder.

Standing at the foot of the stairs, gun still raised, is the king.

King Montes Lazuli killed for me. The evilest man on earth killed for me and probably saved my life by doing so.

And, God, the look on his face. The vein in his temple throbs, and his eyes are cold and resolute. There's no shell-shocked expression, and he doesn't double over and vomit. He's remorseless.

I shouldn't be surprised. This is the king we're talking about. If anything, I should be worried that he'll get a taste for it.

I nod to him. "Thank you."

He takes his eyes off of his victims to nod back to me, finally dropping his aim.

I stand and head to the bodies. Most of the dead are missing appendages. Grenades are a messy way to go. Ignoring the gore, I begin to take what weapons I can. Montes joins me, and together we strap on guns, grenades, and ammunition.

When I begin to drape weaponry across my chest, he stops me.

"Kevlar first," he says. "To protect the baby."

My stomach drops at his words. It's real, this is real. We're in the middle of a shootout and I'm pregnant.

This is some sick parody of real life, and Montes is some twisted version of my knight in shining armor as he removes the bulletproof vest from one of the dead men and slips it on me. The thing's heavy, and the top left breast is soaked with blood.

I don't focus on that. Instead I string ammunition and guns across my chest while Montes dons a vest of his own. I check the men for keys, but come up empty-handed. They must've left them in the car.

Meanwhile the sound of engines is getting closer.

"We need to go, now," he says, and his order actually makes me smile. I hadn't imagined him to be an equal on the field, but it seems that's just what he is.

Together we sprint for the only car out in the driveway. In the early morning light, I make out several unmoving bodies sprawled across the yard. The jeep our attackers drove in is outfitted with a crate of explosives, semi-automatic assault rifles, and ammunition. The keys sit in the glove compartment.

"You drive; I'll shoot," I say.

Montes doesn't argue, which I appreciate.

While he cranks on the engine, I familiarize myself with my new weaponry. In addition to assault rifles, Montes and I lifted machine guns off of our attackers, the kind you can hold and fire continuously. They have a mean kickback, which means that if you're not stationary or bracing yourself well, your accuracy will take a hit. I'm neither of those things at the moment, but the sheer quantity of ammunition we've acquired makes up for it.

Montes floors the gas and the car screeches around the circular drive before cutting down the dirt road off the property. Mud and pebbles shoot out from under the wheels as I make my way to the back of the jeep.

Back here I can brace myself along the vehicle's exposed metal frame as the jeep jumps and dips over the uneven terrain. I peer at the crate filled with explosives. It's a dangerous thing to have in an automobile, especially when there's going to be a shootout in the near future, but I can't bear to dump them. Not when Montes and I are overwhelmed by the sheer volume of enemies.

I flip the lid off another crate, one I haven't yet looked into. Several grenades are nestled amongst wood shavings. I suck in a breath at the sight. This car is a moving bomb. One nicely placed gunshot and we're all going up in flames.

Ahead of us, two more military vehicles barrel down the dirt road towards the estate.

I don't wait for them to recognize us. Bracing myself against the top metal bar of the jeep, I begin to unload my round of ammunition, holding down the trigger as the bullets spray across the vehicles.

The shots tear through metal and glass, but none of the cars slow. If the soldiers were confused about why one of their own vehicles was leaving the estate, they are no longer.

The enemy begins to return fire, and bullets ping against the jeep's metal frame.

"Montes," I call out, crouching down to grab a grenade. His eyes meet mine in the rearview mirror. "Slow down when we pass them."

"What are you planning?" he says, his voice rising to be heard over the engine and the gunfire

"You'll see."

He doesn't show any signs that he'll do as I ask, but I have to trust that he will.

I return to gunning down the vehicles. One enemy bullet whizzes to the left of my head. Another pings against the metal bar I'm holding onto.

"Serenity!" Montes clearly sees who our enemies are trying to eliminate first.

"I'm fine!" I yell, keeping my eyes fixed on my targets. "Worry about yourself!"

I manage to take out the front tire of the first car, along

with its driver. The second slams into it.

We're almost upon them. Out of habit, I kiss the grenade I clutch for good luck. It's a macabre custom of mine, but after you live through enough battles, you become superstitious.

Like I asked, the moment we begin to pass the row of cars, Montes slows. I pull the grenade's pin and throw the explosive into the second enemy jeep, which is now entangled with the first.

"*Gun it.*"

I have time to see the passengers widen their eyes, and then we leave the car in the dust.

The explosion rocks our vehicle forward, and I cover my head as the scorching heat rolls over me.

Once the initial wave of the explosion dissipates, I glance over my shoulder. Both cars are smoldering, and no one inside the vehicles is moving.

I move back to the front of the car and take a seat next to Montes.

He looks at me like he's never see me before. There's a healthy dose of shock on his face, and no little amount of awe.

I work my jaw. I don't want his respect. Not for killing.

At this point, we have two options: to attack our opponents head on, or flee. The problem with the latter is, even if we managed to get to the hangar undetected, Estes has likely paid off the staff that mans the aircrafts. We'd never make it out.

The problem with the former is that Estes has potentially thousands of men backing him. Montes and I, deadly though we can be, are no match to the sheer quantity of our opponents.

It's an impossible situation.

We're quiet for a minute.

My hand slides to my stomach, and I glance down at it. It's rounder than it usually is, but I attributed that to being well fed.

Montes's hand covers mine.

"You are so lucky I have other people to kill at the moment," I say.

"I know."

When I look up at him, I see he's serious.

"How far along—?" I begin.

"About two months."

I pinch my eyes shut. Fighting for your life has a way of throwing things into perspective. And really, what's bothering me is not that Montes kept this from me; it's that I never tried to prevent this from happening in the first place, and now that it has ...

I have few fears left, the king gift-wrapped me a new one.

CHAPTER 24

The King

I'VE ORDERED EXECUTIONS, waged wars, withheld antidotes, neglected people into early graves, and now I've delivered death myself.

I didn't see the soldiers as targets like Serenity advised. I saw them as people. And I didn't distance myself from the violence like I know some killers do. I was there in that moment and I savored watching my enemies die.

Serenity is right to think I'm evil. The last salvaged bit of my soul burns for her. Other than that, I'm cruelty formed into the shape of a man, and I have no qualms about that.

"We need to leave the country immediately," I say.

Serenity looks out the window and rubs her belly absently. It's a knife to the gut, watching her come to terms with what is, and it's making me want to pull over, hold her to me, and force her to rejoice over the news the way I did.

"The hangar may be compromised," she says.

I nod. That very worry has plagued me since we left our villa.

Even if the airport isn't compromised, we could be shot out of the sky.

"And you think all of this is because ..." Serenity glances back down at her stomach.

She can't bear to say it. As much as I would normally enjoy her being squeamish, right now it does nothing but worsen my mood. This is the last thing I want her uncomfortable with.

"You're carrying our child. Is it really so hard to accept?"

She opens the hand that cradles her stomach, staring down at it like it holds the answers. "Yes," she breathes. "I never wanted this."

I give a caustic laugh that does nothing to lessen my blooming fury. "Well you better get used to it because neither of you are going anywhere."

I am the king of the entire world; I picked her, a lowly former soldier and an emissary of one of the conquered lands to be my wife. Queen of the planet. Who is she to reject me and my child—*her* child?

She needs to fucking accept that this is the way things are.

THE KING THINKS he can keep me and this child of ours around. I still can't think about the situation without a fresh wave of nausea passing through me.

"If Estes hasn't already heard that we've survived, he will soon," I say.

I can tell the king hates that I keep changing the subject. I don't give a damn that he thinks I'm being subversive. He has no clue just how terrible the storm inside me is right now. I'm keeping it together only because we're in danger.

"I have a safe house an hour from here," he says.

"Do any South Americans know about it?" I ask.

"Some. You think it's compromised?"

"The WUN—the Americas—don't work the way the Eastern Empire does. Everyone here can be bought for a price, and if Estes is willing to fly in a fighter jet to gun us down, he sure as hell will be willing to pay off people for information."

"I can pay more," Montes argues.

He's thinking like a rich foreigner.

"Yes," I agree, "but Estes lives here. You don't. This is someone else's turf and the people here play by their rules, not ours. Trust me when I say that when we're this close to death, people here are going to remain loyal to Estes for fear of his future retribution."

"Then we're going to have to kill him," Montes says, grim.

"Yes." If we cut off the head of the snake, the orders stop trickling down to Estes's loyalists.

"Let's be clear about one thing," he says, "my first goal is to get you out of here alive. All our actions will stem from that."

I reappraise my husband. He didn't include himself in that statement. If we weren't in the middle of a dire situation, the magnitude of his words might've hit me a little harder.

Something worse than my nausea rises up my throat. Something worse than grief and violence.

I love this broken, broken creature, and damn him to the pits of hell for making me feel it when I should hate him all over again. If I could reason or suppress it away, I would. If I could crush it by sheer force of will, I would.

"Alright," I say, working to make my voice even, "we're clear about that."

"We need to strike before Estes has time to regroup."

Now *this* is the king I'm familiar with.

Already the humidity of this place has my hair sticking to the nape of my neck. I squint my eyes and look at the horizon. "Let's go pay the bastard a house call."

By the time we near Estes's estate, Montes and I have plotted out a rough strategy to kill the man. One that involves liberal use of explosives.

Neither of us know whether the man will be inside, but smug assholes like Estes are fairly predictable. Right now I'm both desperate enough and sure enough to bet all our lives on his being home.

I move back to the bed of the jeep and swap out the machine gun for a rifle. "If we live through this, I'm having a stiff drink," I mutter.

"Better ask those stars of yours to grant your wish, *nire bihotza*," Montes calls out behind me. "I'm not letting you anywhere near the alcohol cabinet when we get back."

I smirk. I don't know if the king's aware of it or not, but banter like this calms my nerves before fights.

The car curves down the road, and ahead of us I catch sight of watchtowers posted on either side of the entrance to Estes's estate. Two grim-faced guards manage them.

"Are you ready?" I say, lining up my sights. Once I shoot, things will happen very quickly.

"Do it."

I pull the trigger.

It takes seconds to shoot down the guards. I watch as one of their bodies tumbles from its post.

"Hold on," Montes warns.

I brace myself against the jeep's frame as we barrel towards the gates. Our car rams into the wrought iron fence. Metal groans and then, with an agonizing shriek, it rips away completely.

It's almost anti-climactic, driving guns a-blazing onto a quiet estate. But it doesn't stop me from taking position once more. I begin picking off guards stationed outside the house one by one as they struggle to grab their weapons and take position themselves. I don't give any of them time to aim. As soon as my sites lock on heads or chests, I shoot.

Our vehicle comes to a halt, and Montes joins me at the back of the Jeep. His normally coiffed hair is wild. Dirt and ash mar his skin and clothes. He has rolled up his shirt sleeves, and a bulletproof vest encases his chest. This Montes belongs on the battlefield; he looks like he was born to the profession. I definitely like this version of him better.

He bends and grabs a grenade. Flashing me a smile that looks even whiter than usual, he pulls the pin and launches it at one of the windows while I continue to take out anything that moves.

The glass shatters, and we hear a surprised shout. Then—

BOOM!

The explosion unfurls out the window, and I can only imagine what it's doing inside.

Montes already has another grenade in his hand, and he drives this one towards a downstairs room.

The screams start soon after that.

I train my gun on the house's main entrance. At some point, someone's going to run out of that front door that might not be evil like the rest of us. My heart and my soul weep for them. All soldiers that have seen considerable action can tell you that there are always these situations—the questionable ones. And often the innocents get caught in the crossfire.

I hope that doesn't happen today. I hope the people that have nothing to do with Estes's power plays are far away from here by the time Montes and I level this building. Because we *will* level the building, and we aren't tak-

236

ing any prisoners.

I draw in a steadying breath when the front door opens, and then I shoot.

Two guards and a woman I recognize from the meetings. No innocents so far.

I periodically flick my gaze to the windows and the sides of the house. That's where counterattacks will come from.

Montes throws a third grenade, then a fourth. The screams are beginning to harmonize, and the house is catching fire.

Now people are pouring out of the building, some on fire. I shoot those ones first; it's one thing to kill, another to watch a human being suffer, and even after all I've seen and done, I don't have the stomach for it.

"*I surrender! I surrender!*" Over the roar of the fire, it's hard to hear Estes's voice. It comes from just inside the front door. "*Don't shoot!*"

Like all good vermin, the rat managed to survive the explosions.

"Come out with your hands up!" I yell.

I cradle my trigger lovingly. I'd love nothing more than to pump this man full of bullets.

Through the smoke drifting out of the front door, I make out Estes's form. Hands in the air, he leaves the shelter of his house. Too late I see the small gun he clutches.

His gun arm drops and he fires off a shot a split second before I fire at him.

I hear Montes shout. Next to me, he stumbles, then pitches forward into the seatbacks, clutching his hip.

I can't breathe. This is my father all over again. The

bullet, the blood, the emotion expanding, expanding, expanding inside of me. It's too large to contain.

Loss, agony, it's roaring, ripping through me, and I can no longer passively kill.

I lunge for Montes just as the South American dictator falls. I grab my husband, and there's blood everywhere.

Not again, please God, not again.

But Montes is breathing. It's shallow, and with every second that passes more blood slides out of him. I don't know where he's hit—whether it's his thigh or his torso; muscle, artery, or organ.

I'm scared.

I don't know when that happened—when this terrible man went from being someone I feared to someone I feared for.

Montes shakes his head as I try to help him. "Finish this," he grits out.

I don't want to. He could still die; every fiber inside me is warring with itself. My training demands that I stand and shoot, my heart is telling me to keep my husband alive.

Vengeance is a poison, and it slithers through my veins.

Estes tried to kill my husband. My monster. Father of my child.

Something cold and resolute settles on my shoulders. Montes *will* survive, and I *will* end this.

I lift my gun. The screams have turned into moans. I shoot at two more people who've caught flame. Everyone else is laying in pools of their own blood. Almost all are dead, and those that aren't will soon be.

I train my weapon on Estes and approach him cautiously.

He's been inching his way towards his gun, which rests several feet away from him. It must've slipped from his hand when he fell.

I reach his gun before he does, and I kick it away, keeping my aim trained on his heart.

The dictator watches me with angry eyes. "You won't get out of here alive," he says.

"We'll see."

I don't shoot. Even though he tried to kill me and Montes, I don't pull the trigger. Not yet.

For all his depravity, Estes is just one more WUN citizen who shares a past like my own.

"What?" he challenges when I don't shoot. "Do you want to know why I did it?"

"No."

I already know why. It's the same reason behind my mother's death, and my father's, and my land's. Power is the worst sort of drug. You can never have enough of it, and you'll give up every last good thing for more.

"Then what are you waiting for?"

It's a good question. I want him to redeem himself. I want proof that a soul as far gone as his—or mine, or the king's—*can* repent.

But he's not going to understand, and it's not going to happen.

"Who are you working with?" I ask.

He tries to laugh but ends up grimacing instead. "You and I both know I won't tell you." He's beginning to sweat. A gut wound is a painful way to go.

Estes has about seven minutes of life left in him. I won't get answers from him willingly or unwillingly. We both know it.

"Did you really think you could ever do what I do?" he says. "You have no idea. You're just a savage with a sad story. And the king wants you to rule the world? I won't be the last—"

I pull the trigger before he can finish the sentence. The bullet hits him in between the eyes. One instant the man was aggressively alive, and the next he's nothing more than bones and muscle and cartilage.

The smoke soaks into my clothes and the wind dries the blood on my skin as I stare down at him. The roar of flames is the only noise out here. The whole thing is a dark baptism.

I don't want to be this way. Killing and killing and killing. I'm a prisoner to violence, and I'll never be free.

I strap my gun back across my body and kneel before Estes. Threading my arms under his, I drag the dead dictator's body to the jeep.

There are a lot of horrific things that I've had to do throughout the king's war. This is just one more of them. The man's body is our ticket out of here. Just as Estes wanted proof of our deaths, I'll need proof of his to sway loyalists who would stop the king and me from leaving.

The stillness of the estate is eerie. All that's left of Estes's great scheming is me, a dying immortal king, and a whole lot of carnage.

I grunt as I pull the body along, pausing when I reach

the back of the jeep to catch my breath.

Montes raises an eyebrow weakly.

I grunt again as I shove first Estes's upper body and then his lower half into the back of the vehicle. Montes's upper lip curls as he stares down at the dictator now lying next to him.

I round to the king's side and remove his hand from his hip. There's blood everywhere. My own hands are beginning to shake; they don't usually do that, especially not in the heat of battle. That's often when they're steadiest.

I take a deep breath.

I still can't tell what the bullet hit, and this is no place to doctor Montes back to health.

We need to get back to the hangar.

I hop onto the driver's seat and press on the gas. Behind me, I hear Montes groan.

A bloody hand grabs my seatback. A moment later, Montes hauls himself over the center console.

"What are you doing?" I say, aghast. "Sit back down."

"You are not leaving me to rot next to a dead man," he says. He grits his teeth as he forces his broken body into the seat next to mine. He didn't once cry out. The guy's made of tougher stuff than I would've guessed.

When I reach the end of Estes's property, I let the jeep idle.

"I don't know how to get to the airport," I say.

I can't meet Montes's eyes. I don't want more proof that my monster-turned-lover is now nothing more than an injured man. He's supposed to defy the laws of nature.

"I'll get you there," Montes whispers. "Just ... look at

241

me."

I don't want to.

"Serenity, please."

I squeeze the steering wheel and force my gaze to meet his. He looks tired. Worn. Weak. All the things I feared I'd see in those eyes of his. And now these might be the last breaths of air he'll take.

"Do you love me?" he asks.

I'm shaking my head. "No."

"Liar."

He can see right through me.

"Now's your chance to kill me," he says.

I work my jaw. "What do you want me to say? That I can no longer do it? I already admitted that to you."

He gives me a wan smile. "Turn right."

I take my eyes off of him to do so.

"There's a Sleeper in my plane," he says. "You want to save me, then get me inside it."

I floor the gas pedal. Anger and guilt and confusion—they all vie for my attention. It's one thing to protect the king from death, another to try to save him from its clutches. I'm truly abandoning my own promise right now. I won't kill the king—not today, and not in the foreseeable future.

I grit my teeth against his groans as the vehicle hits rocks and potholes.

"Left," he says, when the road tees off.

There's a Sleeper at the end of this drive. I just need to get to the hangar, and then we can get Montes inside it. I even my breaths; I'm cool and collected, I can feel myself detaching from the situation.

Until I look over at the king. His head leans against the wall of the jeep, and his eyes are closed.

"*Montes*." I reach over and shake him. "Stay with me."

His head lolls as he tries to nod.

"I swear to God, I will fucking punch you in the dick if you don't."

That actually elicits a shadow of a smile. "Vicious ... woman ..."

Two minutes later, he slips away again. Luckily, I no longer need his instructions. I begin to recognize our surroundings—the skeletal remains of a home nature's reclaiming, streets that are nearly covered by foliage. I can get us the rest of the way there.

By the time I pull into the hangar, Montes is completely unconscious. The place is bustling with activity. I have to assume that all these men are in Estes's pocket. I hop out of the jeep, gun in hand.

"*Estes is dead*." I point to the back of our vehicle with my free hand, where the dictator's body lays. The men peer at the car, and some approach. "Whatever orders he gave you, they no longer apply. The king and I are getting on the king's plane. Anyone who stands against us will be shot on sight. Those that help us will each receive half a year's pay once we safely disembark."

That gets them moving. Men rush around the hangar, preparing our plane for takeoff. Each discreetly looks at Estes as they pass the car.

Once the aircraft is ready to board, two men help me carry Montes onto the plane. His skin is paler than I've ever seen it, and his body is dead weight.

"*El rey está muerto.*" The man speaking has two fingers pressed to the pulse point beneath the king's jaw.

"No." I push aside his hand and place my own where his was. I wait for his pulse. It never comes.

I stare down at the king's face. His head's rolled back, like he's fixated on the ceiling, but his eyes are closed and his mouth is slightly parted. Already the planes of his face are losing shape.

I cradle the side of his head. I don't realize I'm crying until the first tear trickles into my mouth.

People are wrong to say that the dead look peaceful. They just look dead.

"No," I repeat.

This man isn't beyond saving. Not now that I've fallen for him, not now that I carry his child.

The men look at me strangely, but they nonetheless help haul the king into the plane. Montes told me that the Sleeper would be onboard, but I've never seen it before.

"The Sleeper—we need to get him into the Sleeper."

Someone knows what I'm talking about because I begin to hear shouts of "*Compartimiento de carga! La carga! El durmiente! Más rápido.*"

We begin to move again, this time towards the plane's cargo bay. Inside, I can already hear the hum of the machine as it idles. It's bolted to the floor. My heart palpitates a little faster just locking eyes on it.

The king told me once that so long as the brain was intact, the Sleeper could bring the dead back to life. So it doesn't make sense, this irrational dread I feel when I see it. Perhaps it's that such technology seems just as unnatural as Montes. But right now I'm happy to set aside my superstitions if it means resurrecting a dead king.

We get him situated inside and I close the lid. I don't know what to do next, but the machine has a "Power" button. On a whim, I press it.

The humming sound turns into a whirr as the Sleeper wakes up.

I watch the small readout as it begins to assess the king's vitals—his now nonexistent ones. Then it begins scanning his body.

"Come," one of the men says.

"Not yet." I want to make sure that the machine is doing what I need it to. I know that means more time on the ground, more time for a potential counterattack should Estes's allies decide to rise up. I don't care.

It only takes a minute for the machine to get a respirator and something called a cardiopulmonary bypass device hooked up to the king. Five minutes after that, the machine begins cleaning the wound.

A gentle hand touches my upper arm. "Good?" one of the men asks.

I nod, backing away. Leaving is the last thing I want to do, but I need to arrange safe passage with the men here. If the machine can save Montes, it will.

If it can't, then the world will know the undying king can, in fact, die.

CHAPTER 25

Serenity

I STARE OUT the plane's window, my hands resting on my gun and my chin resting atop my hands.

I have all the time in the world and nothing but my thoughts to occupy me. There's plenty to think about, and I don't want to dwell on any of it.

So instead I gaze out at the lonely sky and try to feel nothing. It doesn't work. Last I saw, Montes was dead, and even with the Sleeper's best efforts, he may stay that way. If he doesn't live, I'll be queen.

The world won't bow to me, the young woman who betrayed her land when she married the king. I might inherit Montes's empire, but I haven't earned the right to rule it. War could very well break out again. And I'd be the first to die.

That's no longer an option. Not now that I'm pregnant. I exhale a long breath. I will have to be more ruthless than I've ever been if I want to survive. And I'll have to be willing to get back inside that dreaded machine if I want to live long enough to have this child.

My thoughts turn to General Kline. I couldn't say what I feel in this moment. Gratitude? Grief? Melancholy for the life I once lived? He banished me to this fate the day he made a deal with the king, but I might have died today if not for him.

My thoughts circle back to the king. I'm used to greenies underwhelming me. Montes did the opposite. Before today I couldn't imagine him on the battlefield. I'm used to seeing him in pressed linens and suits, and while he has muscle to spare, I've never seen him exert true force.

Today he did, and he was relentless. He saved my life at least once, but in all likelihood, he spared me from death several times. Had he not so readily killed, we would never have left South America. Of that I'm certain.

The king who killed millions from his ivory tower now left it to kill several himself. That last bit of Montes's innocence was snuffed out today. If he wakes from the Sleeper, what man will rise? Will he be worse? Better? Wholly unchanged?

I find I really don't care. I just want him back.

It seems like a lifetime later that the overhead speaker clicks on. "We're beginning our descent into Geneva. We should touch down in another twenty minutes."

Geneva, the last place I want to be. Only a handful of

months ago I'd fled that city, boarded a plane and crossed the Atlantic to flee the king. Back then I'd mourned the death of my father. Now here I am returning to the very place I'd once loathed, and I'm trying to bring the dead king who'd once tormented my people back to life.

The world has gone crazy, and me along with it.

It's dark outside as we descend, and few city lights illuminate the streets. The airfield, by contrast, is lit up.

When I exit the plane, it's to a crowd of the king's medics and his security team. They try to shuffle me off to look at my wounds. I elbow past them and head for the cargo bay. Behind me, I can hear their protests.

I make it to the back of the plane just as the flight crew opens the cargo hold. I'm the first one inside, despite the commotion behind me. I jog up to the Sleeper and scan the readout.

I blink back tears as I clench and unclench my jaw. Medics and security personnel move in behind me. Some grab my arms and gently guide me out. I let them.

The undying king beat death yet again.

The King

I WAKE WITH a start.

Reflexively, my body tenses. The gold leaf molding overhead is distinctly different from the exposed cross beams of the Spanish villa we've been staying in.

I feel skin beneath my hand. I trace the flesh with my fingers. It's soft, but the muscle beneath it is unyielding.

My hand travels higher, rounding a delicate shoulder. Then the hollow above a collarbone. I feel soft hair slide under my touch.

I glance down at Serenity, who's nestled against my side.

My stomach tightens pleasantly at the sight. Savage woman. She hasn't left me, despite now knowing she's pregnant.

This pleases me immensely.

My last memories involved gunfire and explosions. Somehow I survived it, in no small part thanks to the woman in my arms. Not so long ago she told me she wanted to kill me. But she didn't take her chance when it was offered to her.

My hand delves into her hair and strokes its way down the golden locks. There is no name for what I feel right now. Not awe, not love, not gratitude. None of those are large enough to encompass this emotion that's not quite pleasure and not quite pain.

"Mmm." She moves against my side and opens her eyes. "You're awake."

I expect her to try to move out of my arms—not that I'll let her. When she doesn't, that feeling burrowed beneath my sternum expands.

Her fingers touch my side, where I'd been shot. "Did you know you died?" she says, her voice toneless.

My hand pauses its ministrations.

So my wife not only spared my life, she saved it.

"I don't want to outlive you, Montes," she says.

I squeeze her close and whisper against her temple, "Are you admitting you can't live without me?"

She's quiet for so long I assume she's not going to respond.

"Maybe," she finally whispers.

I'm not big enough to hold what I feel.

I touch the scar on her face and follow the line of it down her cheekbone. "Do you still hate me?"

"Sometimes," she says honestly.

I smile to myself. "Good. I like you feral."

She shakes her head against my chest. "You're twisted."

We fall silent for several minutes.

"I'm going to be a terrible mother," she finally whispers.

I pause. Serenity's *scared*. The woman who's killed legions of men is actually afraid. Of herself.

It's almost unfathomable.

I pull her in closer and kiss the crown of her head. I'm holding my family in my arms; I have literally everything I could ever want.

"You'll be the best mother," I whisper against her temple. She will be because she'll second guess everything and work to get it right. For all of my wife's ruthlessness, she has a wealth of compassion.

"You're not a great judge of character," she says.

I laugh. "When it comes to you, I am."

Serenity

THE DOOR TO our room opens.

"Good morning, Your Majesty."

"Oh, I love the view from this room."

"Look at that flaxen hair of hers. I've tried to dye mine the same color, but I can't quite mimic it."

The female voices fill the bedroom, and I can hear them moving towards the bathroom.

I squeeze my pillow tighter. The cool metal of my father's gun brushes against my hands. I'm not going to look up; that'll make it all real, and I have at least another hour of sleep in me.

The bed dips and I feel a hand on the small of my back. A moment later, the king's lips press against my temple. "Serenity, you need to get ready."

I groan and bury my face deeper into the linen. If the king has it his way, then I am not going to get myself ready at all—a bunch of strangers are.

"Make them go away," I mumble.

One of Montes's hands delves under the pillows and finds me gripping my gun tightly.

"Don't you agree one massacre is enough per week?" he says conversationally.

I turn my head to face him so that I can glare. All that earns me is a kiss on the nose.

He gets up to leave, and I release my gun to snatch his wrist. I'm more awake now, more aware that the only time the king actually calls in a team to get me *prettied* up is when something important occurs. "What's going on?"

He stares down at me, and those conniving eyes of his hold such fondness in them. It both moves me and disturbs me that the king looks at me this way; I'll never get used to it. "Politics," he says evasively.

I squeeze his wrist tighter. "Give me more than that."

He raises an eyebrow. "And what will you give me in return?"

I'm not in the mood for his coy games. "This isn't a fucking exchange. I'm your wife."

Montes leans in. "With me, it will always be an exchange. Of wits, of wills, of affection, and of everything in between." He yanks his wrist out of my grip and walks away.

Two hours later I'm glaring at him as I exit the palace, my hair coiffed, my face painted, my body sheathed in another too-tight dress. He waits to the side of our ride, wearing his coat of arms.

Those deep eyes of his land heavily on me. "My, doesn't my wife look lovely."

"Fuck off." I stride past him and duck into the car waiting for us. I still have no idea where we're going.

He follows me in. "Dark blue is a good color on you."

I won't look at the asshole, who probably took a total of ten minutes to get ready himself.

"Are you going to finally tell me where we're headed, or do I have to guess?"

When I turn to face him, he's pinching his bottom lip and studying me with interest.

"We're going to church."

IT's BEEN A while since I've been inside a church, and not just because I lived in the bunker for most of my teen years. After all, I spent a good amount of time topside when I was doing my tour with the military.

I lost my religion about the same time I lost my city. When it comes to war, people tend to go one of two ways: either they find God, or they do away with him. I fell into the latter category.

I never blamed him, not like some of the others that gave up religion. They seemed more like jaded lovers than atheists. God just never was a man in my mind. He was food, shelter, safety, and—ultimately—peace. And when all that fled, I realized that my world no longer had a place for him.

But now as I enter the cathedral, holding the king's arm like I was prepped to do, I can feel the weight of *something* fall on my shoulders. Maybe it's the dim light, or the silence in the cavernous space filled with hundreds of people, but it prickles the back of my neck.

I'm about to ask the king if we're getting married all over again when I catch sight of a crown at the end of the aisle. It rests on a pillow next to a priest—or a bishop, or a cardinal. I have no idea what title the holy man goes by.

My breath releases all at once.

The king's planning to coronate me.

I pause mid-stride. I want no part in this. It's one thing to be forced to marry a ruler, another to accept the position yourself. And this isn't just some parliamentary affair; this is a spiritual one as well.

No good god would sanctify this.

"Montes," I hiss. "No." That's all I'm willing to say in this place of silence.

"*Yes*," he insists.

I'm still fighting him, even as he drags me forward.

"Do it for our child," he whispers.

My heart pangs. I have a new weakness, and Montes just exploited it. If he thinks a crown will protect the baby, I'll go along with it. After all, I was willing to do much worse when I didn't know if Montes would survive the flight to Geneva. So I stop fighting him.

We're halfway up the aisle when he leans into me. "Once we get to the altar, kneel," he breathes, his voice barely a whisper. "When you rise again, you'll be a crowned queen."

Montes leaves me at the foot of the altar, where I do as he says and kneel.

The rites are read in Latin, and they go on and on and on. My eyelids are drooping by the time the holy man grabs the crown.

I blink several times as he approaches me with it. Lapis lazuli circles its base, and dozens of gold spikes branch off of it. I've never seen anything like it.

The holy man speaks more Latin as he places the crown on my head. He makes the sign of the cross before re-trieving a robe made of velvet and ermine. The material settles over my shoulders, and he clasps it at the base of my throat. The weight of it all presses down on me; I'm sure the effect is intentional. This is very much a burden.

He gestures for me to stand. I do so, and the two of us lock eyes. I think for a moment we are wondering what kind of person the other one is. What kind of woman marries a tyrant ruler? What kind of religious man ordains a killer as queen? Staring at him, I realize we might both simply be decent people cornered into powerful roles. Everyone can be bought, but the price is not always power. I wonder what his was.

He speaks again in Latin, makes the sign of the cross again, and then indicates for me to face the crowd.

I swivel and find hundreds of faces staring back at me. But there's one face my eyes seek out. He's the only other person besides me and the man behind me who remains standing. His dark eyes gleam with approval.

For the first time since I entered the Cathedral, the man behind me speaks in English. "I present to you, Her Majesty Serenity Lazuli, High Consort of the King, Queen Regent of the East and the West.

"Long live the queen!"

CHAPTER 26

Serenity

I'M STARING OUT the window of my room at Geneva's broken city. It presses up against the edge of the palace grounds and fans out to what I can see of the horizon.

I don't like this place; it holds too many bad memories. I keep wanting to hunt down the suite my father and I stayed in. It's macabre, but I feel like if I went there, I'd run into him—or at least see the stain his blood left on the carpet.

I touch my crown and prick myself on one of its points. They might as well be thorns. They look like thorns, they feel like thorns, the only difference is that these thorns are golden and shine in the light.

I pull the thing off and stare at it.

"It's not going to bite you."

I don't turn around when I hear Montes's voice. He'll demand attention soon enough—he always does—but I won't give him any immediate gratification. I've been whittled down to petty acts of rebellion.

"How long have you been planning that?" I ask.

"The coronation? Since we returned," he answers.

"I'm actually impressed," I say, running my thumb over the spires of my crown. "You coordinated an entire ceremony, a feat you managed to keep me in the dark about, and you executed it all without making me look like a fool."

I think he recognizes what I'm not saying.

You deceived me.

You made me vulnerable in a room full of wolves.

You forced my hand.

"Our enemies already recognize your position as my wife; it's time the people recognize it as well."

I rotate to face him. His eyes glint as he watches me. He wears a crown of his own, and the sight of it brings back all those months and years when he was just an evil so unnatural that he defied the very laws of nature. He seems just as inhuman now—just as dark, just as beautiful, just as untouchable.

I should renew that old vow and kill the king where he stands. My gun is holstered against my inner thigh. It would take seconds to pull it out, aim, and fire a lethal shot. Hit that terrible mind of his and destroy all chances of him ever being revived.

I won't act on the fantasy. This evil man has awoken

my heart. I don't understand why or how, but he has, and even my ironclad will doesn't stand a chance against it.

Montes strides across the room and takes the crown out of my hand. He studies it.

"Whether you like it or not," he says, "you were always a queen. You were this morning before you woke up, you were the day I slid my ring onto your finger. You were the first time I laid eyes on you. You were queen the first time you drew blood, and the first moment you drew breath." Very deliberately, he places the crown on my head. "The coronation makes no difference because here," he touches my temple, "and here," he touches my heart, "you've always been this way."

He has no idea that while he waxes on about queenship, I've been debating whether or not I could kill him.

"I'm calling bullshit," I say.

He laughs and extends his arm. "Come, Queen Regent, you have a coronation banquet to attend, and our child needs to eat."

And there it is, the final nail in the coffin: he has compassion, and now we share more than just bloody, deadly love between us. We share life.

WE HEAD DOWN the hall, towards the ballroom where I first met the king. The doors leading to it are closed, but muffled conversation and laughter still filter out. I'm hit with a powerful wave of déjà vu. Not so long ago I walked down this hall with my hand tucked into the crook of another man's arm and together we faced the same pair of closed doors. But then it was my father, and the dreaded meeting was with the king.

Now the very monster I feared is the one lending support at my side. I breathe in deeply.

"All you have to do is eat a little and nod to people you don't know," Montes says, misreading me. "Oh, and don't stab anyone in the eye with the utensils."

"Montes, I'm not going to stab anyone with anything." That's what my gun's for.

We stop at the doors and wait for the guards to open them. "It'll take an hour," he says, "and then we'll leave."

The doors swing open. The moment the room comes into view, the guests fall silent even as they rise to their feet. I wonder what they see when they look at me and the king. Their nightmares swathed in silk and crowned in gold? Or are we more benign in their eyes than that? I know what I see. This place is the bastion of extravagance and corruption.

"May I now present you with Your Majesties the King and Queen Montes Lazuli, Sovereigns of the East and the West."

Applause erupts and amidst the noise I hear shouts of "Long live the king! Long live the queen!"

Montes leads me down the stairs. As I pass by our guests, they bow.

The whole thing is more than a little unnerving.

The ballroom is now an expansive dining room. Everything that's not gilded at least gleams. The clothing, the jewels, the candlelight, even the guests' eyes and smiles.

There's a table at the far end of the room and at its

center are two empty seats. I just need to make it there and then converse with people I despise.

It's times like these that I'm almost positive I somehow already died and this is my hell.

When we get to our designated table, the king pulls out my seat, just as he always insists on doing. I sit—and just about scream when I realize who is across from me.

I *have* died. This *is* hell.

"Congratulations, Your Majesty," the Beast of the East says.

I don't see him; I see a string of broken women.

This monster is going to die before the dinner is over.

I glare at the Beast—Alexei is far too innocent a name for this *thing*—until he looks away. Even that's not good enough. I begin tracing the serrated edge of my steak knife with my finger.

I don't care at this point that nearly a dozen cameras are capturing every second of this dinner. I'll kill this monster where he sits, and then I will stand on his corpse and laugh.

Not five minutes after we've taken our seats, the waiters begin bringing out dinner. The sight and smell of all that red meat ...

I think of the grenades tossed at Estes's estate. The smell of charred humans that drifted in the air. The sight of those bodies ripped open, their innards exposed.

My nausea is climbing up my throat. I press the back of my hand to my mouth. I thought morning sickness behaved its damn self and stuck to mornings.

"Are you alright?" the Beast asks.

260

I ignore him while Montes drapes his arm over the back of my chair and rubs my neck. He leans in. "Do you want me to send back the food?" he asks quietly, reading my reaction.

I look over at him. Is he seriously considering wasting every single plate of food all because of me? It's horrifying, this power I wield, this power the king seems happy to bestow upon me.

I rear back as I assess him.

The psycho is serious.

"Don't you dare."

"Very well." Montes still flags down a waiter and discusses something with him. The waiter's eyes focus on the Beast as he listens. Finally, he nods to Montes and leaves. A short while later a bowl of soup and a basket of bread are set in front of me.

I glance over at the king. He goes on talking to the men on his left, but the hand still resting on my neck gives a light squeeze.

He ordered me soup so I wouldn't have to eat the meat. It's just one more considerate thing the king's done on my behalf.

I break the bread and dip it into the soup. This I can palate.

I'm halfway through it when the king's lips brush against my ear. "Better?" he asks.

I turn into him, my lips brushing his. "Much."

This might be the first time I've been genuinely affectionate with the king in public.

"Good," he says, his voice roughening.

Someone begins clinking a knife against their glass. When Montes smiles, I feel it low in my belly.

"Do you remember what that means?" he asks.

I do. They want us to kiss.

I lean in the remaining distance and press my lips against his. I can feel his surprise in the way he returns the kiss and the slow smile that gets incorporated into it. Our audience begins to clap, and though my skin prickles uncomfortably from the attention, I don't pull away until the kiss is done.

We break apart slowly. Montes is gazing at me, his brows slightly pinched, his mouth curved with amusement. He leans in and steals another brief kiss. Then he lounges back in his chair and reaches for his wine glass. Lifting it, he surveys the room, but it's me he looks at when he takes a lazy sip from it.

I grab my glass of water with a shaky hand. Either it's all the eyes on us, or my own actions, but I'm not nearly as composed as the king.

"How does it feel to be the queen regent?" the Beast asks, drawing my attention to him. He cuts into his steak as he speaks. Blood seeps out of the nearly raw interior.

My eyes drift from his plate to my own. I take a sip of my soup and pretend he doesn't exist.

Only he won't let me.

"I mean," he continues, "technically you were queen since you married our king, but today he handed over part of his empire to you." He shakes his head. "I never thought I'd see the day he shared his power with anyone. You must be something." His knife scrapes against the

262

porcelain as he cuts into the meat again.

I can't take it anymore. The smell of the meat, the sight of this abomination, the stifling civility of these people. We're all barbarians here, and we know it.

I'm done pretending.

I lean forward. Somewhere along the way, I released the soup spoon and exchanged it for something a little sharper. I'm now gripping the steak knife in my hand and not wholly sure how it got there.

"I'm going to tell you this just once," I say. "If you so much as look at me wrong, I will castrate you with the nearest object." My voice is low and angry. "Then I will throw you into the worst prison I can think of. One of the ones where they'll have fun with you—and I'll make sure they do. And if I ever catch wind that you've *raped*"—I hear a gasp from one of our nearest guests, and feel Montes's eyes immediately on me—"anyone else, I will do all that and worse."

Other than looking a little pale, the Beast appears unruffled. Either he's schooling his features well, or he can't bother to be intimidated by me. It's probably some mixture of both.

He stares at me for a long second then inclines his head. "Understood."

"Good." I release the knife and return to my soup.

Conversation, which had quieted for a moment, picks back up.

My left hand rests on the table, and I feel the king cover it with his own. He leans in close. "I'd been almost positive I'd have to dig a knife out of Gorev's skull," he says quietly, eyeing the Beast, who is now in a conversation with the person to his left.

"This isn't funny."

The king's hand tightens around mine. "No, it isn't. Save the killing for when the cameras aren't around."

I give him an exasperated look, but I relent. The Beast is safe.

For now.

I WAKE UP in the middle of the night to terrible, throbbing pain. At first it simply stirred me from sleep. I'd roll, reposition myself, and go back to bed.

But now my eyes snap open as the pain rips through my abdomen like a knife wound to the gut. My skin is slick with sweat, and the sheets stick to it.

My hand drops my lower stomach, where it hurts the worst. Several seconds later another wave hits. I let out a groan and fist the comforter as it cramps up my muscles.

"Serenity?" Montes's voice is thick with sleep.

When he tries to pull me to him, I let out a gasp.

"*What's wrong?*" Now he sounds wide awake. He clicks on the bedside lamp and turns back to me.

I shake my head. "I don't know."

A healthy body shouldn't be doing this. Montes and his doctors have been swearing up and down that I'm alright, but right now I don't feel alright. I feel wrong.

Very, very wrong.

My pelvis cramps so sharply that I release a strangled sound. I'm being wounded from the inside out.

264

One of Montes's arms slides behind my back. The other touches my cheek and tilts my head to face him. "Do you need a doctor?"

I shake my head, then nod. I don't know. I grip Montes's upper arm as the cramps intensify.

Oh God, dear God, I think I know what's happening.

I squeeze his arm. "Montes," I say. "Our child ..." This is the first time I've openly acknowledged the baby as ours.

His expression doesn't exactly change, but I see it—fear.

I choke on a silent cry as the pain somehow gets worse. Warm, wet fluid seeps out between my thighs. I can't look away from him as it's happening.

Montes's eyes search mine, and there's such desolation in them.

He begins to pull away.

I latch onto his upper arm. "Don't leave me."

"Serenity, I need to call a doctor." He's pleading.

A tear slips out before I can help it. "I think it's already too late," I whisper.

CHAPTER 27

Serenity

SOME DAYS I want to live, and other days, like today, I want to die.

I shouldn't feel this sadness, this overwhelming grief. I hadn't even thought I wanted a child. Especially not this one. Only once it was too late do I find out I did. Now I can actually admit that I might've even been excited.

But just like everything else in my life, all roads lead back to death.

I lean against the pillows propped up behind me like I'm some kind of invalid. The sheets have already been changed, the bloodstains removed like they never existed. I've now lost two family members within these walls.

This place is cursed.

"... These things just sometimes happen," the doctor is saying to Montes.

The king paces, one of his hands squeezing his lower jaw almost painfully. Other than that single tear I shed, neither of us has cried. We bottle up our emotions because to dwell on them might just destroy us, and the king and I, we won't let anything consume what's left of us.

I stare at the far wall, study the gilded edges of the molding. The impersonal art painted by an expert hand that hangs just below it.

"Serenity ... *Serenity*."

I blink and refocus my attention on the king.

He takes my hand. I don't realize that I've been fisting it until he smooths the fingers out. Each nail has left bloody, crescent-shaped wounds in the pads of my palm. "You're going to need to get into the Sleeper so that everything's been properly flushed out—"

"I'm not getting in your fucking machine ever again."

That's probably a lie. I'm speaking from my heart right now. The weight of this terrible existence is pressing down on me, and I can barely breathe through it.

I don't want more of this.

Montes's hand squeezes mine. "I'm not giving you a choice." He sounds as close to losing it as I've ever heard him. "Either you get into the Sleeper on your own free will, or it happens by force."

I narrow my eyes at him. He's not the only one close to the edge. But anger lifts the fog I've been under for the last couple hours.

What's happened to me today can't happen again. I

won't let it.

Montes will force me into the Sleeper, that I don't doubt. But if I go willingly ...

I run my tongue over my teeth. "I'll do it—on one condition."

Montes and the doctor wait for me to finish.

"I don't want to get pregnant again."

The King

THEY GIVE HER a birth control shot. It won't last forever like she wants it to, but it will keep her sterile for a while. Long enough for both of us to grieve and move on.

My hand covers my mouth as they sedate her and place her in the Sleeper.

Now I've lost two people in mere hours. Serenity will be fine in a few days, once her body has purged the last of the fetus and the Sleeper has expunged the most recent flare-ups of her cancer.

But I won't.

I leave the medical wing because I can't bear to look down on her sleeping face and envy her fate.

I head to the palace's training facilities, which I share here in Geneva with my soldiers and guards. When I enter the weight room, several of my men are already there lifting. They stand and salute as soon as they recognize me.

"Out," I say. It's all I can manage.

I wait until I can't even hear the echo of their boots.

I don't wrap my hands or change before I begin laying into the punching bag. It feels cathartic, releasing emotion this way.

I slam my fists into leather until my knuckles split and my body's covered in a sheen of sweat. Even then I don't stop. My grief is turning on me. I never did well with feeling helpless.

I embrace the rage that's willing to take its place. This is one of the fundamental ways I understand Serenity. Death makes us both vicious. It burns through us like fuel and we consume it before it can consume us.

Another hit. I pretend I'm hitting skin and bone and not unforgiving leather. The chains clang and the bag swings.

Such a little thing, this life we lost. Just a spark of a possibility, really. And that was snuffed out before it could grow into something more. I was warned. I didn't listen. And why the hell would I? I played God for the past thirty years. It's a rude awakening to realize I can really be powerless.

I slam my fist into the bag—left, right, jab, uppercut. The metal chain that it hangs from continues to shiver, the sound echoing in the empty space.

Eventually I stop and steady the swaying bag. I'm a bloody mess; it drips from my hands, and it's smeared into my clothes and on the leather.

I catch my breath, watching droplets of blood and sweat spill from me onto the floor. And then I begin to laugh. Two of the world's most terrible people lost a fetus—or is it an embryo? Whatever it is, it couldn't have survived on its own. It didn't have a gender—it might not have even had a heartbeat. It lived instead off of Serenity's scarred one. And we *mourn* for it—us, the two people who have staggering death counts to our names. This grief is madness.

And yet I can't shake it.

My laughter turns to ragged sobs. Not a single tear falls from my eyes, and yet my entire body weeps. I tried so hard and for so long to not feel this way. You can heal your body, but not your mind or your heart.

And how they bleed.

Serenity

SOMETHING'S WRONG. I know it's wrong before I even fully wake. As I blink, I try to figure out why I feel so ill at ease.

The first thing I see is Montes. He grips my hand in his, and he's kissing my knuckles one by one. He looks troubled.

I sit up and look around. I'm back in our room, in our bed, and—

The last lucid hours of my life come back to me. I now have a name for that wrongness; it's called death.

The nausea comes on suddenly, and I run for the bathroom. Maybe it's the grief or maybe it's the physical aftereffects of a miscarriage, but everything hurts. My back hurts, my stomach hurts, most of all, my heart hurts. I heave and heave, but nothing comes. Even after the nausea passes, I don't bother moving from where I kneel in front of the toilet.

I hear Montes make his way in. He places a hand on my back. "*Nire bihotza*, I need you to get up."

I bow my head. Take a deep breath.

Keep moving. One of the many soldier creeds I learned in the military. So long as you focus on placing one foot in front of the other, your demons can't catch up to you.

Reluctantly I stand and turn to Montes. My hair's in my face. He brushes it away and cups my cheeks. Our eyes meet, and then he pulls me into a tight embrace.

The king hugs me like I might slip away if he doesn't hold on tightly enough. He doesn't say anything, and I appreciate it. When it comes to grief, words have no balm strong enough to soothe the soul.

His fingers run down my hair, and he buries his face in my neck. I breathe him in. How had I ever thought this man inhuman? He smells real enough, he feels real enough, he bleeds, he hurts.

I turn my head into him, my lips skimming his jawline. He pulls away and our eyes meet. I can feel his mortality beneath my fingertips, his anguish batters against mine. For perhaps the first time ever, I wish to consume him the way he consumes me.

His brows draw together as I lean in. And then I'm kissing him, marking him, making him mine. I grab the collar of his button-down and—*rip*. Seams split and buttons fly. The hard skin of his stomach is bared to me. I touch it, luxuriate in it.

My monster.

He nearly died. We all nearly died. I will hurt because of what we lost, but it could've been worse.

So much worse.

And now I want to savor what I didn't lose.

His hands grip my upper arms. He's staring at me like he doesn't know me—but he desperately wishes to. I like the look. A lot.

Montes backs us up, helping me out of my clothes and his. He doesn't dare speak. This side of me, the one that pursues him—he must think it's some sort of apparition. Smart man is not going to ruin the moment if he can help it.

We fall together onto the bed. Neither of us bothers kicking off the top sheets before I slide down onto him.

I close my eyes and exhale as I relish the feel of him inside me. One of my hands finds his corded shoulder. I run my palm over the muscle. Real. Alive. Mine.

He holds my hips tightly to his own. We both need to move, but neither of us wants the feeling of being connected to slip away.

"Open your eyes, my queen."

I do.

His dark, mesmerizing ones stare back at me.

No one ever warned me about feelings like this. That I could see something worth redeeming in the world's evilest man, or that he could see something worth saving in the scarred, dying girl he holds in his arms.

I touch his cheek. My hand looks pale and delicate against his olive skin.

Had I once despised the way his presence could overwhelm me? Now the way he envelops me, fills me, devours me is what I love most about this life I lead. He is what's

272

real.

"Make me forget," I say.

And he does.

CHAPTER 28

Serenity

LONG AFTER MONTES and I finish, I lay in bed awake.

Outside our windows, the night is dark. The city gives off no light, and for once it feels like the darkness is pressing in on me, rather than beckoning me away.

Next to me the king's breaths are deep and even.

My throat works as I gaze at the ceiling.

Event one—the king's palace comes under siege. I lose my memory in the process. Event two—I catch a strain of plague concocted in one of the king's laboratories, a laboratory nations away. A strain of plague no one else catches. Event three—the stabbing. Again meant solely for me. Event four—an ambush meant to end my life and the king's.

Four events spread over a couple months. All of them took place in areas the king deemed safe. All around people the king trusted.

There's a traitor amongst us.

My heart beats faster. The more I mull over it, the surer I am. No average Resistance member could know where the king's blast door was, the door Marco and I never made it inside. Nor could an average Resistance member know our movements enough to try to stab me or ambush me and the king. And to acquire and transfer a super virus like the plague—for that, one would need a scientist or, perhaps, a doctor ...

I bolt upright in bed.

Dr. Goldstein? Is it possible?

A terrible, terrible thought clutches me. On the evening of my coronation, I had a miscarriage.

Panic seizes up my lungs.

What if ... ?

The king reaches for me in his sleep, murmuring something. I move out from under his hand.

I need to know.

I slip out of bed, dress, and leave our room.

My boots click against the marble floors as I stride down the hall.

I touch the gun I holstered to my side. If what I fear is true, there is no place my enemies can hide where I won't find them.

It takes me almost ten minutes to reach the royal medical facilities, which are housed belowground. Even here guards are stationed along the hallways. They look on, impassive, as I pass them.

Ahead of me are two double doors. When I reach them, they're locked shut, but next to the door is a fingerprint scanner. I place my thumb against the surface. In theory, being queen essentially grants me access to anywhere I want to go, but this is the first time I'm actually testing that power.

A light next to the scanner blinks green and the door unlocks.

I don't question my luck.

I flip the lights on, and a moment later the fluorescent bulbs flicker to life.

The royal medical facilities are some strange hybrid of hospital and palace. The walls have gilded molding and the floors are made of marble, but the smell of the place is exactly what you'd find in any hospital.

The soles of my boots sound deafening against the floor, but there's no one here to startle.

I'm looking for the proverbial needle in a haystack. The chances of finding anything are slim, but I won't fall back asleep again until I know for sure whether the doctor has been compromised.

I move through the first set of sterile rooms towards the labs, using another thumbprint scanner to make my way into another room.

I hear the hum before I see the Sleeper. This machine holds none of the answers I seek. Still, I feel compelled to approach the hated device.

Over the last several months, I'd been in one of these things longer than I'd been out of it. At the end of this particular Sleeper is a window, similar to a porthole on a ship.

I hesitate. The machine's on; I have no idea what I'll see if I peer through that glass pane, and I'm not here to sightsee. But curiosity gets the better of me. Who else is important enough to incubate in one of these coffins?

My shoes click as I near it, I tilt my head and peer down.

I inhale sharply.

Dear God.

I recognize the dark, close-cropped hair and that hateful face that's so serene at the moment. I watched that very face kill my father, and then, later, himself.

Marco, the king's former right hand.

He's supposed to be dead.

But apparently he's not.

MY HANDS BEGAN to tremble. First the king's immortality, now this—resurrecting a dead man from his grave. Where I come from, things are simple: you live, you age, and then you die—in that order.

I back away.

This is unnatural. More than that, it's wrong.

"I see you found Marco."

I'm reaching for my gun before I fully recognize the king's voice.

When I turn, he's carefully watching me. His hair is swept back; he wears slacks and another button-down, the sleeves rolled to his elbows like he's ready to get his hands dirty.

Had he watched me as I dressed? Waited for me to leave before he dared to follow? I keep forgetting that no one can even sneeze in this place without the king learning of it. And when it comes to me, he always wants to learn.

"You sick bastard," I whisper. "What have you done?"

The king steps up to my side, but his eyes are focused on the Sleeper. "He was my oldest, most loyal friend." He touches the glass fondly, his eyes sad. "When you and Marco were sealed off—and then I found out that at least one of you was dead—" he shakes his head, "I wasn't willing to lose either of you."

"You can't change these things," I say.

Montes is shaking his head. "Do you remember what I told you?"

I furrow my brows.

"So long as the brain survives, the Sleeper can save him."

"Marco put a bullet in his brain. I saw him do it. By your own logic, Montes, the Sleeper can't revive him."

"You're right," the king says, leaning against the machine. "The man you're staring at is a vegetable. My friend is gone."

I shouldn't be affected by how desolate his voice is. Not after witnessing this.

I don't bother asking how Montes secured Marco's body. The king has his ways; if he wants something badly enough, he'll get it. I'm firsthand proof of that.

"Would you do this to me?" I nod to the Sleeper. "Leave me in one of these things rather than letting me die?"

This is an important question because I *am* dying.

The king doesn't say anything, just continues to gaze down at his fallen friend.

"Montes, would you do this to me?" I repeat.

His eyes flick to mine. And then very deliberately, he turns on his heel and walks away.

I STAND THERE for several seconds, processing that. I hear the far doors open and close. My husband left me with his silence. And in that silence, I have my answer.

Heaven help me, that was a yes.

He'd shove me into one of these coffins and prevent my body from dying.

Now I'm faced with the very real prospect that at some point in the near future, I'm going to need to take matters into my own hands. I rub my eyes. My heart's heavy.

After every sacrifice I've made, must I make this one too? Is it wrong to not want immortality? That the price I'd have to pay would be too steep?

My hand drops. I stare down at Marco as unease settles low in my belly. Had he known the king would do this? Had he rejected the idea as well? Was that why he took the bullet instead of the serum?

I force myself away from the device. I didn't come here to ponder Montes's plans. I wanted answers.

I begin rifling through everything. No one comes back for me—not Montes, not the guards. I'm sure someone's got eyes on me, but I don't much care.

I move out of the lab and deeper inside the facility. Back here the doors have bronze name plates fastened to them. I stop when I come to Goldstein's.

Using the thumb scanner, I enter his office.

Stacks of charts sit in piles around the doctor's desk. But it's the one sitting right in front of his computer that captures my attention.

It's mine. I read my name clearly along the tab.

Serenity F. Lazuli

On the front, a note's been paper clipped to it. I pick up the folder and begin to flip through it. The first page appears to be a form for a prescription. The only thing that's written in at the bottom of it are two drugs I can barely pronounce.

Behind this page are the latest readouts from the Sleeper, mostly x-rays of my brain and body. The doctor's gone through and circled certain sections. Malignant tumors, by the looks of them. Not that I know anything about this. I was trained to kill, not to heal.

As I flip through the x-rays, they appear time lapsed. Each gets smaller, but then, the dates get older. My eyebrows pinch together.

That can't be right. I spent weeks upon fucking weeks in the Sleeper in an attempt to reduce these. The machine might not be able to cure cancer, but it can remove a tumor.

I recheck the dates. My eyes aren't deceiving me; my cancer hasn't been treated.

If anything, it's been expedited.

CHAPTER 29

Serenity

A SHAKY HAND goes to my mouth. The warm breath of anger is pushing against my shock, and I welcome it. Dr. Goldstein tricked me and Montes.

An inside man.

I need to find the good doctor, but first I have to figure out the depth of the deception.

I fold the x-rays and scans in half and shove them into the back of my waistband. Carefully I put my file back on the desk where I found it.

My eyes move to the note paper-clipped to the front of the file.

I grab a pen and notepad from the doctor's desk and scribble down the series of numbers written on the note, followed by the medication I read on the first page of my file. Once I finish, I rip the sheet of paper from the notepad and, clutching it in my hand, I leave the palace's medical facility.

But I don't go back to my room. Instead I head to the office I've been using here in Geneva.

I sit down at my desk and boot up my computer. Time to find out what else the good doctor's been up to.

The King

SERENITY NEVER CAME back to find me. I'm pissed, both at her refusal to simply accept her situation and at my own burgeoning dependency on her.

Two hours after I left her, I leave my office. I thought that work—rather than lying in bed awake—would better take my mind off of her; I was wrong.

I'm going to find my wife, and then I'm going to make her understand that I am not a monster for wanting her to live.

I head for the medical facility, almost dreading the possibility that she's still there.

She has to know that I won't give her up to death. For Christ's sakes, she should be more desperate to live than I am. Why would she want it to all end when she knows I have the power to keep her alive, and that, one day soon, I'll have the power to cure her of her cancer?

Another thought chills my blood: what if she's already tried to kill herself?

282

She's the furthest thing from depressed, but if she got it in her head that she had to take her own life, she would. Without hesitation. It wouldn't be suicide to her; it'd be a mercy killing.

Now I'm running, my footfalls echoing against the marble. I can hear my pulse between my ears.

When I burst into the medical facilities, the lights are still on.

"Serenity?" I call.

Silence.

My heart rate continues to ratchet up, and the cloying sensation of dread floods my veins. I find myself holding my breath briefly each time I enter a new room, fearing that this will be the one that contains her lifeless body.

I should've hid Marco better. I should've simply known she'd react the way she did. I scour the facility for her, but she's not here.

Relief doesn't come.

Where would she go once she left this place?

Short of death, she might try to escape.

That thought sends me stalking towards the palace gardens. I consider asking the guards if she's passed this way, but I don't want to shed light on the fact that I can't control my queen. I'm not that desperate. Yet.

She's not outside. Not in the gardens. Not near the fence.

I head back inside, scrubbing my face. Where could she be?

Her office.

I go there at once. The lights are on, the computer's

running, but Serenity isn't here. She's leading me on a goose chase.

I head over to her desk and pick up the thin pile of papers sitting on top of her keyboard.

At first they don't make sense. I'm looking at a rib cage, a pelvis. Another rib cage, another pelvis. Someone's gone in and circled orbs—tumors. As I flip through the scans, a horrifying pattern shows up. The tumors are becoming bigger, and more numerous. Some disappear, but those are the minority.

The last image I see is not an x-ray; it's a color-coded image of the brain. A small cluster of color is circled.

I nearly drop the papers. As it is, I stop breathing.

I'm almost positive that I'm looking at Serenity's cancer. The Sleeper should've minimized or altogether eliminated the growth of malignant cells. But these images suggest a different story.

The papers crunch in my hand. I bring my fist to my mouth.

While the Sleeper can't cure someone of cancer—yet—it is capable of controlling it. Yet I hold proof it hasn't done that.

This was a deliberate act of sedition. And it will cost Serenity her life.

Usually I'm a cold, calculating bastard. Not this time. My wrath is a living, breathing thing. Every ounce of fear I feel—and I feel a great deal—fuels it.

Goldstein is a traitor.

"Guards!" I bellow.

They come running into the room.

284

"Collect Dr. Goldstein and take him to interrogation," I order.

They leave just as swiftly as they came.

I promised the man that his life was tied to my child's. Not only did he ignore that warning, he also tried to take Serenity away from me. And he might have succeeded.

It's time to let him know just why no one crosses me.

Now I MUST find where Serenity went. She's a smart woman, she knows I won't let her die, and it appears she's figured out before me that Goldstein played us both.

All this time I thought Serenity's symptoms had been the result of her pregnancy.

Fool.

I'd been had.

The thought brings on a wave of rage so strong an animalistic cry forces its way out of my mouth. Without thinking, I grab the back of the bookcase next to Serenity's desk and topple it over.

I do the same to the filing cabinet. I hurtle a paperweight across the room, and it punches a hole through the drywall. I can hear my guards running back towards this room.

"Stay out!" I yell.

So help me God, I will kill the first man that comes through the door, and I'll enjoy it. Lucky for them, they listen to my order.

The quiet drone of the computer catches my attention. The screen is dark but all it takes is a jiggle of the mouse and it comes to life.

Two windows are up on the screen. The first is an informational page on two drugs. A single, chilling word pops up repeatedly throughout the article.

Abortion.

I taste bile at the back of my throat. For one sheer instant I believe my wife rid herself of our child.

Anger, betrayal, and soul-searing fear all move through me, and for one second I feel the devastation Serenity always alludes to. I feel as though I'm losing everything all at once.

And then I remember. The x-rays, the scans. She found her medical file. The site she left open gave her only a definition.

She didn't seek out the drug; she must've found evidence of it in her medical records.

The second wave of my rage rushes through me. Her miscarriage was no accident.

Goldstein killed my child.

I almost leave then. I already know that Goldstein will not die quickly, and I'm eager to see that man suffer as none have before him.

However, the second window catches my eye. On the screen is the palace's directory. It's listed in alphabetical order, and about five people and their corresponding contact information fill the space of the screen. Four of the names and faces mean nothing to me. But the fifth one, the fifth one I see almost daily.

It's my newest recruit. The Beast of the East. Alexander Gorev.

DR. GOLDSTEIN AND the Beast of the East. Two traitors who are in communication. Two traitors who are sharing my personal information. Two traitors who've tried to kill me—if my assumptions are correct—and succeeded in killing my child.

I smile viciously as I head to the office Gorev uses while in Geneva. This is one of the few times I'm actually pleased with my fractured conscience. I wanted an excuse to kill this sad sack of human flesh. Now I have it.

The random assortment of numbers scribbled on Goldstein's note referred to Gorev's fax machine, a number registered in the royal directory.

I don't bother going after Goldstein. Not yet. The doctor will face my wrath later, once the Beast is nothing more than ashes.

Do these men not realize what I did when my father died? Did they think it would be any different with my child? How cocky both must be to think I wouldn't find out.

I reach Gorev's office. Another thumb scan and I'm inside. I make myself at home. Immediately I begin to flip through his drawers. In the first one I find cigarettes, a fancy metal lighter, and a bottle of 186 proof whiskey.

A man's most important professional items are those closest at hand. Alexei's are his vices. He's not a man plagued by his demons; he's ruled by them. It actually makes me more curious about the Beast. What his motives are for getting involved in treason when he's just about as high up as one can be?

Then again, in the king's world, all roads lead back to greed.

I pocket the lighter and uncap the whiskey, taking a swig as I continue to peruse the traitor's office. I almost choke on the stuff. My eyes tear up as it burns its way down.

I glance at the label again. This stuff isn't alcohol; this is lighter fluid.

I find nothing else of interest in the office. Gorev is less careless than Goldstein when it comes to leaving damnable breadcrumbs.

I kick my legs up on the desk, and then I wait.

When the Beast walks in, I'm playing with fire.

I flick Alexei's lighter open and closed. Open. Closed. Open. Closed.

He stops.

My gaze is focused on the fire. "Do you know why I'm here?" I ask.

Alexei steps into the room and closes the door behind him. He leans back against it. No one in the WUN would be so stupid as to lock themselves in a room with the person they were betraying. When you live amongst casual violence, you never underestimate people. Not even a young, dying queen.

Especially not a young, dying queen.

But perhaps the infamous Beast of the East sees me as just another meek woman.

"You wanted to speak with me?" he says, one side of his

mouth curving up. His eyes fall on the bottle of whiskey.

My mouth curves upward as well. "You're good, I'll give you that. Even when you know that I know."

He tenses, and it's the signal I need. Grabbing the 186 proof alcohol, I saunter around the desk. I stop in front of him.

He has no idea what I'm going to do next.

I tilt whiskey bottle to read the label better. "You know, what it really comes down to is this: you killed my child."

My eyes flick up to him, and before he has a chance to react, I backhand him with the bottle. Glass shatters against his cheekbone, and the force of the impact throws him to the ground. The alcohol soaks his face and his hair, and it drips down his neck and seeps onto his chest.

The Beast cradles his injured cheek as blood drips between his fingers. I must've cut him with the jagged edge I still hold. I drop it to the ground and smash it with my boot.

Then, ever so slowly, I stroll towards him.

He's drenched in whiskey and glass shards, and he's losing his calm facade as he crawls away from me.

"The attacks on my life—those I could've forgiven. The attacks on Montes's—well, you know my history. But you involve an innocent?" I kick him onto his back and flick open the lighter I still hold. "That'll bring out the sadist in me."

Now I'm seeing this hateful man's fear. Wrapped up in it is anger and incredulity. I'd like to think that last one has to do with my gender.

I hold the lighter over him. "Just how fast do you think

you'll go up in flame?"

The cocky man who entered his office is gone. Alexei keeps swallowing, and I think he's desperately trying to hold back vomit.

"There's alcohol on you," he says. "If you drop that on me, I'll make sure you catch fire as well."

I flash him an indulgent smile. "You think I'm scared of death? Goldstein's been informing you on my health. You know how advanced my cancer is," I say. "The king can't stop it. I might be squandering ... oh, a few months if you do manage to kill me. But you know just as well as I do that with cancer, the final months are the worst.

"You, on the other hand," I continue conversationally, "probably have decades left." My gaze moves back to the flame. "I've heard death by fire is the worst way to go."

I let him see my eyes. My empty, empty eyes. I am the result of a life of loss. This is what happens when you live through every fear you've ever owned.

"Please," he says.

"Please what?"

"I don't want to die."

I stare down at him. My hand is practically shaking from the need to drop the lighter on his body and see him go up in flame. Vengeance is whispering in my ear, and it's such a seductive lover.

"Who else?" I ask.

He's looking at me with confusion.

"Who else is in on it?" I doubt his word is any good, but every once in a while someone squeals who's actually telling the truth the first time around.

He opens his mouth, but before he has a chance to talk, we both hear footfalls approaching the door.

"This could end very badly for you depending on who enters," I say.

Several seconds later the door bursts open. I shouldn't be surprised when I see Montes, but I am. Sometimes I forget just how resourceful my husband is. And this time, he's come alone.

His eyes take in the scene. He's seen me kill, but this is the first time he's ever seen me truly cruel.

"Do it," he says.

My eyes move back to Alexei. He knows he's a dead man.

"I'll tell you everything, just please don't kill me."

And then he begins to list off names.

CHAPTER 30

Serenity

IT'S WORSE THAN we imagined.

The Beast and the royal physician aren't the only traitors amongst us. There's a whole ring of them, and most Montes meets with on a daily basis.

His advisors betrayed him.

He'd been right all along to begin that witch hunt amongst his councilors. At the time I'd been horrified at the thought of him killing one of them. I'd even saved one from death, an advisor whose guilt the Beast admitted to several hours ago.

I saved the man who helped plot my assassination. Who facilitated the death of my child.

I have to work to keep my features expressionless.

The advisors trickle in, all but Alexei. The king's newest advisor will never again take his seat, or walk, or eat, or conspire.

He's now nothing more than a lump of cooling flesh, and my only regret is that he didn't die slow enough. Those women he raped and tortured, they deserved better justice than I gave them.

I pick out a bit of glass from underneath a fingernail. My eyes flick to the king's remaining advisors. These fuckers, however, we haven't dealt with. They sit down in their expensive suits and chat idly as they wait for the king.

Next to me, Montes lounges in his chair, watching them all, a small smile on his face. He's utterly still—no bouncing legs, no drumming fingers. Whatever fuels my husband, he doesn't waste it on tells. Not even that vein in his temple throbs at the moment.

Suddenly, Montes's chair screeches as he slides it back. He stands, bracing his hands against the table.

The room falls silent.

"For the longest time I believed the Resistance was behind the attacks on Serenity's life," he begins. "But a king has many enemies." His gaze moves over his advisors, and the men eye one another uneasily.

The door to the conference room opens, and the king's soldiers storm inside. They head up either side of the conference table, boxing the advisors in.

It's a nice show of force; the soldiers even have their guns out.

"Half of you have committed high treason. Traitors do not get the benefit of a fair trial. I am your judge, jury, and executioner."

I glance over at Montes.

Executioner?

I'm about to stand when the officers aim their guns. It all happens so quickly. I only have a second to take in everyone's shock before half a dozen guns go off at the same time.

I jerk back at the deafening sound. Blood sprays across the room and mists in the air.

Foreheads and eyes are missing from a handful of the world's evilest men. The smell of meat and gun smoke fills the room as their bodies slump over. The rest of the councilors stare at their dead comrades with horror.

I draw in one shallow breath, then another.

Slowly I turn my head to Montes. He meets my gaze, and I see rather than hear him say, "I did what I had to do to keep you safe." And then he leads me out of the room.

He's holding my upper arm, and I realize it's because I'm weaving. I'm so goddamn tired.

I shrug his hand off me and walk ahead of him.

He grabs my arm again. "I did that for you—and for our … child." He can barely even say it, now that it's gone. For once we actually created someone rather than destroyed them. In a sea of old experiences, this is a new, intimate one, and it binds us together in a way that nothing else can.

"I'm not mad," I say, weary. "I wanted them to die. Horribly." That's the problem. "I don't want to be that ruler, Montes. I don't want to be what you've become."

NOT TWENTY-FOUR HOURS later we get wind that the rest of Montes's advisors—as well as several of his staff, including Dr. Goldstein—have fled the king's palace. The next day, the king's intel alert us to their whereabouts.

South America.

The land of Luca Estes and now over a dozen more traitors.

The king's council has dissolved. I'll never have to attend another ridiculous dinner party with his men because they're either dead, or they've absconded to the wilds of the West.

Montes and I are all that's left of his inner circle: two enemies brought together by war and bound by peace. I was wrong when I believed that the king and the Resistance were two sides of the same coin; in reality, it's the king and I who are. The East and the West, the conqueror and the conquered. We complement each other nicely in all things, even ruling.

Montes and I sit next to each other in his cavernous map room. He hasn't taken down the assassinated men or his intricate war strategies plotted out across the map. I eye the web of thread and the crossed out faces with unconcealed disgust.

"It still bothers you?" Montes asks, not looking up from the paper he's reading.

"It will always bother me." But tearing down distasteful wallpaper is a battle for another day.

Our thighs brush as I return my attention to the latest reports, and concentrating on work becomes a task in itself.

"All seven of your advisors have been spotted in South America," I say, once we've gone through the documents.

They hadn't just been spotted in South America, they'd been spotted near the former city of Salvador. It's awfully close to a Resistance stronghold and the city of Morro de São Paulo, where the king and I nearly lost our lives.

Too close.

The vein in Montes's temple throbs, and one of his hands is curled into a fist so tightly his knuckles are white.

"Alexei gave us the wrong names." The Beast's final bit of treason.

The last laugh is on Montes—or us, rather, since I'm involved in this feud as well. Alexei tricked the king into killing his honest advisors.

"Do you think they were aligned with Estes? With the Resistance?" I ask.

"It doesn't matter." The king's quiet voice raises the hairs on my forearms. "They'll all die, along with every single person they have ever loved."

THE KING IS slipping into violence.

Whether it's the personal cost this war is finally having on him, or that he just can't bear to lose what he worked so ruthlessly hard for, he's falling deeper into that abyss.

"Leave the innocents out of this, Montes."

He turns his head to me slowly. "You are my equal in many ways," he says quietly, "but I am the man who conquered the world, and you will not tell me how to carry out my will."

What he is proposing is abominable. I know he's done this before, leveraged loved ones to force a person's cooperation—hell, he's done it to me—but even bad men have a code, and targeting innocents goes against that code.

I push up from my chair. "Yeah? Well you better make damn sure you kill those innocents. Because the survivors, they'll turn out just like me."

I walk away from him, my boots clicking against the floor. As far as I'm concerned, this meeting is over.

"In that case," he calls out to my back, "I have no need to worry at all."

His meaning is clear: I, and anyone like me, are fickle with our vendettas.

He is so wrong.

Swiveling back to him, I pull out my gun, cock it, and fire. The bullet buries itself into his right shoulder. It all happens so fast he doesn't have time to react until blood is blooming onto his expensive suit.

Shock and pain mingle in his eyes as he clutches the wound. Blood drips over and in between his fingers. "You shot me," he gasps out.

Normally I'm not this stupid. To draw blood from the king but refuse to kill him—that sort of thing doesn't go unpunished. With all that I've endured, I've just guaranteed myself more pain. But these days, pain is the only thing I really feel. Without it, I might as well not exist.

I holster my weapon. "Look into my eyes, Montes."

He's clenching his teeth, his breath coming in quick pants, but he makes eye contact.

"This monster, the one you created, the one you love so

much, this is what I can do."

I can hurt those I love.

Montes doesn't need to know that my windpipes are tightening up at the sight of his agony. That even now I have to steel myself from running to his side and soothing the very hurt I caused.

But I don't do that. I need him to know the extent of my depravity.

Soldiers burst into the room right before I say my final piece.

"You don't want more of me around," I say, "and you should never, ever forget exactly what I am."

CHAPTER 31

Serenity

I'M ON HOUSE arrest until the king's released from the Sleeper. That pretty much means I just have a shit ton of soldiers guarding me at all hours. And my gun's been confiscated. Again.

Because there are no more advisors to help govern the world, I find myself running the globe by myself.

I want to laugh that I did what so few could: I shot the king and received a promotion for it.

That all ends the day Montes is removed from the Sleeper. It's my turn to sit at the king's side and wait for him to wake. Of course, guards flank me. They no longer trust me alone with the king, but since he's given no orders to punish me for my crimes, they can't stand against the queen until the king wakes.

They won't let me touch him, but my fingers twitch with the need. I try to tell myself it's just curiosity, that I want to feel the smooth expanse of skin where his bullet wound was. But if I'm being honest with myself, what I really want is to stroke his dark hair back from his face. I want to run my fingers over the stubble that's grown on his cheeks and chin.

His eyelids twitch, then one of his fingers moves the barest bit. It takes another several minutes before his eyes flutter open. They immediately lock on mine.

Before he can help it, he smiles, and it's free of any duplicity. He's just happy to see me. His attention shifts from my face to the soldiers that flank me.

His eyebrows draw together.

I help him out. "I shot you. You've been recovering in the Sleeper."

His expression grows distant as he searches for the memories.

Montes sits up. "Wife doesn't bluff," he mutters. He looks to me again, and I can see him trying to make sense of me. His gaze flicks to the guards. "Leave us."

They hesitate.

"I gave you a direct order. *Leave.*"

Reluctantly, the guards do so.

"Am I no longer on house arrest?" I ask.

Montes's eyes burn. "Oh, your punishment is far from over."

The King

I STARE INTO my wife's mesmerizing blue eyes. I'm still wrapping my mind around the fact that she looked me square in the eye and shot me. But I always knew what I was marrying. I'd seen the bodies in my palace back when she was just the daughter of an emissary.

I will admit that I had underestimated her. I didn't believe she would hurt someone she loved.

"I know what you were trying to prove back in the map room," I say. "I could've passed on the demonstration, but I understand."

She leans back a little in her seat and I think I actually managed to make her uneasy. I doubt she expected her tyrannical husband to see her side.

"Have *you* been in the Sleeper?" I ask.

"Montes," she warns, "I'm never going in there again."

Her tumors are growing, the cancer has spread to her brain, and while I've been recovering, she grows closer and closer to the grave.

"You *are*," I insist.

"I will shoot you again before that happens."

She doesn't realize it, but she just sealed her own fate.

I reach out and cup her face. For a girl who has lost much, she seems awfully entitled. Queenship suits her all too well. "You won't shoot me again," I say, my thumb rubbing the corner of her mouth.

She glares at me, her lower jaw working. She might as well have just agreed. Whatever proclamations she's made about her lack of a conscience, hurting me cost her.

I frown to keep from smiling. I'm pleased beyond measure. I never meant to tame this creature, and to some extent she'll always be a wild thing, but she's given in to me—to us—far more deeply than I initially imagined she would.

A knocking on the door interrupts us.

"Come in," I say, not bothering to look away from my wife.

"Your Majesties," the soldier bows low to us, "I have word on your former advisors."

My mind is still a bit foggy from the effects of the Sleeper, but it sharpens at that statement.

"What about them?" I say.

"We think they're attempting to take over South America."

SERENITY AND I storm towards my conference room. It doesn't slip my notice that she's having trouble keeping up. She may be in denial, but I'm not. Her body is shutting down; her muscles and organs aren't working as they should.

Her illness has robbed me of the last of my fury. I cannot find it in myself to be angry with her when I fear for her life. I have no intention of punishing her, but what I do intend—she'll think it punishment.

I've been in denial, thinking that because Serenity acted strong she physically was. But no longer. As soon as I deal with this freshest calamity, I'll deal with her.

302

When we arrive at my conference room, several of my aids have already pulled down a large screen from the ceiling. A slideshow of photos and grainy video clips stream across the screen, many of them capturing my advisors in the middle of treasonable tasks.

Some of these men had been on my council for decades. We shared more than power and ambition.

Over the next twelve hours we hear from the band of traitors. The message is written in red. South America's militia and the Resistance turned on my soldiers. My government officials have almost all been summarily executed.

Serenity stumbles back when she hears the news that the Resistance has sided with my councilors. She should know by now that the Resistance holds no allegiance to her, that they crave power just as much as I do. Just as much as my former advisors do.

I rub my mouth with one hand and cradle my elbow with the other. I've nearly worn a hole in the rug where I've been stalking up and down. It's taken me most of the day to grow detached. Strategy doesn't come to those blinded by emotion. My young queen knows that on the battlefield, but she still struggles with it inside these walls.

I stop and stare up at the footage still being projected on repeat.

"Ready as many troops as you can—I want them coming from the air, the water, and the land," I say. "We'll need to disable their lines of communication first—satellites, radio towers, and whatever electronics we can. And then we'll descend on them."

This needs to be stopped immediately.

Serenity

IT'S NEARLY FOUR in the morning by the time we finally make it back to our bedroom. I roll my shoulders. My muscles are tight from holding them rigid for so long.

Just when the king thought his pretty war was over, it reared its ugly head again. And for once, the king didn't orchestrate the bloodshed. In fact, most of the violence that occurred since the war ended has been reactionary, and all these events have been set off by a single catalyst—me. The moment the king found something other than his power to care about, the world began to plot.

One of the king's hands touches the back of my neck and he rubs the base of it. I lean into his touch.

My eyes fall to the bed. I've been running on nothing but caffeine and adrenaline for the better part of the day. My body still buzzes with the need to do something. It doesn't understand that in this situation, I can't fight or flee. Instead I have to watch from afar as more men fight and die senselessly.

The last thing I want to do right now is sleep.

Montes's hands slide down my back. He kisses the juncture where my neck meets my shoulders as he squeezes my waist.

My mind still remembers all the black deeds he's done, but my body is pliant beneath his hands, and my heart forgives, even though it shouldn't. Even though it knows a man like Montes never changes, not really.

I'm someone who will never really change, either. And what we have, it works. This twisted love that's endured so much more than it ever should've.

"Are you tired?" he asks.

It's a loaded question. I already know where his mind is.

"No," I say.

Montes's fingers grip the edge of my shirt and, pulling it over my head, he trails kisses along my now bare shoulders, and then my arms. He removes my bra and his hands smooth over my skin.

"Neither am I."

He releases me to remove his own shirt and toss it aside. The look he flashes me is all predatory. He makes quick work removing the rest of his clothes, and then he saunters towards me.

I back up until my skin brushes the ivory and gold wall trimmings. Montes follows, pressing his sculpted torso against mine. Already the sensation of skin meeting skin has me turned on.

His dark eyes are trained on mine, and as that alluring stare of his bores into me, he reaches a hand between us and flicks open the top button of my pants. The zipper goes next. His hand delves into them and—

"*Montes.*"

"Are you going to take your boots off, or am I?" That silken smooth voice of his is now coarse, husky with the first stirrings of passion. I like him the most when he's like this—untamed.

When I don't answer him, he crouches at my feet and begins unfastening my boots. He slides one off, then the other. My socks go next. Lastly, with one quick pull, he draws down the last of my garments.

Montes rises to his feet slowly, drinking in my nudity. My own eyes appraise the tight, flowing muscles that wrap themselves lovingly around his frame.

We're both naked from head to toe. My heart gallops as he grabs my hand and draws me to the bed.

Sometimes, when we're together, we're feverish. I don't have time to reflect on what exactly my heart's caught itself up in. But now, every move of ours is deliberate, and it gives me far too much time to savor each drawn out second.

With those depthless eyes trained on me, he drapes his body over mine.

"My vicious, hardened queen," he murmurs, cupping my cheeks, his thumbs stroking the skin beneath my eyes. "You are not so terrifying in my arms."

I know I'm not.

Devoid of my gun, my clothes, and my anger, I'm nothing more than a troubled, broken girl. And here in the king's arms, when all his intensity bears down on me, it's easy to pretend that nothing else besides his skin and mine matter. He's my Romeo, and I'm his Juliet, and even though we're star-crossed and our time's running out, we might fall into each other's eyes and live forever in this moment.

He enters me, and where there was two, now there's only one. Montes rocks his hips against my pelvis, moving languidly in and out.

The whole thing's gentle and slow, and he watches me the entire time.

The king has a growing habit of making love to me. It's more than a little disquieting, and it makes me feel like what he sees when he looks at me and what I see in the mirror are two very different people.

His chest slides along mine as I pull him closer.

His Serenity seems like a better person than the horrifying one I've known since war changed me.

Montes picks up the pace, and I begin to lose the last of my composure.

A wicked grin spreads across his face. "Say it."

I already know what he wants. "No."

He squeezes one of my hips. "Say it."

When I don't respond, he leans his forehead against mine. "Do I have to do it first?"

My eyes widen. I've never considered that the king could fall in love with me. Caring for me? Yes. Obsessing over me? Yes. Loving me? Not in the truest sense. Love takes too much selflessness for that.

But now he's essentially admitting as much.

He likes that he's shocked me.

He rubs one of his thumbs over my lips. His eyes move to mine.

"I love you," he says.

Instinctually, I cover his mouth with my hand, like I can push the words back inside him.

My eyes prick with moisture.

I don't want to know this. I don't want to feel hope

like this. Happiness like this. He's going to ruin it, or I'm going to.

He moves against me, just enough to remind me of how intimately connected we already are at the moment.

His ruffled hair hangs down around his face. He removes my hand from his mouth and presses a soft kiss to my lips.

"I never meant to," he whispers against me, "but I do."

A tear drips down my cheek, and he kisses that away too.

"Tell me you love me," he breathes against my cheek.

I shake my head.

"Stubborn woman," he says, thrusting into me harder, "I *will* get you to say it."

He forces my orgasm out of me with several long strokes, perhaps just to prove how easily manipulated I can be. I don't care. I hold him close as my climax works its way through my body.

He comes on the heels of my orgasm, his body slick with sweat as he moves against me.

Once we break apart, Montes gathers me to his chest and holds me there. "Stay with me, just like this," he says, kissing my shoulder.

I press my hand to his heart as I lay against him and savor the thump of it beneath my palm. This is where happiness sneaks up on you, and you forgive evil people for unforgivable things because they give you a taste of a future you always thought was beyond your reach.

I wait for the king's breath to even before I whisper my secret in the dark. "I love you too."

CHAPTER 32

The King

SERENITY AND I have maybe been asleep for an hour when I'm awoken by one of her rattling coughs. The thing has got ahold of her body. Her entire frame shakes as she desperately tries to clear her throat.

"I'm sorry," she says in between the hacking coughs.

It's only after she says that, that I realize my hold on her tightened the moment I woke. She's clearly too sleepy to realize she's apologized to me—something she's made a point of avoiding at all costs—and my constricting grip is only making it harder for her to catch her breath.

I relax my hold and begin rubbing her back soothingly. I'm still not used to the tight ball of fear that's made a home for itself in my stomach, or the slow release of its poison.

I'm also not used to being caring, affectionate. The previous women I have been with can attest to that. But with Serenity, it comes naturally, perhaps because I know just how unused to it she is as well. It's easier to give another something that's never been demanded of you.

She's still coughing, and at some point several droplets of her sickness hit my chest. Concern trumps any disgust I might have. She hasn't stopped coughing; if anything, it sounds like it's getting worse. She rolls away from me.

I pull her back against my chest and press my lips to the back of her slender neck. "*Nire bihotza*, I'm not letting you go." I'm not sure whether I'm referring to this moment, or the larger trajectory of her life. She's mine. Her life is mine, her heart and her soul are mine.

"What does that even mean?" she rasps, choking down her cough to talk.

I swallow the golf ball sized wedge that's taken up residence in my throat.

A reluctant smile tips the corners of my mouth up. "'*Nire bihotza*' means 'my heart' in Euskara—Basque."

"That's your native tongue?" Her voice sounds painfully rough.

I run a hand down her arm. "Mhm."

"You've been saying that for a while."

My hand comes to the end of her arm, and I thread my fingers through hers. "It's been so since the moment I met you."

Even now I want to wrap myself up in her and make her the air I breathe and the earth I stand on. But she's not earth or air.

She has been and always will be fire. She's my light and my death, and I couldn't escape her unscathed even if I tried.

Serenity falls quiet after that. With relief I realize that her coughing fit is over, for now.

Finally she breaks the silence. "Montes?"

"Yes?"

"Bury my body in my homeland."

My hand tightens around hers. A single sentence shouldn't be so devastating. This one levels my heart.

No.

No, no, no.

I want to shout my answer at her. She's not leaving me. I won't let her.

"Go to sleep, Serenity."

She sighs.

I wait for her body to relax before I leave her side and go to the bathroom. Turning on the faucet, I splash water on my face then settle my palms heavily against the marble countertop.

War comes at steep costs. Everyone I've ever held in high esteem has told me this. I just never felt the breath of it until recently. Things I've never had trouble holding onto are slipping through my hands—friends, loyalties, countries, *lovers.*

When I glance back up at my reflection, I notice the blood speckled across my chest. I touch my fingers to it and look down at them. The crimson liquid is smeared across the pads of my fingertips. It hadn't been saliva that

Serenity had coughed on me.

My last straw just broke.

I return to our bed and pull her back into my chest, attempting to get as much of her pressed to as much of me as I can.

"Fuck you and your bravery," I whisper. This hurts worse than the bullet she buried in my shoulder.

She murmurs against me.

For the first time in what feels like eons, tears spill from my eyes.

My eyes had burned when I found out Marco died, and they'd watered when we lost our unborn child, but it's Serenity who gets my tears. This is the first time since my father died that I let them freely fall.

I bite my lip to keep a sob from slipping out, and it takes most of my self-control to not squeeze her to me when it might trigger another coughing fit. I can't, however, stop my body from shaking as premature grief consumes me. It's almost unbearable, watching someone die. I've callously killed millions, but when my victim is my lover and she's dying in my arms, I can't bear it.

What I told her earlier was true. I never planned on loving her, but I do. I never planned on losing her either.

I still don't.

Serenity

I GROAN AS I wake, stretching my limbs out and wincing when I feel a sharp lance of pain in my abdomen. I tilt my head to the side and stare tiredly out the window. The sun has an orange glow to it. For a moment I relish the fact that I can wake to the sun at all. Aside from my stint with the military, I've lived belowground for the last five years. I'm used to waking to total darkness or the bunker's sickly fluorescent lights.

Then I noticed that along with the deep orange light are the beginnings of shadows.

How late did I sleep?

I look over my shoulder. The other half of the bed is empty. And now that I think about it, I vaguely remember Montes bending over and kissing my lips.

That snake.

He slipped away before I woke to resume his post and help his troops fight the rebellions in South America. He left his weak, sick wife to sleep in.

For all his good intentions, he left me here, out of the action. I hate that. If there's trouble on the horizon, I don't want to be left in the dark about it.

I push back the covers. That's when I notice the blood. It speckles the sheets and my pillow.

Had the king seen this?

He couldn't have, otherwise he'd be riding my ass to get in the dreaded Sleeper. Even now I shiver at the thought of it. Months spent in stasis as my body heals and no memory to account for that lost time. Could you even call that living?

When I glance down at my hands, I see more droplets of blood.

Cancer's a frightening way to go. I always wanted a swift

end for myself, for death to take me quickly. Not this.

I quickly change into a black shirt and pants. When given the choice, I will always reach for the outfit the leaves me the most mobile.

In the middle of dressing, I have to pause to run to the bathroom and vomit. After I rinse my mouth out several times and brush my teeth, I roughly comb out my hair.

Good enough.

I tuck my tight black pants into a pair of lace up boots and leave.

When I arrive at the king's conference room, it's empty. I try him in his map room next. Again, the room is completely vacant.

Where is everyone?

I run into a group of aides talking in the corridor. They glance up from their readouts and monitors.

"Where is the king?" I ask, glancing at each one.

"Your Majesty," the aide nearest me says, bowing as he does so. The rest of them murmur the greeting and dip their heads. I wave the title off.

One of the aides pulls me aside. He bends in close for a private word. "Last I heard, he was discussing the possibility of another aerial strike with some of the men upstairs. Third floor, east wing, fourth door on the left."

I leave then and follow the aide's instructions.

I climb up the stairs and head for the east wing. From the windows I get a panoramic view of the palace grounds and a glimpse of the world beyond. That world still represents freedom, and now that so many have seen my face, that freedom seems farther and farther out of my reach.

314

When I arrive at the room the aide referred to, I don't bother knocking. I simply storm inside.

The tea room—or whatever the fuck they call delicate little spaces like this one—that I walk into is devoid of life.

My first thought is that I've entered the wrong room, but I head back out into the hallway and recount the doors. I'm in the east wing, and the tea room is the fourth door on the left. I re-enter the room.

A few papers rest on one of the couches. I glance down at them. All appear to be printouts of the latest activities in South America. A cold cup of coffee rests on the side table next to the couch.

My second thought is that this is a trap, another intricately rigged situation designed to lead to my death. My heart palpitates at the thrill of it all. Bring the carnage, bring the destruction. I could use a good showdown at the moment.

I no longer have my gun, but half the objects in here could be weaponized.

I'm considering all the ways one can bludgeon someone to death with the bronze figurine resting on a nearby stand when I hear a familiar noise. The rhythmic stomping comes from beyond the windows.

Walking over to them, I peer outside. Two rows of soldiers cross the palace gardens, heading towards the east wing. I back away from the windows.

Something feels wrong about this situation. It shouldn't be unfolding the way it is.

I hear an echo of the footfalls in the hallway heading straight for this room. Understanding sets in. This is a trap, and it's one my enemy did set.

I just forgot for a while who my enemy really was.

I can taste bile at the back of my throat, and I realize I'm grimacing. My throat works and my eyes sting.

Oh God, I'm actually hurt by this.

Like this is anything compared to the atrocities the king's already committed. It was only a matter of time before he turned on me like he had everyone else close to him.

Still, when the door opens and Montes walks in, I have to physically swallow down the emotion rising up the back of my throat. Behind him I can see two armed guards, but I know there's more that I can't see.

I watch him warily.

"Serenity," he says, and the monster's eyes are actually sad, "don't look at me like that."

"Like what? Like you betrayed me? You never did." No, the blame lies with my own weak heart.

"I can't let you die," he says, and his voice breaks. The man is begging me to understand. "Not now when you're so close to death and my enemies are more aggressive than ever."

My muscles tense. Here I'd thought he was coming to dispose of me. That's usually what happens when someone betrays you. This betrayal, I realize, is much deeper and more intrinsic than I imagined.

He doesn't want to kill me, he wants to keep me alive in that Sleeper of his.

"How long?" I ask.

His shoulders relax. He thinks I am actually considering this. "Just until we find a cure." Looking into his eyes, I know it will be long enough to horrify me.

I nod, and I'm sure to him it appears as though I'm ruminating over this.

The idea of being in that machine for months or—heaven forbid—*years* has my breath picking up. I've lost my family, my friends, my land, my freedom, even my memory for a time. I can't lose this last sliver of my free will.

Montes's eyes are flat. He's already detached himself from what's about to happen to me.

My muscles are twitching, telling me I need to run, now. I take a step back, towards the windows. Then another. "What will happen to me between now and then?"

This is the man who married me. The man who held me when I was sick. This is the man I'd begun to fall in love with, the man who told me he loved me.

But he is also the man responsible for the death of countless people. He's the one who killed my parents, leveled my hometown, gave me cancer and the scar on my face.

He's the one that made me the monster I am.

I'm already studying the exits. We're on the third floor, which is probably intentional on the king's part. If I try to leave through the windows, I will surely break my legs. That leaves the door behind Montes.

I don't have a gun, and by now, there are probably over a dozen guards on the other side of the door, all waiting for me to try to escape.

If I want to leave through that door, I'm going to have to get past the king and many more armed guards who I can hear positioning themselves in the hallway. They're outside too, and they're getting closer.

Montes must see the realization in my eyes. He takes a step forward, then another. "Serenity, look at me."

That was why he called so many guards into such a futile situation, to smother any wild ideas I might get. He's the leader of the world; he knows a thing or two about strategy.

"You led me in here like a lamb to slaughter." I'm moving around the room. Resting on one of the side tables is a vase. On another is a lamp. Both are potential weapons.

He folds his arms, tracking me. "Are you seriously considering smashing that lamp over my head?"

"It doesn't have to be this way, Montes," I say. "Everything can go back to the way it was."

He takes a step towards me. "It will," he says. "Eventually."

Adrenaline buzzes just beneath the surface of my skin. "I will hurt you," I say. "I don't want to, but I will."

It's that, or hurt myself, and nothing in this room would kill me faster than the king could save me. Not even falling through those windows, I realize.

That's why the soldiers are outside. Not to prevent escape, to prevent a potential suicide.

The king turns away from me and glances at the door. "Guards!"

I begin to move before the words are fully out of his mouth.

I grab the lamp, but rather than throwing it at the king, who would surely duck, I lob it at the window.

Glass and porcelain shatter as the lamp obliterates it. Behind me, the door is thrown open.

I sprint away from the king, towards the broken window.

"Serenity, don't!" the king yells.

He thinks I'm trying to kill myself; he still doesn't really know who I am or else he'd know that this is my last desperate chance at survival. Then again, I can't blame him. Even after all we've been through, I don't really know who he is either.

I leap over furniture, ignoring the shouts coming from the guards.

I can hear them behind me, flooding into the room now that the charade of civility is up.

I reach the window and kick the last jagged bits of glass out before throwing one foot over the side. I swing the other leg over, and then I push off the sill.

"*Serenity!*" the king yells.

This is the second time I've exited the king's palace through one of his windows. And there's a moment after each leap of faith where I feel blissfully free. My hair whips around my face, my shirt flaps manically, and the ground rises up swiftly.

This time, like the last, there is someone here to catch me. Several someones. I land hard in their arms. I grip their starched uniforms as I try to right myself.

Brushing my hair from my eyes, I glance up. More soldiers peer from the room I exited. Distantly I can hear shouting, and people are running towards me.

A half dozen hands hold me in place; more join in as

I struggle.

I bite my lip hard enough for it to bleed. The odds are now stacked far against me. I'm not getting out of whatever twisted plan the king has in store. There isn't a car waiting, nor are there Resistance fighters to protect me.

The normally stoic soldiers are yelling, trying to contain my struggles. Eventually they do, leaving me gasping out of anger and incredulity.

Servants are watching, the ladies of the court are watching, the men who might be politicians or just more elite individuals are watching. I have captured all their attention. And they look horrified. The queen who jumped three stories only to fall into the arms of her husband's waiting army.

I have a clear line of sight to the palace's rear doors. It only takes a minute for them to open and the king to come storming out.

This man who I have come to know intimately looks larger than life as he strides towards me, a doctor in a white lab coat at his heels.

He's really going to do it.

I renew my struggles. A handful of wild, animalistic cries slip from my lips as I vainly try to get away. The entire time my eyes stay locked on the king's.

His rove over my body. I can only imagine what he must see—the tangled locks of my hair, the whites of my eyes, the angry set of my jaw.

I grit my teeth as he steps up to me. This is it.

"What were you thinking, Serenity?" The vein at his temple pounds, and God does he sound angry. Angry and desperate.

"Montes, don't. Please." I have desperation in my voice to match the king's.

He tips my chin up. "I *love* you, Serenity. I'm not doing this to hurt you. I'm doing it to save you."

After all this time, he still doesn't understand. "This was never about me," I say as he steps back so the man in the lab coat can get closer. "You're not saving me, you're saving your own chicken-shit heart—"

The man in the lab coat presses a damp cloth against my nose and mouth, and a sweet, chemical smell wafts from it. I buck against my captors and try to shake the hand. It grips my face harder.

I know whatever they've doused the material with is a sedative. As soon as I lose consciousness, I don't know when—or if—I'll wake up.

I try to hold my breath, but it's a lost cause. I last for maybe a minute and a half before I'm forced to breathe in a deep lungful. I breathe in another. And another.

The soldiers are lowering me to the ground, and someone's brushing my hair back. I follow that arm to its owner. My husband truly appears upset.

Is there no room for my own suffering in that heart of his?

The drug's beginning to affect me. My focus drifts, and when I move, the colors of my surroundings blur for a second too long. But I haven't passed out yet.

A surge of anger has me redoubling my efforts against the hands that hold me down, but I'm too weak and too outnumbered to make much headway.

Still, I don't stop fighting.

"Serenity," Montes says, continuing to pet my hair. "I would never hurt you. It's going to be okay."

Those five lying words. I've said them to soldiers as their lifeblood drained from their veins and their souls slipped from their eyes. It's a statement you say to someone who's lost hope, a lie you voice to make yourself feel better. But the person who is forced to hear it? They alone know the truth.

Sometimes, there is no hope to be had.

An angry tear trickles out. I can't tell if my rage comes from this strange betrayal or from what will happen to me once I'm unaware.

Montes's eyes focus on the tear, and the bastard strokes it away with his thumb. "Don't cry, *nire bihotza*," he says, his voice hoarse—as though this is tough for him. It makes me want to scream.

He has absolutely no idea what pain and loss feel like. The narcissist in me hopes that the king cares for me enough to regret this mistake for a very long time.

But I'm not counting on it.

"This isn't forever," the king says.

My eyes try to focus on him, but the sharpness of my reality is slipping away. I don't know how much time has passed—minutes maybe—but I can tell the drug is working. Darkness is licking the edges of my vision.

The last thing I see is the king's face, and the last thing I hear is his voice. He leans over me, and I feel a hand stroke my face. "We'll only be apart for a short while. Once we cure your sickness, you'll be mine again."

322

EPILOGUE

The King

1 week later

I TELL THE world she's dead.

My enemies don't believe me, but it doesn't matter. She's locked away in the Sleeper far below the surface of the earth, the machine healing her advanced sickness one malignant tumor at a time.

My fierce, violent queen.

I ache for her. This is different from the other times she'd been hospitalized. Now I know she's not coming out until we cure her cancer. That could be years, decades even. That entire time I have to endure it with one side of my bed cold. I have to carry this nation solely on my shoulders after catching a glimpse of what it would be like to have a true partnership with the woman I love.

I gaze into the window of the Sleeper and press my hand against the glass. She looks too serene. I'm used to my queen's frowns, her glares, her narrowed eyes. The way she studies things with cool detachment, the way those old soul eyes of hers assess the world.

This woman does not look like my wife.

I don't think I can bear staring at her face much longer. It's cruel to want something and know you can't have it.

Serenity believed that I never felt the wounds of my war. That I was above it. If only she knew how goddamn bad my heart hurts. Sometimes I can't catch my breath under the weight of all this grief. I lost my closest advisors, my oldest friend, my child, and the love of my very long life all within months of one another.

The world doesn't realize just how fragile their immortal king is at the moment.

But my enemies do. Of course they do.

6 months later

THEY STILL MOURN her, my people. They hated her while she was alive, but her supposed death has made her a martyr. It helps that the rebellions in the West are responsible for some of the most heinous atrocities to date. The devil the people know is better than the one they're learning about, the one the Resistance is regretting aligning with.

It also helps that I've encouraged Serenity's martyrdom. I've leaked a series of clips, much the same way the Resistance once did. But rather than degrading her character, these video segments show the world the Serenity I knew—a woman who wore violence alongside benevolence. I have clips from her interrogation, security feeds from the palace, even rare footage from her time as a soldier and an emissary of the WUN.

They're scrubbed down and shortened so that they cast her in a positive light, and they do the trick. Too late my people want to know about this woman that fought for them, who not only claimed to be one of them, but *was* one of them. And they love me for loving her.

I watch the clips over and over, until I've memorized every word, every expression, every movement of hers.

I'd hoped it would bring me peace.

It only brings more heartache.

2 years later

"CHRIS KLINE, YOU are a hard man to track down."

The man in question currently wears shackles and sits sullenly on one of my couches. He's much rougher around the edges than when I first met him. Hiding does that to a man. Makes him lean and shifty-eyed. But the former general's sanity is still intact, and I can see he's just as hardened as ever.

My guards flank him on either side. If he so much as moves a finger wrong, they'll load his body with bullets.

I settle myself on the couch opposite him and prop one

of my ankles over my knee. A butler comes in with two glasses of aged Scotch. He dips down, and I take one from the tray. My butler then turns to Kline, who's watching this all unfold with wary eyes.

I gesture to the drink. "Go on. I'm not trying to poison you. I have far more efficient ways of getting rid of people than that."

Reluctantly he takes the tumbler off the tray, his cuffs clinking together as he does so. It's an awkward maneuver, drinking while shackled, but the former general manages it with ease. He takes a swallow and exhales, his eyes closing for the briefest of seconds.

"That's good stuff," he says.

"It's near the best," I say.

"Why are you sharing your best Scotch with one of your prisoners?" he asks.

Blunt and to the point, just like my wife. I wonder if this is where Serenity picked up some of her personality traits, or if this is just a feature of all North American citizens.

"I'm hoping by the end of this conversation you won't be my prisoner."

The man squints his eyes and leans back. "I reckon that's not going to happen," he says. "I don't like you very much. See, you killed my son, destroyed my country, and married the closest thing I had to a daughter, and now she's dead too."

I swirl my Scotch. "I'm not here to apologize or discuss the past. It's your resume that interests me. How long had you been the general of the WUN?"

"Six years."

"And before that?"

"I was the Secretary of Defense for two years."

I nod. "And you remain loyal to your homeland even now?"

Kline leans forward, resting his forearms on his thighs, his drink still clutched in one of his hands. "From where I sit, you've got me by the balls. Do you really think I'm going to answer that honestly? Add treason to the growing list of charges against me?"

I set my glass of Scotch down carefully on a side table, then I, too, lean forward. "This isn't your old world. I can kill you now just because I feel like it—if I were so inclined. I'm not. I know you're now heading up the Resistance, I know you love my wife, and I know you still want to help your people."

South America has fallen into my enemies' hands, and North America is set to follow. Serenity's beloved homeland is far worse off now than it was two years ago when they surrendered to me.

For the first time ever, someone's taken land from me. I intend to get it back.

"'Love'?" Kline's still stuck on my comment about Serenity.

"Come," I say, standing. "I want to show you something."

He doesn't get a choice. His drink's taken from him; my guards yank him up to his feet and force him to follow me.

I head down to some of the lowest levels of the palace.

Here, the drone of many different machines fills the air. It doesn't take long to find Serenity's. I open the outer shell. Inside it is another glass case—a sort of incubator. And inside of that, the woman that holds my heart.

I haven't laid eyes on her in nearly a year, and I have to lock my knees to keep myself upright. But for my purposes, Serenity's old general needs to see this.

"Holy fuck!" Kline reels back soon as he catches a glimpse of her. "She's alive?" There's a strange note in his voice.

"She never died to begin with. But she will if I take her out of this machine."

Kline regains his composure and creeps closer. I can still read the horror on his features, however.

"Why keep her like this?" he asks. "Why not just let her die?"

My eyes are transfixed on that scarred, beautiful face. "Because I love her."

He's shaking his head like he thinks I'm crazy, that what I feel for my wife is something less pure than love. But what does he know? He gave away this very woman to a man he considered his worst enemy.

I'd level the earth before I'd let that same fate befall Serenity.

"I'm working on curing cancer—and repairing radiation-damaged tissue," I say instead. "I'm going to save her life. Once I do, I will have the ability to heal the sick. And I *will* heal them.

"You are a good man, Kline. I believe you have an honest heart. I need men like that. Will you help me repair what I've broken?"

It's been a long time since I've done something that's felt right. Like power, this feeling is addicting. Maybe I'll rewrite my own history along with Serenity's. Maybe one day people won't see me as a man who ruined the world, but the one who saved it.

That won't happen anytime soon, but time is something I have plenty of.

"I worked for you once," Kline says. "I never will again."

Before the sight of Serenity can break me, I close the lid. I turn to Kline, a man who was once my enemy, then my ally, then my enemy again, in hopes that he will be my ally once more.

Serenity trusted this man. I will too.

"I'm not asking you to work for me. I'm asking you, and the Resistance, to work with me."

7 years later

MY TRAITOROUS FORMER advisors have stolen my technology. For the first time ever I feel the anger that comes with trying to kill something that just won't die. That's how I find out they're utilizing the Sleeper.

I've never received direct evidence that they're taking my pills, but while under my rule, I watched their hair thin and their skin wrinkle. Now their thick heads of hair and their youthful faces are all the evidence I need that they're taking the pills.

I am now fighting monsters of my own making.

10 years later

NANOTECHNOLOGY.

That's how we save her.

24 years later

ANOTHER FAILURE. AND just when things were looking up. We'd begun human trials on the latest drug, too.

When I find out, I cradle my head in my hands and I sob.

It wasn't all a loss, I suppose. The drug is able to cure certain types of cancer—just not Serenity's. And, selfish bastard that I am, hers is all I really care about.

I have to accept the fact that even after all this time, I'll have to wait longer.

That doesn't sit well with me, and I take out my aggression on the WUN. I imagine that Serenity would hate me for it. But then, I wouldn't be giving her enough credit. She always had a way of parsing down issues fairly. Maybe she'd understand that the WUN I fight today is not the same one she left.

29 years later

I SIT IN front of the Sleeper, my hands in my pockets.

"My queen, I think we've found the key to curing your cancer."

It's not the only news I have, but it's the one that consumes my thoughts. My hands practically shake from excitement.

Three decades, three long, excruciatingly lonely decades. Three more decades of war. My depravity has gotten worse. And now, finally, I'll be able to hold her in my arms again.

Will we be the same once she wakes? All this work I've done for her, and sometimes I fear that I've changed too much. She will still be the Serenity I left thirty years ago, but will she see me as the same man she gave her life and heart to?

"You're getting moved. I'm rebuilding my Mediterranean palace," I say to her. It's the place where we were first married. Far below the palace there's to be a secret room—more of a temple really. And right at the heart of it my queen will rest until the last of her illness is obliterated.

53 years later

THE PLAGUE HITS again, and the death toll this time around is just as merciless as it was the last time it swept through the Eastern Empire.

The WUN and my old advisors who rule it are responsible. We traced the origins back to a series of contaminated food supplies smuggled in.

I've now lived through two epidemics. The first one fashioned me into a wealthy ruler when I sold the cure for profit. I thought I was evil then, but compared to current events, I've actually had to reassess my own suppositions.

Unfortunately for the WUN, a mutated strain of the virus made its way back West. The numbers of our dead are nothing compared to that of the WUN.

It's times like these that I'm glad my queen still sleeps.

Her cancer's been cured, but there are other mutations to her genome caused by radiation that the Sleeper is fixing. It's a slow process, providing gene therapy, and just when it appears all is well, some new issue pops up that the Sleeper must deal with.

I rub my face. Most of the time my thirst for life vanquishes all those things that haunt me. But late at night when I'm alone, like I am now, they come pouring in and I feel the weight of all my regrets and sorrow.

It's moments like these when my skin feels most alien. I'm far too weary for the young body I live in.

I leave my study and head down flight after flight of stairs. The mausoleum is finally complete.

Once my architects finished the project, I delivered a refined version of the memory loss serum to them. No one can know about this place. And for the unfortunates that I hired, that was the price I exacted.

My footsteps echo against the marble stairs as I enter the cavernous, subterranean chamber. The room is covered completely in marble and embellished with gold, lapis lazuli, and indigo tiles. I head down the walkway that leads to Serenity's burnished sarcophagus. At least, that's what it looks like by all outer appearances. But beneath the golden designs that cover it is state-of-the-art machinery. This Sleeper is not only the most beautiful one in existence, it is also the most advanced.

It sits on an island of marble, surrounded by a pool of water. Columns ring the edges of the circular room, and the ceiling arcs high above us.

My shoes click as I head down the marble walkway that bisects the pool. The water is still and smooth. It reflects the dim lighting and, beyond that, the artificial night sky set into the ceiling. So she'd always have the stars to gaze up at.

I sit at the bench that overlooks her sarcophagus.

I still miss her, but already I've forgotten the sharp ache of our love. Now, like the rest of the world, she's more myth than woman. I wouldn't even know what to do with the real Serenity if I were to meet her again.

64 years later

I'VE DONE SOMETHING unforgiveable—two things, actually. Two twisted deeds I already regret. It's times like this when I need Serenity's ferocity. I need her to aim her father's gun at me and demand I change my ways on pain of death.

As fucked up as we were, she tempered the conscience-less part of me.

No one else bothers to stand in my way.

My loneliness is to blame. It eats away at me. Some days I'm not sure I'll survive it. But I'm too afraid to die and too afraid to resurrect my queen.

"I'm sorry, Serenity."

I miss her.

73 years later

SERENITY IS HEALED. Completely.

Every single strand of DNA mutated by radiation has been repaired. Externally she retains her scars, but on a cellular level, she's flawless. It took the better part of the century, but I did indeed cure her.

So why does it feel so wrong?

I rub my mouth with my hand as my stomach contracts, sickened by where we've ended up. I'm still no closer to reclaiming my lost lands and she's still enshrouded by glass and metal. My vicious Sleeping Beauty. This is our violent fairytale.

To the world, she's a martyr and a mascot of all that is good and free.

The irony isn't lost on me.

Dear God, it isn't lost on me.

I stare at her golden sarcophagus.

Not dead, but not alive.

I pinch the bridge of my nose. I need to wake her. I need to let her see sunlight for the first time in nearly seventy-five years.

But.

I can't go back there. Back to a time when I had a weakness. When I lost control, and lost loved ones and territories in the process. The WUN still remains out of my hands. If I woke her now, what would I lose next?

I don't want her to see the man I've become. I don't want to fall for her all over again. It took decades for the pain of her absence to dull.

334

Here my wife's safe. And so is my heart.

So is my heart.

104 years later

I SLIP DOWN the passageway and head straight for Serenity's subterranean temple. This visit should be like the thousands of others I've made over the last century.

But it isn't.

The sarcophagus lid is askew, and the chamber inside—it's empty.

Serenity's gone.

Keep a lookout for the final book in the Fallen World
series

The Queen of All That Lives

Coming May 15, 2016!

Be sure to check out the Laura Thalassa's young adult
paranormal romance series

The Unearthly

Out now!

She's dead.

Samantha, her wavy caramel-colored hair, her little Bambi eyes, her angel face...dead.

Killed in a car crash at 1:45 a.m. last night.

But what if there was a way to save her? What if there was a way to send back a warning? What if there was a way to undo it all? The crash. Us. Falling in love. All the way back to the beginning.

What if there was a machine?

Be sure to check out book one in a brand-new contemporary YA time travel series by Dan Rix

A Strange Machine

Be sure to check out Laura Thalassa's new adult science fiction series

The Vanishing Girl

Out now!

Are you Fan X?

Six authors. One newsletter.

All-in-one access to your favorites.

Authors included:

Scarlett Dawn, Laura Thalassa, Ashley Stoyanoff,
Stacey Marie Brown, Rachel E. Carter, and Amber Lynn
Natusch

Form: http://eepurl.com/bBFVlX

BORN AND RAISED in Fresno, California, Laura Thalassa spent her childhood reading and creating fantastic tales. She now spends her days penning everything from young adult paranormal romance to new-adult dystopian novels. Thalassa lives with her husband and partner in crime, Dan Rix, in Oakhurst, California. For more information, please visit laurathalassa.blogspot.com.

CPSIA information can be obtained
at www.ICGtesting.com
Printed in the USA
LVHW091948261021
701602LV00006B/986